A Collection of Strangers

POSTSCRIPT TO NIGHTMARE

THE MAN WHO CRIED ALL THE WAY HOME

THE BANK WITH THE BAMBOO DOOR

THE ABDUCTOR

FOOTSTEPS IN THE NIGHT

THE WATCHER

By the same author FOOLS' GOLD

SLEEP WITH SLANDER

SLEEP WITH STRANGERS

BEAT BACK THE TIDE

TERROR LURKS IN DARKNESS

NETS TO CATCH THE WIND

STAIRWAY TO AN EMPTY ROOM

A Collection

of Strangers

DOLORES HITCHENS, (Birk) 1907-

G. P. Putnam's Sons
New York

A Collection of Strangers

1

The first phone call came on a Saturday in September.

Thomas Stoddard, dressed in an old shirt and khaki pants and sneakers, was out at the pool doing some cleanup jobs. Under the warm early-afternoon sunshine, dust showed on the redwood decking, and the eucalyptus trees had shed leaves which had drifted to the rim of the water. Stoddard was tall, thin, a little stooped, with touches of gray over his temples. He glanced toward the house once in a while. It was a long, low, rambling house with walls of cream-colored stucco and white brick. The decking led from the pool area to big double glass doors in the house wall.

When he was through raking leaves, Stoddard sat on a poolside bench to smoke a cigarette. He watched the smoke drift away with an expression that seemed to contain a thoughtful sadness. He was too far from the house to hear the phone ringing.

There was about a quarter acre of land here on the flank of the rise, enclosed in corral fencing, with the big round valley to the south, hazy now, and to the north behind the house, the sharp rim of hills, burned brown with toothy skylines, and the barranca slicing down through, a dark V-shaped trough full of old wild palms and sage and broken tumbleweeds. Jackrabbits and possums and quail lived up there. The hills had a wildness, loneliness, not disturbed by the presence of houses below.

The phone rang in the kitchen, where it was answered by Davie Stoddard, who was twelve and a half. He was a tow-haired boy with his father's thoughtful long face and rangy shape, but with a promise of more heft to come through the shoulders and torso.

David had just finished putting the final touches to a cheese and tomato sandwich, had just poured a glass of milk. He put the half-gallon container back into the refrigerator, wiped moisture off his hands onto his pants, and stepped past the end of the counter where the phone hung on the wall just above his mother's little desk.

He put the phone to his ear and said, "Hello," politely, and added, "This is the Stoddard house, Davie Stoddard speaking," and was planning, even as he spoke—it would be for Vicky, and she was downtown with Mom, looking at new curtains or something; lately it always seemed to be changes made in the house. Or it would be for his grandmother, and he'd have to say, "She's in her room, I'll call her on the intercom." And in that moment, waiting for a voice on the wire, he found himself looking past the open end of the kitchen into the big shadowy room the builder had kept calling the Family Area, a shiny-floored room with a TV set and a game table, scattered chairs, two couches, and at the far side the big double glass sliding doors that gave a view of the eucalyptus clumps and the edge of the pool. There was safety glass in the doors now, scrolls etched in the glass, and the decals his mother had added, black blobs now against the light outdoors. He took his eyes off the glass with an effort, and then somebody was speaking to him.

It was a quiet, even voice. An anonymous voice, though for an instant something seemed to tug at him, some shred of reminder. The voice said, "Hello, Davie," so he knew that this was somebody who knew him, knew *them,* and he felt easier, and then the voice added, "I have a very confidential thing to say to you. Are you alone? Are your sisters there? Your mother, maybe?"

"I'm all alone here in the kitchen."

"Good, then. I want you to listen very carefully."

David half frowned, half grinned, felt a touch of embarrassment, and looked over at his sandwich and the glass of milk. The house seemed awfully quiet. Of course it had been quiet, a strange quiet, for some time now—

"You love your sisters quite a bit, don't you?" the voice asked.

David thought: *It's a crazy question, and this is a kind of crazy telephone call, and I don't like it all at once. And I wish this—*

this person would tell me a name. "Sure," he said awkwardly, and added, "Which one?"

"I'm guessing Suzie is the one you're the fondest of. Vicky is sort of grown up. Twenty. But Suzie's fifteen and she helps you a lot with your schoolwork, and she's . . . fun. Isn't she?"

"Well, so—so what?"

"And you wouldn't want anything bad to happen to her, would you?"

The words came kind of slick and slow, and Davie found for a minute that he didn't want to understand, this wasn't the way people behaved on the telephone, not this—

"You've had a couple of bad things happen to your family this past year. Isn't that right? I won't mention what happened, but I think you must remember. What I want you to understand, Davie, is that these things, the kind of things that have already happened, aren't really the *worst kinds* of things. Of course, they seemed pretty bad at the time. And maybe all of you thought that nothing that bad could possibly happen again. Only, what might happen to Suzie could be a worse thing, worse, for instance, than just sudden death, or falling down stairs and breaking bones. Suzie might have . . . well, experiences, let's call them experiences, that she'd have to remember for the rest of her life. Experiences that she couldn't forget, no matter how hard she tried. Things that could keep her awake at night. Or that she'd dream about— Do you want me to describe some of these things, Davie?"

Davie wanted to cry *no, no*—but the sound stuck in his dry throat, and there was only a whistling stillness in his head, in his straining ears, and his hand moved, trying to hang up the telephone; only, with all the quivering slowness, it was still close enough for him to hear the voice.

The words that came over the wire seemed to suck their way down into his mind the way water corkscrews out of a drain, with a slimy coldness, slowly, almost in a crazy way, regretfully. The voice seemed really sorry, almost, to be telling him these things that could happen to Suzie.

"I'm going to call again," the voice promised at last, "and perhaps I'll have a little errand for you to do, a favor I'll ask, and meanwhile, you can keep an eye on your sister and make sure she's all right. I don't think anything will happen for a while."

And that was the end.

The click came, and he was listening to an empty line.

He found himself walking stiff-legged toward the big glass doors. He passed the TV set, big and dark, and the end of a couch, and he crossed a rug and bumped a corner of the game table. He turned around. He didn't want to go back through the kitchen, past the telephone, but he couldn't go out through those double doors and have to skirt the pool and perhaps meet his dad. He would go back the other way and head for the barranca. He slid past the phone, aware of it, not looking at it, on through the rest of the kitchen to the hall that led to the back entry. He passed the stairs that went up to his grandmother's part of the house, her bedroom and parlor, and for a moment he thought, with a sense of panicky relief, of going to her. But then, Grandma was not her old self these days. She was quiet, almost totally silent, and there was at times a look of anger and outrage in her face that she never put into words. And sometimes she winced, also silently, and you knew that her injured leg was hurting her.

Before the bad things had happened here, Grandma used to sing and tell jokes, get her hair done in smart ways, and buy new dresses. But not anymore.

Davie let himself out at the back entry, the part of the house that faced the lonely hills and the steep cut of the barranca. The barranca was always a refuge, a removed and pocketed place where you could sit and be alone to think. He crossed the planted areas, a graveled slope, and opened the gate in the fence, went through, fastened the gate behind him. Ahead of him now was the wild rocky slope that led up to the beginning of the hills.

It was cleared for a short way, the result of an old fire and of his dad's preoccupation with neatness. The walls of the barranca were lower here, worn away by the rains of winter. Up ahead the barranca was choked with dead tumbleweeds, random palms, some sage mixed with stunted cactus. But Davie had found a way through, long ago, an old trail—he imagined that it had been made originally by sheepherders. There had been sheep up here in the hills above the green floor made by the orange trees. Before the houses had come.

He shouldered his way into the narrow opening, the weeds pricking and scratching through his knitted shirt. After about fifty feet of tangled brush, a dirt fall from the bank had left a cleared way, and here Davie had made his camp. There was a little fireplace made of rocks under the sheltering bank, two old blankets rolled up and kept in a discarded laundry basket with some worn-out pots and cans of soup and a big jug of water. This was his private place, and now he stumbled into it, knowing that he was beginning to cry, not wanting to cry, but filled with the terror and dread left by that voice over the phone, and not able to do anything about it except to shed tears.

He threw one of the blankets on the dusty ground and got down on it, and curled himself, and stared through his tears at the old brush around him and the shining blue sky above. The thing to do, he told himself fiercely, was to *think*—only now he couldn't because the words he had heard in that unknown voice kept beating around in his head. And they were horrible. He wouldn't think of those things as happening to Suzie, though the voice had said that he must.

He lay for what seemed a long time, not moving, clutched by the cold feeling of helplessness.

A big old jackrabbit came down the barranca from above, moving silently, his rump bobbing up and down above the big hind legs, his nose twitching and his ears up. One ear had been torn, the tip shredded off, probably by a hunting shot, and the edge of the tear always looked newly healed and sore. Davie had seen him before, many times; they shared the private secrets of the barranca, its sense of refuge. Davie knew where the big jack had a hole, farther up, and sometimes he had left apples and oats beside it.

The big eyes studied Davie for a long minute; the jack seemed curious but not afraid. He was shedding, preparing to grow in a winter coat, and his brown-gray fur looked rough and patchy. A gnat or something equally small, almost invisible, drifted down and bothered him and he shook his head hard and then turned and nibbled experimentally at some leaves on a dwarf bush.

Davie felt a sudden rush of envy. In that instant he sensed the simplicity of the animal's life, its preoccupation with the primal basics of food and survival. There was nothing to be afraid of except target shooters with .22 rifles and an occasional dog. There were no threats in that world, and no lingering terrors.

The tears came again, bitter tasting.

. . . perhaps I'll have a little errand for you to do, a favor I'll ask. . . .

The words returned, crowding out the uglier suggestions that had gone before, and Davie almost sat up. *A favor.* A trade is what the voice had meant. You'll do this errand, this little thing I'm going to ask, and nothing will happen to Suzie. You can forget all the things that *might* have happened to Suzie.

What would it be?

He had no idea what it was going to be, but the feeling of coldness came back worse than ever.

It wasn't going to be anything nice or easy.

The old jack heard the horse before he did. The rabbit stopped nosing and nibbling around the little green weed and put his chin up, and the big eyes grew still, fixed on nothing, while the ears twitched.

Then, leisurely, the rump rising and falling with the pistonlike motion of the big legs, the jack went back a little way and then turned right, tucking himself in under the brush, and was gone. Meanwhile, now, faintly, Davie began to hear the horse coming down the barranca, the hard thud of the hooves echoing in the ear he had against the ground, an occasional grinding sound as a hoof slipped, the hollow noise when the horse dislodged a stone. The sounds grew louder, and Davie nervously pushed himself up, crossed his legs on the blanket, and folded his arms. It would be their neighbor Mr. Warren on his gray mottled gelding.

Mr. Warren had come down this way before, once, while Davie was here in camp, so he wouldn't be surprised to find Davie here, and the horse was too placid to be startled. A quick hard digging with his fingers removed the last of the tears.

The gray gelding became visible in the distance, head high and pushing himself impatiently through the brush down the half-choked trail. But Mr. Warren wasn't in the saddle; it was someone with a blue scarf on her head. Davie suddenly realized that it was Suzie. Suzie had borrowed the horse again and gone riding. She did this every once in a while, but now, seeing her there in the wilderness of heavy growth, bracing herself against the horse's swaying, Davie had a moment of frozen panic, followed at once by anger. She had no *right*. She had no business being out where it was lonely like this, where no one could see her or hear her, unprotected, unwary.

He had thought that Suzie must be with their father, out helping around the pool.

He got his feet under him, half-crouched, tempted to run. The feeling of anger had sent a rush of heat through him. His heart was pounding. He wanted to cry again; something like tears collected in his mouth, and he had to swallow.

Suzie had seen him now. She waved a hand and hollered his name. The echoing sound of her call was a shock in itself; he realized, stunned at the insight, that he had tried to be very quiet ever since the phone call. He had tried to move without sound, keeping small and still.

The horse pushed its way down the last few feet of brushy trail and emerged into the little sloping clearing. Davie trembled, his breath sticking in his throat and his face burning, and then he attacked with a rush. He tore over to Suzie; he pounded his fists on her leg, the only part of her he could reach, the leg flattened against the skirt of the saddle. And moisture was running from his eyes and his gasping mouth, and he was grinding out what were for him obscenities. "You dirty old . . . you dirty old *bitch*—"

"*Davie!*"

The horse shied mildly, his hooves slipping in the sandy soil, his skin prickling. He lifted his lips to show his big yellow teeth and tossed his neck a couple of times until Suzie reached down firmly to touch him.

"I'm going to tell Daddy what you called me! And you needn't get mad just because I came here through your silly old camp—"

She was beyond reach, and anyway, what he'd done had been crazy. It wasn't Suzie he was mad at or afraid of. It was someone else, someone he didn't even know.

He stood there, head hanging. The crying wouldn't stop, and he refused to lift his clenched, shaking hands to hide it.

Suzie pulled up the reins as if to go on, but then she dropped her hands on the saddle horn to gaze down at him. "Look, Davie, if I surprised you, I'm sorry. I thought you knew I was coming; that's why I yelled from up there. I know this is your place."

He wanted to say, "That's all right," but the words wouldn't come.

After a minute she asked, "Is anything else the matter?"

Muffled and choked, he got it out. "No."

She was looking around, he sensed, trying to figure out what could have happened to make him act as he had.

"Have you been up here long?"

He shook his head. He had to tell her, though; he had to spill it, the terrible warning. "You mustn't go out by yourself anymore." He mumbled it, head lowered, and she wasn't sure of what he'd said, and she answered, "What?" and he had to repeat it, through all the wetness in his mouth and the difficulty in breathing right. The sobs kept catching at and distorting his voice.

"Why mustn't I go out by myself?" she asked, her tone patient.

"It's dangerous."

"How? How is it dangerous?"

"Things—" How he hated this part of it; it reminded him of the voice on the phone; instinctively he put his hands over his ears as if to shut out what might come back again, the dreadful words. "Things could happen to you." Almost, he wanted to be sick.

"What things?" She was still patient, but now her attitude was frowning, attentive. "Bad things, you mean. Like what?"

He looked up at her, his gaze swimming. She was a silhouette against the pale sky, but he thought, too, all at once, there was a kind of huskiness about Suzie. She was strong, and she went in for a lot of games at school—she could run, too. She could run faster than he could.

"I don't know," he whispered. He couldn't tell her what the voice had said might happen to her. She was his sister. He could never tell her that.

2

The second call came on a Tuesday, more than a week later.

It caught Davie totally unaware. The intervening days had been peaceful and ordinary. There had been shopping, going with Vicky to buy school stuff—school opened in a couple of weeks. Mr. Warren had paid him to do a few jobs around the stable, jobs he would have been glad to do for nothing just to be close to the horse. Mr. Warren even promised that sometime soon Davie could learn to ride. He was plenty old enough, in spite of what his mother said.

Suzie hadn't gone on any wild-country jaunts. She, too, was thinking about school now, and calling up some of her friends, and checking to find out which teachers would be back and what courses they'd teach. She got a kind of excited glaze to her and looked pinker and bigger-eyed and even more able to look after herself than ever.

Vicky was still trying to make up her mind about the University of Arizona. She was all enrolled and everything, clothes bought, and knew where she'd be living in Tucson and which of her friends were going to be there, too, but there was this hitch, this uncertainty and though nobody spoke about it—her dad just looked wisely weary and her mother stunned—it was all because of Jeff Norbert.

Jeff Norbert was a junior at Cal Tech. He was a brain. He did physics in his head. He was smarter than Mr. Lafferty, who taught sixth grade. He was tall and blond; he had a blond beard, kind of a showoff sort of beard. He wore green shirts and he could surf and he drove a big new sports car. Once he had let Davie drive it a whole block, coming to their house, and Davie had done it perfectly, had turned into the drive and stepped on the brake without a single mistake.

Jeff Norbert lived in a big place across the valley. His mother was active in art societies, and his dad spent a lot of time in Chicago.

Jeff had his eye on Vicky, and Vicky was looking back. It was as if they were on either side of an invisible mirror, looking through it at each other and seeing things in that vision that nobody else could see. There was a kind of magic about Vicky even when Jeff wasn't around. She wore an atmosphere of secrets.

She took Davie to the downtown stores for boy stuff, pants and shirts and shoes and school supplies, but when they passed the men's outfittings, Davie noted her sidelong looks.

She's thinking how Jeff Norbert would look in that, David told himself, growing wise.

The only time he had been on the verge of telling anyone about that other phone call had been in the evening of the day it happened.

At dinner his grandmother had seemed quiet and serene, hadn't frowned or gone off into that angry dream even once, and had even looked directly at him and smiled. And so, still full of that cold terror and lostness, he had waited a little while and then headed for the stairs that led to her rooms.

He put his hand on the smooth varnished banister, and then above, coming down, was his mother. Her face was tight, her mouth clenched, and when she saw Davie, she said, "If you're thinking of bothering Grace, don't. She doesn't feel well."

"Uh . . . she looked okay a little while ago."

"Davie, obey me and leave your grandmother alone."

Davie could only wonder, when had they stopped being friends? Had it been when Cootie had died? He shrank aside as his mother passed. She seemed to give off a freezing rejection; she was back in that world where nothing mattered except whether the draperies matched the rugs, or some sofa didn't fit, or a picture was all wrong.

He hung there at the lower edge of the stairs, undecided. But then, finally, he hadn't gone up to talk after all.

Maybe the man on the phone wouldn't call again.

But he did call, on Tuesday. It was later than the other time. The draperies had been pulled shut in the big room beyond the kitchen, the place the builder had kept calling the Family Area, and Davie and Suzie were there with the TV set on, something going, a rerun they'd seen before, and Davie was fooling around with a crossword puzzle. Vicky was over at a desk looking through a pamphlet, probably one describing the courses at the University of Arizona or maybe one telling how you managed to study when it was one hundred and ten degrees in the shade and with your mind full of Jeff Norbert.

The phone rang in the kitchen.

It rang in their father's den, of course, too—and in their parents' bedroom, though usually their mother kept that one tuned so low it was practically silenced. It didn't have a chance to ring a second time, because Suzie jumped up and ran for it. Vicky lifted her head; she never ran, or jumped for it, or seemed terribly interested, which was all a fake, Davie sensed; actually she was on pins and stuff supposing it might be Jeff.

Suzie laid the phone down with such a prompt loss of interest that Davie was sure it was Jeff, all right, but then she said to him, "Hey, squirt, it's you they want. Li'l ol' you."

Something cold slid up his spine, a feeling so definite that it seemed something real must have touched him. It was like a warning; it was as if the person waiting on the other end of the wire had reached into the room, ghostlike. He put down the crossword puzzle and got up.

"Well, come on, slowpoke," Suzie said. "Your pal is waiting."

"Who is it?"

"How should I know? I don't keep IBM records on your wee friends. Just come and answer the phone, that's all."

He went drag-footed, unwilling, filled with a deep sense of disquiet. "Hello," he said into the receiver, and in the moment of silence, of waiting, he knew. He took a deep breath and started to put the phone back into its cradle.

"Davie, how are you?" said the hateful voice. "Are you keeping watch over Suzie the way I suggested? You remember some of those bad things I said could happen to her, don't you? Or maybe even all of them? You know, Davie, you're old enough to understand a few things. Things about anatomy, for instance. A young girl's body."

The thick cottony tongue glued to the roof of his mouth wouldn't come unstuck; if it had, he would have begged the voice not to continue.

"There are parts of the body, parts of a young girl's body, which are very tender. Very sensitive. Easily hurt. It would be hard for a girl, even a girl as athletic and as vigorous as Suzie, to defend herself against getting hurt like that. I guess you might not understand exactly what I'm trying to explain. You see, it's—"

Davie managed to croak, "No. No." And he stared helplessly at his two oblivious sisters, Vicky's blond shining head bent over the pamphlet about the University of Arizona, and Suzie— He couldn't endure to look at Suzie. He shut his eyes.

The voice went on; it added up detail upon detail as if in some lesson in anatomy. How Suzie was made inside became quite clear. Given the right materials, Davie felt that he would be able to build that part of Suzie from scratch.

"Of course, nothing may happen to Suzie, nothing at all," the voice added, pretending to comfort him. "It depends on you. It depends on how good you are at keeping a secret. And how careful an observer you are, and how clever. I want this thing, this job you're going to do, done just right. To keep Suzie from being hurt."

"You wouldn't!" Davie gasped.

"I didn't say that *I* was going to do anything, did I?"

"N-no."

"I was just explaining what bad things could happen to Suzie if she wasn't careful. Girls should *be* careful."

Davie couldn't answer. The voice shifted from terror to pretending to a lie, but it was burned into his brain, the threat as bald as a lifted ax.

"So you see—don't be putting words in my mouth."

The tone was so mean, so full of ugly promises, that Davie tried to say, "I won't. I promise I won't," but he couldn't get it out. He was afraid the phone would slip from his sweating hand.

"What I want you to do—and this is the beginning of the job I told you about—what you're to do is to keep watch and find out what your father does with his keys when he gets home at night. Where he puts them, are they locked up, and if there's a time you could get them for an hour or so without his knowing about it. I may have to tell you the time to get them, the time I'll need them."

There had been a slight noise, cutting across the mutter of the TV set, and one of the glass doors all the way down the big room had slid open, and his father's figure parted the draperies there. Beyond the darkened silhouette of his father's form he caught a glimpse of the twilight, gray and misty, before the draperies dropped shut.

His father walked forward slowly, glancing at the TV set and then over at Vicky. It seemed to Davie, suddenly, that his dad seemed older and more tired, all at once, and then he tried in that agonized moment to remember when had been the last time he had seen his father smile.

"Are you listening, Davie?"

"Yes."

"Do you understand what you are to do?"

"Get the keys."

"No." The voice was sharp, mean. "You don't touch anything; you make no move until I tell you."

"You're going to ask me to steal my dad's keys," said Davie, wanting to end the hateful pretense that there was some kind of cooperation between him and this monster at the other end of the wire, "but right now I'm just supposed to watch what he does with them and if I could get them if I wanted to."

There was an offended and angry silence, and Davie found to his horror that he was beginning to cry. He turned hastily from the scene in the big room, concealing his face by cupping the phone closer and higher. His dad had stopped and was talking to Suzie, who was sitting cross-legged on a round rug, looking at the TV and pulling the fringes of the rug through her fingers.

"You really must want something to happen to your sister," the voice said finally, dropping a notch, sounding more dangerous than ever.

"No, I don't!" Davie strangled on the unwilling tears, and then something in the voice woke such a chord of memory that he cried without thinking, "Wait—I *know* you!"

Again a silence, filled this time with the sound of heavy breathing. The silence drew on and on while Davie waited, trembling, searching his mind frantically for that lost flash of knowing.

When the voice came back, it was almost a growl. It was a bear's mumble. Again Davie knew that the man was trying to sound different, trying to disguise who he was. "So you know me, do you? Well, who am I?"

"I—I thought . . . there for a minute, I kind of thought—"

"You'd be awfully smart not to go on thinking along that line," said the growl.

Warned by something undefined, Davie turned and gave a start of terror and surprise; his dad was standing just a few feet away, looking at him with mild inquisitiveness. "Who is it, Davie?"

Davie covered the receiver. "Just a—somebody I know."

"Oh, all right." His dad started to go on, and then paused. "If you want me for anything, I'll be in the den. Mr. Ralston is coming over and we'll be going over some papers, but if you want me—"

"Sure, Dad." Davie remembered Mr. Ralston, a big red-cheeked man who wore black suits and smelled of rich strong cigars. Bald-headed. Eyes that twinkled the way Santa Claus' were supposed to. Mr. Ralston worked for a firm that bought land for subdivision, and he often came over to talk to Davie's dad about some legal angle or other.

His dad patted Davie on the head as he passed, a gesture out of old, old memories, out of the days when Davie had been very little. The patting ended in a little squeeze on top of the scalp, and this too was out of the long ago, except that once his dad's hand had covered his whole head and the scalp squeeze had left a pleasant tingle all over his skull. Such an aching lump rose in Davie's throat then that he half turned; he almost thrust the hated telephone into his dad's hands and said, "Here, Dad, you take care of this—this thing—" Only he couldn't. There was Suzie, Suzie all oblivious of her terrible danger, sitting there playing with the rug fringe, thinking about school and her new clothes and the friends she'd be running around with every day again.

Mr. Stoddard left the kitchen with a last glance back at his son.

Davie looked at the phone in his hand. "Hello," he whispered. "I had to talk to my dad. He was passing by—"

The phone was dead.

He looked at it in quick fear, and the first idea was that somehow he had been disconnected, through his own fault, by leaning on the hook or something. But no, the hook was too far, away over on the wall over the desk—he couldn't have done it. The caller had hung up.

Slowly he put the phone back on the receiver. He went into the Family Area for a few restless minutes, walking around, staring at things without seeing them. Vicky looked up to give him an absentminded smile. Suzie went on watching television.

He went back through the kitchen to the hall where the stairs were that went up to his grandmother's rooms. He crept up the stairs without a sound and stood on the little landing. There wasn't much light here, just the reflection of the glow through the open door of the kitchen.

From inside his grandmother's place he could hear muted talking and laughing. She had *her* television set on, too, and for a moment he felt so rebuffed, so shut out by everyone in the house that he almost went back down the stairs. But then all at once her door opened.

The room inside looked warmly lit, comfortable. It lacked the look of space and openness that characterized the rest of the house, but this was not because the rooms were small but because there was somewhat too much furniture in them. Mrs. Stoddard had kept most of the furnishings, the precious old things shiny with memories, from her own home.

"Davie," she said, looking at him a little sharply, "aren't you coming in?"

"How did you know I was here?"

"Oh, I just knew somehow."

He went in and he saw that she was still watching him. She was a tall woman, and during the last year she had lost weight, and her hair had grown noticeably whiter. She was almost like a stranger, with the quietness that had come over her and her way of watching people to see if they were thinking about Cootie. She had been to blame for what had happened to Cootie; she was supposed to have been watching him that day. No one had ever said, "You're to blame"—neither his father nor mother, nor any of the men who came during the investigation, nor Suzie nor Vicky, nor Davie— but *she* knew. And now she didn't put her arm around Davie's shoulders the way she would have a year ago. She sort of led him in and to a chair, and she switched off the noise from the TV set, and she sat down, all without touching him, though he sort of wished she would.

Davie couldn't think of a way to start talking, and as if she sensed this, she began, "Well, I suppose you're thinking a lot about school starting. When is it? Next week?"

"Week after next," he got out.

"And you'll be in seventh grade. Beginning junior high school. Think you'll like that?"

"I guess." He tried desperately to think of a way to get off the subject of school, to get to the fearful reality of this other thing. The idea of school seemed as far away as the moon. What was going to happen to Suzie was a bursting sickness right inside him.

"Do you need money for anything?"

A sudden dazzling glimpse of an idea—he'd buy the man off; he'd pay him to leave Suzie alone. His grandmother would give him the money, and he would—

The man didn't want money. He wanted his dad's keys. Eventually. When he was ready for them. And if he *had* wanted money, it would have been far, far more than Davie could have raked together, even with his grandmother's help. Thousands and thousands.

Davie discovered to his surprise, and in spite of the shortness of those contacts over the phone, that he knew some very definite things about that man who had called him twice. The man asked for exactly what he wanted. And he wasn't worried about whether you were going to give it to him. If you didn't, it was just too bad —for you.

"I—I wanted to ask you about something," he said, after drawing a deep breath.

She nodded a little, a look of thought in her face, as if the offer of money had been some kind of test, or experiment.

"What would you do if . . . if somebody called you up on the phone and"—his mouth was so dry that he had to stop, let it get wet again, and lick his lips—"and told you things?" he finished lamely

3

There wasn't any expression on his grandmother's face, no surprise, no worry, just a kind of sudden blankness, and the only move she made was to pull her knees closer together under her skirt and to rub her right hand slowly down the leg which had been broken so badly in the fall down her stairs, one month to the day after Cootie had died. "Told you things? What kind of things?"

"Something bad that—" Davie felt a great rush of heat, all over, as though he had been doused with fire. He *couldn't* tell her those things that might happen to Suzie. He *couldn't*.

She waited, and then she moistened her lips and said, "Something bad happening here?" Her eyes looked kind of dry and tired, and he saw how thin her face had become and how much older-looking. "You have somebody teasing you about troubles we've had?"

"Not exactly. It's like . . . going to happen," he managed to say.

"More things that might happen?"

"Yes."

She thought about it for a minute. "Who's calling you?"

"I don't know."

"The calls are pretty mean?"

"Yes." He felt such relief. She was going to understand, after all. He wasn't going to have to tell her all of it, but she was going to get the idea, and she would know what to do. She'd know what to do about the danger to Suzie.

But then, what she said next surprised him completely. "Do you miss Cootie?"

He said uncertainly, "Yeah. Sure."

"Do you think of him often?"

He tried to figure out how much he really thought about Cootie these days. He remembered Cootie vividly, the round three-year-old face and the fair rumply hair and the hands always sticky and warm with life. "No, I guess not a lot. Not anymore. I mean, I'm not walking around, crying inside because of my brother, the way it was at first. It's the house that makes me remember, when I do. Every once in a while I notice how quiet the house is, and then I look around and I half expect Cootie to be there, even though it's the quietness that tells me he's gone. He made a lot of noise, when he was awake, when he was running around getting into things."

She sat even more stooped, and her hand was rubbing the leg that must hurt her all the time. He had heard the doctor telling his mother and father that the break had been such a bad one that she might always have trouble over it.

"When people suffer terrible things . . . things like what happened to my little grandson," she said, "there are always others, wicked ones, evil ones, who are—for some reason known only to God—glad about it." She looked meaningfully at Davie, and to show that he understood, he nodded. "These bad ones are so constructed—made, Davie—that the agonies of others are their pleasure. Their sport. When Cootie died, you remember, the police finally put a man out in front of the house to keep the gapers, the morbid watchers, from coming around to look at the glass doors." She swallowed something in her throat. "To look at where the glass door had been."

"Yes, I remember that." He had actually forgotten it until just now, but now he recalled the straggling crowds of strangers, some shabby, some driving old wrecks of cars, people from someplace away off, who had come and sauntered around the house and stared at the plywood his dad had put up temporarily where the glass door had been at the end of the Family Area. One girl about his own age, he remembered, a frowzy-haired blonde in a boy's T-shirt and denim pants whacked off at the knees, had picked herself a bouquet of flowers from stuff his mother had planted out there, and she had seen Davie watching, and she had grinned. The grin had been a shock.

The cops had finally put up sawhorses in the driveway, with a cop to motion the people to move on.

Suddenly Davie remembered something else that had gone on at the same time. His grandmother had insisted that someone had been standing out in the yard when Cootie crashed the door, standing there indistinct in the half twilight, almost past her angle of vision as she rushed through the kitchen. It was as if, in the way she told it, the mysterious person outdoors had lured Cootie in that last dash on his tricycle.

His grandmother had told the story over and over, and Davie could see how the others reacted. They didn't believe it, and they were embarrassed, even his dad, who had been most gentle and protective about his mother in her guilt and grief. And then, after a day or so, his grandmother quit telling people about the person outdoors, the watcher who had just disappeared when the great shattering of glass filled the air, and she got quiet, the way she was now, and so far as he knew hadn't mentioned the story since.

But the newspapers had printed it all, because it made a mystery and helped sell the papers. And maybe that was why all the strangers had come in such a stampede. His grandmother had drawn them here with the story that no one else could believe.

With sudden insight Davie thought: *Maybe I'd have done the same thing if I'd been left with Cootie and he died that way. Maybe I'd have made up somebody out in the yard, so people would think Cootie had seen another person and that person had caused the accident. It hadn't happened because I wasn't taking care of him.* He looked at his grandmother in surprised understanding and felt sorry for her in a way that he hadn't before.

She was speaking, slowly and distinctly. "What has happened, Davie, is that someone very evil thinks that we may have begun to forget. He thinks that our sorrow is dying, that perhaps we aren't each in our hearts blaming ourselves. Me for being here with Cootie. The others, for not being. My son and his wife are beginning to quit tormenting themselves, what was so important that they had to leave Cootie that afternoon—"

She seemed drawn tighter, there on the chair, almost bird-shaped, the gray head thrust forward, a hawk with a gray head and sad dry eyes. Davie wanted to interject something, to remind her of what he'd come here to ask. But his thick tongue didn't respond.

"So something must be done to remind us. Choose the youngest among us, the most vulnerable. You. And make dirty phone calls. Torment him so that he turns to the others. The cruelest way of all to make sure our grief never dies."

Davie felt chilled, sunk into some freezing despair—she didn't understand at all. She connected everything he had told her with what had happened to Cootie, not with a new threat at all.

And then he understood that the accident to Cootie was so terrible, so unforgettable to her, that it made a kind of horizon over which she couldn't see to grasp anything else. There was no further real danger, because the greatest danger was over, could never happen again.

"Somebody else could get hurt," he stammered, still knowing that he couldn't tell her what was supposed to happen to Suzie if he didn't obey that man on the phone.

"We have been hurt," she answered, "in such a way that we can laugh at any further dangers." She waited as if hoping that he would say yes, he understood, but he sat mute, frozen with the new awful feeling of helplessness. "So if any creature calls you on the phone, tell him that. Or tell *her* that. And then laugh; somehow manage to laugh. And then hang up."

She got out of her chair and brought out the cookie crock, the old brown crock shaped like a fat man, whose head came off for the lid. It was years and years old. His father had eaten cookies out of it when he had been a kid, so it must be about a hundred, Davie remembered. The cookies in it were store-bought now, not fresh and full of crunchy surprises the way they used to be, but Davie took one and thanked her for it and tried to choke it down his dry, tormented throat.

He had better go hang around his dad and see, or try to see, what his dad did with his keys.

He stood up, holding the last softening part of the cookie, and his grandmother came close, and then without warning she hugged him. She hugged him with such broken loneliness that he wanted to cry. The cookie vanished into fragments toward the floor.

His dad was in the den with Mr. Ralston, so Davie headed for his parents' bedroom to see if the keys were there. The door of the room was open, no lights on, but he could see his mother in the dressing room beyond. It was brilliantly lighted. The top half of one wall was mirrored, with a marble counter below and a pink velvet stool, and the counter was crowded with bottles of perfume, creams, lotions, and foaming bath powders, and his mother was there, still dressed in the suit she had worn to town. She was holding an enormous bouquet of paper flowers in a vase, and she was trying them in various locations on the counter. The flowers were red and orange. They threw reddish reflections into his mother's face and made a great flamelike dazzle in the mirror.

He remembered then—his mother hadn't eaten dinner with the rest of them. This was happening kind of often lately. Had that been the reason his grandmother had smiled at him, had seemed more friendly and less absentminded? His mother had rushed in from shopping and had said she had things to do and had drunk a cup of coffee standing up, looking at them through the dining-room door.

In the dressing room she wasn't aware of Davie at all, didn't notice him while he circled the wide bed, under its plum-colored quilted spread, and the chaise, all silver brocade with a couple of dresses flung down on it now, fresh from their boxes, tags still trailing from them. She didn't see him until he stood in the lighted doorway. When some movement caught her eye, she gave a start and turned quickly, frowning. "Davie! Well, what do you want?"

He searched with some hope of patience, willingness to listen, the end of the kind of frenzy she lived through these days, but her face was smooth and had nothing in it but the frown, not even any real surprise or displeasure. It was as if his mother didn't allow herself to come to the surface anymore. The hurry and the busy, busy ways concealed her.

Davie put his hands in his pockets, hesitating, wishing he hadn't come here. "Why didn't you eat dinner with us?" he blurted, surprising himself.

"Why didn't—" She bent one of the flower stems so that the paper blossom hung at an angle. "Isn't that an impertinent question, David?"

"You'd ask me if I didn't," he said, skidding off toward some point of danger he only half realized. "You'd make me eat."

"I am an adult," she said coldly.

"It's as if you don't want us around anymore. You don't want to be near us."

"You're being ridiculous, as well as impudent. Please go, until you feel in a better humor."

He stood mute, willing her to look at him, not with this new brisk unmoved way of hers, but with that soft searching glance she used to have. It used to make you glad, he thought, when she looked at you that way, because it seemed that she was summing up everything she saw and that maybe it wasn't all perfect but that she loved you very much anyway. And in those days he could tell his mother anything. There were no secrets, there was nothing in the world you couldn't take to her for explaining or for comforting.

She had the big paper bouquet in a corner of the mirrored wall now. She pushed some of the fancy bottles together and then picked them up and shoved them into a cabinet below. She arranged the remaining bottles in bunches, and Davie saw that she was trying for some effect, something she already had in mind, and that this effect was going to transform the little dressing room so that it would look as if someone very, very stylish used it.

Davie turned to go.

"Wait a minute." She looked with narrowed eyes at the paper flowers, the groups of bottles. Then she came out of the dressing room and turned on a lamp beside the chaise. "What did you come for, David?"

"I don't know."

"There's no problem about school opening, is there? Clothes all bought? Supplies?"

"I've got everything."

"Well, then, what is it?"

The way she stood, as if pausing between things that were important, and the expression on her face, the look of haste and annoyance, brought the words out of him. His voice was angry and uneven, but the words were plain enough. "What would you do if somebody—someone you don't even know—kept calling up and saying that something bad was going to happen?"

"Going to happen where?"

"Here. To—to one of us."

The annoyed look softened into thought. "Do you mean that someone is actually doing this? Is calling and making threats?"

What had the voice said? . . . *don't be putting words in my mouth.* "Not threats, not exactly. It's more like telling a story. A thing could happen. Not that it *has* to happen, you see."

"If anyone is trying to play tricks on you over the phone, David, you can just hang up the moment you hear the voice."

He wanted to say, "I'm afraid. If I hang up, it could happen to Suzie." But then his mother would want to know what might happen to Suzie, and he wouldn't be able to tell her.

"Just remember," she concluded, her tone final, "that you don't have to listen to anything you don't want to hear."

He clenched his hands in frustration. He felt hot and tired, and tension was like a red wire drawn from his brain down through all the nerves of his body. The flowers in the mirror swam in a mist, and his mother's figure wavered.

She bent and picked up one of the dresses on the chaise and began to strip it of tags. He turned toward the door.

He rapped softly at the door of the den, then turned the knob and went in. Mr. Ralston and his dad were at the desk, papers were spread out, and the room smelled of Mr. Ralston's cigar. Neither his dad nor Mr. Ralston looked around when he came in. Mr. Ralston's teeth were clamped on the cigar, and there were two spots of color, kind of angry color, in his dad's face.

Davie said, "I'll just be a minute. I want to look for a book," and crossed to the bookcases that lined the far wall. It was the family library, a cheerful unplanned mixture of school reference works, book club fiction, adolescent mystery and horse stories, Dickens and Shakespeare and Stevenson, along with some of Stoddard's old lawbooks. Davie stopped in front of the section nearest the desk and took a quick glance over there; the silence was peculiar and seemed to have dropped the moment he rapped, though the rapping couldn't have had anything to do with it. It was as if the two men had run out of words.

They weren't paying any attention to him, but they weren't going to continue the conversation until he was out of the way.

There were no keys around that he could see. If the keys were on the desk, they were under all those papers. Perhaps his dad had the keys in his pocket. Or maybe he kept them in a drawer of the desk. Davie had no idea where his dad habitually kept his keys or how many there were.

Thomas Stoddard cleared his throat. "Get your book and go, Davie. We're busy right now."

From somewhere came the crazy inspiration; he got the words out breathlessly. "Did you lose your keys, Dad?"

His father frowned. "No, of course not."

"Are you sure? Are you real sure you didn't lose them?"

His father glanced sharply at him. He didn't examine the inside of a desk drawer, nor did he pat any of his pockets. Mr. Ralston took the cigar out of his teeth and tapped the ashes off with meticulous boredom.

"If you've found any keys, Davie, check with your mother or with Vicky."

"How do you know you haven't lost them?"

"Because I know where my keys are," said Thomas Stoddard firmly.

4

He went wearily back to the Family Area. Vicky was alone now, staring dreamily into nowhere, the stuff she'd been reading lying in her lap. She looked awfully pretty, Davie realized; she looked grown up, completed, softly shining and clean, a lady. For a moment, with all the lonely lostness and fear that filled him, he was tempted to tell her about the phone calls. But then he thought of Suzie.

"Where's Suzie?"

"I guess she went to bed," Vicky said, as if noticing all at once that Suzie wasn't here.

"Are you sure she went to bed? She didn't go outdoors or anything, did she?"

"Why would she go outdoors?" Vicky rose, covering a yawn.

"I—I don't know."

He went to his room, went in, and shut the door without turning on the lights. Across the room the windows faced the back of the property. The glow of a city on the other side of the broken hills made the sky light enough so that he could see the paleness of the white fence, dark clumps that were shrubs and trees, and even the slash of the barranca. He went there to lean on the windowsill, smelling the night smell from the hills, a combination of dusty sage, dried earth still giving off the long heat of the sun, and something that seemed a ghost of empty distance. Time ticked by, a long somber time.

"I've got to find the keys," he whispered to himself.

But how?

Maybe, in the middle of the night, he could get up—

There was a sound from outside, from the yard, a sound that began as a kind of wooden knocking and died to a whisper, a whisper that dragged itself through leaves or sand. Davie dropped instantly, hugging the carpeted floor beneath the window, breath stopped and pulse pounding. At any other time, his flying thoughts reminded, he would have thought of a possum or woods rat, or even the big old jack, pulling a leaf off a shrub, the shrub rebounding with the knocking noise—but now everything was terror, chilling him with what might lie in wait.

Nothing came to scratch at the wall, at the open window whose screen let in the sounds and smells of the night. After a couple of minutes, Davie got to his feet, still bent low, and got over behind the draperies and peered out. There was nothing new that he could see. The dark blobs of shrubbery, the pale fence, the glow of the sky were exactly as they'd been before.

It could be Suzie . . .

A fierceness, a hotness and rebellion beat through him, and he reached into the closet for his baseball bat. He left the room and stole through the house, all the way to the back entry. He unlocked the door and went outside. It was much cooler out here, the wind icing the sweat on his face and throat; he slipped along the rear of the house and then stood still and listened.

The bat trembled in his hands.

Suzie, if it's you, you'll be sorry— Hatred made a burning wetness in his mouth, shook down through his arms to his trembling hands. *Oh, Suzie, Suzie . . . how could you? How could you come out in the dark when that—that thing is waiting for you?*

He threw away the bat and turned to the wall and sheltered his weeping eyes.

Nobody was out here. His fright and his guilt had tricked him. An animal, the lonely old jack perhaps, had been searching for something to eat.

And leaning on the wall, hating himself, Davie could see how the twisted ugliness of the words he'd heard on the phone had boiled up into this strange hatred for Suzie, this blaming of her, so that the anger turned not toward the unknown tormentor but toward his sister, whom he loved.

In her room Vicky moved away from the dressing table, where she had brushed her hair. At the bed she tugged down the pink silk spread from the pillows, evened it neatly in folds across the foot, and then drew down the blanket and sheet together. It made a neat and pretty bed, a bed all smooth for dreaming. Her eyes were already touched by dreams, and her lips held a wry and bemused smile. On the dressing table in its silver frame Jeff Norbert's photograph looked out, not smiling and yet not unsmiling, ironic with a "So what?" kind of expression.

Vicky brushed the soft hair back toward her neck and glanced at the photograph. "Good night, darling," she whispered. She clicked off the bedside lamp, and the room was dark. In the darkness Vicky said, "Good night and God bless you, Cootie."

Face up, pulling the smooth sheet over her breasts, she heard the noise from outside, a kind of rubbing and fumbling at the wall, and she thought of Mr. Warren's stupid horse, who liked to get out at night—Mr. Warren claimed the animal knew how to work the latches—and roam around sampling the shrubbery. But then she heard crying. A low, lost kind of crying. She lifted on an elbow, knowing all at once that the one outside was Davie. She was reaching for the bedside lamp, but stopped and slid out of bed instead.

How stupid I've been. There's been something wrong about Davie for days. For a week. He's been—a succession of images, fragments of encounters, glimpses, rushed through her mind as she groped for words to complete the thought—*he's been* afraid.

She went to the window. The pane was open, but the curtains had been drawn. She pulled them aside. The crying had stopped, but she sensed a presence out there, someone standing close.

"Davie?"

There was a brief sound as if he had moved with a start.

"Davie, is that you?"

"Yeah," he said hoarsely

"What are you doing out there?"

"I thought I heard . . . uh . . . something."

"Mr. Warren's horse?"

"Nothing's here."

"Come inside. Come to my room. I want to talk to you," Vicky said.

"It's nothing," he insisted. "I just imagined a noise."

"No, come on in."

She thought: *He's been crying and he won't want me to see.* She switched on a light in the bathroom that reflected only dimly into the room when the door was almost shut. After a couple of minutes, Davie came in, and she noted that he was dressed; he hadn't gone to bed yet. "Did you go outside right after I talked to you?"

"No. I was in my room when I heard it." He sat down gingerly on the bench to her dressing table; Vicky sat on the side of the bed.

"What sort of noise was it?"

"I don't know."

"You thought it was someone . . . a person. Didn't you?"

He stared back in such frozen fear that in spite of the dimness, the carefully shielded light, she saw the change in him.

"A person," she repeated. "Who, Davie?"

"I don't know," he stammered.

"Is somebody giving you a rough time?" she asked, trying to think of any recent quarrels, fallen-away pals, disruption of the clique—if he had a clique. And suddenly she realized that she knew nothing of Davie's world. Yes, they'd spent hours together in the big stores, choosing clothes and supplies for the coming school year. But she hadn't really looked at Davie, not to see him, she thought with a self-accusing fear. She hadn't really been thinking or noticing Davie at all, because behind everything she did now was this shiningness, this wonderful promise and preview of happiness. Of her happiness with Jeff Norbert.

And that's how it had been with Cootie, her accusing thoughts ran on. *You didn't have time for Cootie because the end of high school had been such a whirl . . . and then Cootie had been dead.*

And you had hardly even seen him.

Her hands were clenched hard enough to ache, in the lap of her fragile gown. *I won't let it happen again. I won't be too deliriously wrapped up to see somebody. Like my brother, here.* "Tell me all of it," she commanded. "Tell me what you have on your mind. And we'll figure out exactly what to do." *We'll give a party,* she thought, *and we won't invite the creeps.*

He hesitated, as if her suddenly firm and commanding tone had scared him. But, then, what he said in answer was so far from what she had expected that it might as well have been in another language. He was rubbing his eyes, tiredly, and then he began, "I almost told you tonight. Earlier. I wanted to say, somebody called up. The man called up tonight, and he called a week ago. He doesn't say who he is . . . just that something awful is going to happen to . . . happen to"— Vicky saw how hard it was for him to get the name out, and then she thought: *It's my name.* But he caught his breath and went on—"happen to Suzie. A bad thing, and don't ask what it is, Vicky, because I can't tell you. He told me, and he described what would happen to Suzie and what it would do to her . . . remembering—"

"I see, Davie," she cut in, aware of his rising anguish.

"And if I do what he says—"

"What's that?"

But then this, strangest of all, was the end of what he had to tell. He looked at her mutely across the shadowy space, and she thought how much older he seemed. He was like somebody in his teens, facing the world, trying to find an answer for a problem leading to adulthood.

"What are you supposed to do?" she demanded.

"I can't tell you."

She tried to imagine what it might be, and then her thoughts flew back to a single word. "You say it's a *man,* Davie?"

"Yes, I'm sure. And somebody we know—*I* know—somebody I've heard before—"

"Who?"

The silence hung between them, something light and gossamer and ready to shatter at a word, at a name.

"Who, Davie?" Vicky repeated, a sense of dread filling her.

"I don't know. I made a mistake, I told him—'I've heard you, I know your voice'—and he didn't like it. He told me I'd better quit thinking about it."

"He's called you twice?"

"Yes."

"Did he give you a deadline, a date, you have to do this thing for him by a certain—"

"No." Davie slumped on the bench, his arms hanging tiredly between his knees, hands clasped, the knuckles bony and big with promise of the growth to come. "I have to get ready, that's all. That's all for now."

"Get ready . . . doing what?"

"I'm scared to tell you. You'll go to—to Mom or Dad."

"No, I won't. I promise I won't," she cried. "You can't handle this alone. Can't you see that? This is why he called *you,* and nobody else. You're the youngest here, the most defenseless, the one he can frighten—"

"He'd frighten anybody," Davie said.

"Please tell me what he wants you to do."

"I'll have to think about it." Davie got up off the bench and went over to the door, quickly, as if he had to hurry before he spilled all of it. He didn't look at Vicky before he went out; he seemed to be staring into some future of cruelty and despair.

She remained sitting on the side of the bed. The sounds made by Davie in the hall whispered away, and there was silence. Night air was seeping into the room from beyond the curtains; there was a feeling of strangeness, the scent of the out-of-doors.

Vicky tried to rub away the feeling of goose bumps on her arms.

She looked around in the dimness. This had once been a place completely safe and protected. Nothing ugly or threatening could enter here. That sense of safety had been upset for a while when Cootie had died, cut by falling shards of glass, and then again, but more briefly, when her grandmother had been hurt. Then the feeling of security had built itself up again. Now in being destroyed, it was taking everything, all warmth and trust. There was great danger; it breathed through the house like the night wind.

She went to the closet for a robe. Standing there, the pencil-thin glow from the bathroom falling on her cheek and down the shoulder of the thin gown, she stopped to think. Davie said he had to spend the time *getting ready*. How do you get ready to obey an anonymous threat over the phone? What do you do, say, arrange?

She put on the robe, tied the silk belt slowly.

My room feels cold, full of menace, hateful. I've got to see how the rest of the house feels.

She went out into the hall. There was no trace of light under any of the bedroom doors. She went past her parents' bedroom, turned right, passed the louvered doors of linen closets and other storage places, turned left, and came to the front entry of the house. The front door was flanked by ornamental glass panels, thick and heavily frosted and etched, which let in enough light from outside, dim as it was, for her to make out the expanse of flagstone paving and the big boxes of tropical greenery, fernlike and black against the white walls.

It was empty, quiet, smelling only of moss and dampness and planter mix. She continued to the door of the living room. The big room stretched away in darkness. She touched a light switch, and a couple of lamps came on. It was a subdued room, a formal room, with gray velvet carpeting and pale-blue couches and chairs. The scattered occasional tables were white and gold. The lamps matched them. This was not a place where the family spent any time. When they had first moved here, her parents had entertained quite a bit, mostly old friends that Thomas Stoddard had made over the years through his law practice. Then they used the room, and with all the lamps lit and with flowers—pink roses and blue delphinium—it had looked quite impressive. *Expensive, too*, she thought. *And perhaps this man who's calling Davie now, perhaps he was one my parents entertained here, and he got the idea Dad might have a lot of money.*

It must be money he's after, she decided, switching off the lamps and pausing there in the dark. *If he were really some kind of sex freak, if he really meant to do this to Suzie, this thing that makes Davie look sick to think about, he wouldn't warn us.*

"It's money," she whispered to herself. "And so, how does Davie help him by getting ready? Is Davie supposed to open the door some night? But that takes no getting ready at all."

There was a night-light in the kitchen to guide any hungry ones who searched for a snack and to save barked shins or spilled milk. It was plugged into the baseboard near the refrigerator, and since it was almost at the floor, it cast shadows upward, made shadowy angles on the ceiling, and distorted the shapes of cupboards and range.

Vicky looked at the phone on the wall above her mother's desk. She could call Jeff, ask him to come over. Davie might listen to him, might even tell him what the getting ready consisted of. She put a hand on the phone, hesitated for a moment, then lifted the receiver. To her astonished disbelief there were voices on it. She took the phone from her ear to stare at it. She felt as if she had picked up some inanimate thing, a kitchen tool, for instance, and found it coming to life in her hand. And this was silly, because voices were what a phone was for. . . .

She recognized her father's voice at once. She hadn't passed the door of his den on her walk tonight; it was in a cul-de-sac beyond the bedrooms. He must still be up, still working in there. The other voice was that of Mr. Ralston. She wrinkled her nose. Mr. Ralston, the promoter and would-be land baron who had been here earlier, and he sounded harsh and offensive.

She didn't catch Mr. Ralston's remark but caught what her father said in reply. "And even if I knew I couldn't tell you. You know that Whitney has been our client—Mr. Bowman's client— for years." Mr. Bowman was the founder of the law firm of which Stoddard was a partner. "I couldn't betray a confidence."

"You can just give me an idea of what the old man would consider a fair bid. And how well he's satisfied with what Jemmerson and Marks are offering. That's not much. For God's sake, I've been *your* client for a long time, and this is the first time I've asked you for anything like this!"

"I'm sorry," her father said wearily. "I hate to turn you down, but this time I just have to."

5

There was silence from Mr. Ralston. When he spoke again, he seemed to be making an effort to be calm. "Well, I shouldn't have called you, Tom. You gave me the word there in the den tonight. I should have accepted it as final. No hard feelings, huh?"

"No, Vince, of course not." Her father sounded tired, relieved. *He must be thinking of going to bed by now,* Vicky thought, *and glad to have done with Mr. Ralston.* She hung up the phone softly. *What a sneak I am . . .*

And then she thought: *Before Davie came tonight, I would never have snooped on the phone. But I'm glad I did.*

There was something new to think about. Her father had things of value . . . not money. As an attorney he must be in on many private affairs, secrets—secrets that could be important to others if they could just find them out. Was Davie's tormentor someone who needed to know a secret? And how could Davie go about getting ready to help? This was a secret *she* needed to know!

She poured a glass half full of milk and went into the Family Area and curled on a couch. Heavy draperies closed out the view of the yard and the edge of the pool that were visible through the glass doors. She sipped at the milk and tried to unravel Davie's secret. She remembered that she'd wanted to call Jeff, but now the thought of sharing anything before she did some more mental picking seemed a little unwise.

Her father had a desk in the den, but she wasn't sure whether he kept it locked. The door was never locked. Would he keep highly confidential papers here at home? Somehow she thought not. True, Mr. Ralston and a few others came to see her father here at the house, in the evenings, but these were men whose businesses kept them on the go during the day—like Mr. Ralston, who roamed the hinterlands searching for acreage to turn into shopping centers.

If her father kept papers here, what would they be?

Could she hint around, ask questions, without making her father suspicious and in the end betraying Davie's story?

Or should it be told at once, what she knew of it, and the rest forced out of Davie?

Davie would never forgive her . . . never share a secret with her again. She rubbed her head, wondering what to do.

Someone was in the kitchen—

She swiveled quickly, gripped by an instant of fear, but it was her grandmother who had entered the room without a sound and was now opening a cupboard. In the shadows Vicky saw her take down a bottle—aspirin, Vicky thought—and cross the kitchen with it to the sink. Vicky was stunned to see what a limping, crippled gait her grandmother had. She didn't walk like this around the family.

And what an effort that must take.

Her grandmother leaned on the edge of the sink, drinking down the aspirin and water. Her white hair was pulled back gracelessly, braided at the neck. She wore a robe over her gown, a blue robe faded with wear and washing. She took the glass from her lips to cough.

Vicky leaned forward, frowning. This old, coughing, crippled woman was someone she didn't know, a stranger. *And when,* Vicky asked herself, *did I quit looking at* her?

"Gran . . ."

Mrs. Stoddard jumped, turned fearfully. Her hand faltered, holding the glass; she set it down on the tiled sink with a cracking noise. "Who is it? Oh . . . Vicky. I didn't know that anyone was here—" She pulled the robe over her bosom, wrapped her arms tight as if to make herself shrink small.

"Gran, do you feel like talking for a few minutes?"

Her grandmother looked so uncertain then, kind of disbelieving—and Vicky thought: *Has it been so long since we paid any attention, since we asked her, and* listened? The moment of insight hurt.

"Talk?" Mrs. Stoddard echoed. She moved then, coming into the big dark room and sitting down in a chair that faced the couch. "Of course. We can talk."

How to begin? Vicky decided to plunge in, get it said. "Have you noticed how nervous and worried Davie seems? As if he had something on his mind—"

"Oh, yes." Mrs. Stoddard nodded. "He came to me about it."

Davie hadn't said a word about this. "He told you about the phone calls?"

"Yes, and I told him what to do. How to cut them off."

"What did you tell him?" It hadn't been an answer, Vicky sensed; it hadn't helped Davie.

"I told him to laugh into the phone and to hang up."

"Laugh?"

Her grandmother moistened her lips nervously. "Of course. And above all, not to act as if it mattered or as if you cared. I explained to Davie what was behind it, someone who was mean and who enjoyed the unhappiness of others and who was afraid that we might be forgetting our grief. And not blaming ourselves—"

Vicky didn't get the connection, though her grandmother seemed to expect an instant understanding. "I don't seem to catch what you mean—"

"These phone calls, according to Davie, kind of hint around—"

Cootie, Vicky thought, wondering why she hadn't grasped it before. Her grandmother, wrapped up in never-ending self-blame, tied every threat, any promise of sorrow, to what had happened that afternoon when Cootie had died.

"Suggesting that we could have further trouble. More heartbreak." Mrs. Stoddard's voice trembled and grew hoarse. "Isn't this what Davie told you? You *have* talked to him, haven't you?"

"Yes, and he told me about the calls. But I don't think the motive is just to torment us, Gran. Davie is supposed to do something, a favor, a bribe, to keep this from happening to Suzie."

It was her grandmother's turn to be baffled. "To Suzie?"

"Something so bad he can't tell me about it."

"And what's he to do, to keep it from happening?"

"He won't tell me."

Her grandmother started to rise. "Well, let's go to Thomas. He'll get the story quick enough."

"No, Gran—please wait! No one is going to get this out of Davie. He's too terrified—"

Her grandmother hesitated, then sat down again slowly. "It must be a trick of some kind. Something mean cooked up by some boy who's mad at him. Either that or—or Davie's misunderstanding it. He's seeing things in it that aren't there."

Vicky considered briefly. True, Davie had a lot of imagination. His teachers had commented on his originality in composition, storytelling, and dramatization. But then she remembered the sobbing sound from outdoors, the crying when Davie had thought no one could hear. She opened her lips to say, "No, Gran —Davie received two phone calls that frightened him almost out of his wits. Certain things could happen to Suzie, dreadful things —and to keep them from happening, he had to do something, some favor, in return."

But looking across at her grandmother, Vicky never said these things. Her grandmother looked small and frail; the shock and grief of Cootie's dying had changed her, made her old almost beyond belief. It was wrong to add to her burden.

"I'll talk to Davie again in the morning," Vicky told her. "I'll find out exactly what this is all about."

Her grandmother nodded in relief, her tired eyes brightening. "Yes, be sure to do that. And we can always talk to Thomas if we have to." She got up, bracing herself on the arm of the chair, drew a deep breath as if pulling on some reserve of courage. She walked into the kitchen almost without a limp at all.

She inspected the glass at the sink and, apparently finding it cracked, put it into the trash container below the sink. "Good night, Vicky."

"Good night, Gran dear."

When her grandmother had gone, Vicky returned to the other part of the house, pausing in the hall outside Suzie's door. She listened there; everything was silent. Softly she opened the door and went in. The bedroom draperies were pulled wide, exposing the windows. One pane had been drawn back, and through the screen came the clean smell of the night. There was enough of the faint light so that Vicky could make out Suzie's shape on the bed, curled into a lump. Standing still, she could hear the even breathing.

Tomorrow she must warn Suzie. She went out, shutting the door, trying to figure out what she must say. How could she tell Suzie that someone wanted to hurt her, that a terrible danger existed, without almost doing as much harm as the thing happening? To Suzie now the world was a great big wonderful circus, full of mad music and a new school year and new clothes and old friends. Along with, of course, boys whom she must study and size up and discuss with other girls because before too long there would be the exciting world of dating. It was all glorious, the beginning of being almost grown up, and it had to be smirched and dirtied and made small.

"I feel sick," Vicky whispered in the silence.

In the morning she would call Jeff before doing anything else.

He came right away. The morning fog lay in ragged patches along the flanks of the hills, and the eucalyptus dripped. The big, rakish black car swung into the driveway.

Vicky had risen early. She noted that Suzie was busy in her room, sorting out the contents of a closet, and that Davie took some buttered toast and a can of peaches and headed for the barranca. He avoided her, didn't speak or look at her, and she respected his silence. He was trying to forget the unforgettable, and a sudden red lash of hate flared in her, that someone had chosen Davie for the part he was supposed to play.

She put on pink Bermuda shorts and a sleeveless sweater and went out to wait beside the pool. She could see the driveway from here, where it curved up from the street to the front of the house.

When the black car appeared, she quickly got up off the poolside bench and went out to meet Jeff. He was getting out of the driver's side, unfolding rather; when he stood beside the car like this, he made it look lower than ever, distortedly so. His blond hair looked damp, as if from the fog; there even seemed to be faint droplets in his short, clipped beard. He was quite tanned, and his blue eyes squinted down at her, looking bluer because he was so dark. His hand felt warm and rough on hers. "Hello, wild one," he said. He bent and brushed her lips with his.

"Jeff . . ." She put her arms around him, and he enfolded her, and all at once there was all this warmth and safety and the feeling that everything must be all right in the world, that things like what had happened to Cootie, and was happening to Davie, didn't really exist.

"Always call me early like this," Jeff said into her hair, bending because he was so tall. "I'm at my best, my very best. I can positively do anything. I can even balance mixed-up checking accounts—"

"I don't have one. Only savings, and only what Grandpa left me. Come and sit down. Or—no, wait. Let's drive a little."

"The woman is impetuous. We'll have to be careful; it's daylight. Any passionate lovemaking will have to be—" He stopped and put a hand under her chin, chewed his upper lip with his teeth. "Wait a minute. You're serious. You're very serious, and it's taken all this time to register." In mock disgust he hit his forehead with his free hand.

"We must talk a little," she answered, hating to lose that sense of warmth and protection. "It's about something that's . . . that's happening."

He stood quite still. "You've made up your mind?"

"No. It's not about us at all."

"Oh."

She pulled him by the hand toward the car. Then the idea came —he might tell her they must go to the police; the police were the logical ones to take it all over—and then memory flooded back over the wall she had built against it, the intrusion that had come on the heels of the police that other time, the hateful milling and watching and trampling of the mob that had descended after Cootie's death.

No, he mustn't say, "Bring the police." The police must never come here again.

Bitter, bitter. She remembered her grandmother seated in the room where the big glass doors had been replaced with plywood, a patch job done by her father. Her grandmother had been there with two detectives, big, patient, hard-eyed men, who had taken her over and over the details of what had happened when Cootie had died, and one of them had kept saying, "Now, Mrs. Stoddard, will you describe this figure again? The figure you saw outside, in the twilight. Would you say that the figure was in motion? Lifting its arms? *Beckoning,* maybe?" And when Mrs. Stoddard had made some weak effort at an answer, he'd broken in again. "Lifting a hand, say, like this?" and had looked ridiculous, had made the story foolish and improbable, by the way he'd put up his arm, the coat sleeve pulling down into wrinkles, and crooked a finger toward those ominous doors.

Her grandmother had looked around with sick eyes, searching for escape. But there had been no escape. The detectives had questioned her for a long time, and then again the next day, and the next, and her grandmother's voice had gradually died into whispers and then to silence. And the story of the figure outside had split into tatters and blown away.

That's what the police would do to Davie.

"You—" Jeff said, shutting the car door beside her. "Those aren't tears? Not real tears?"

"Yes."

He looked at her with perplexity and then said, "We'll drive into town and have coffee somewhere. And find out where those tears are coming from."

The big car rushed backward out of the driveway, turned, and began to wind down off the heights. The patchy fog blew past, frosted the windshield, and dampened her hair, and she tasted it along with the salt taste of the tears.

In the back booth of the little café she told Jeff about the phone calls. She tried to keep calm, keep her voice under control, not seem hysterical.

He interrupted her before she had finished. "This isn't what you're crying about?"

"But it is!" *Don't say that we must call the police,* she thought. He shook his head. "But it's— What does it amount to?"

"Don't you see, Jeff, he's playing on everything that has gone before—banking on it, figuring he has us all in a corner where we can't make a move?"

"Yes, that's right," he agreed slowly. "Go on. Who else knows about it? Your dad?"

"No, Dad doesn't know." She finished the story. "The mystery is what he expects Davie to do. And how Davie is to get ready to do it. I thought right away of—of opening a house door at night or of leaving one unlocked, a burglary. But there's nothing in the house worth the trouble, really. Furniture. Dad doesn't keep cash there that comes to any real amount. And that kind of thing wouldn't require any getting ready. Whatever the man wants is more complicated. And uglier."

Jeff sat quiet. Then he said, "You'll have to keep Davie away from the phone. I don't think anything's going to happen. The threats against Suzie are just a bluff. And don't cry anymore over it, darling. I can't stand to see those tears."

6

Davie saw the paper right away. It was white, type-writer size. There was typing on it, and it was fastened to a dried bush under the bank near his little stone fireplace, by having a twig thrust through the top edge.

He put down the can of peaches and balanced the buttered toast on it carefully, took a blanket off the top of the laundry basket, and spread it on the ground, and all the time he could see the paper out of the corner of his eye.

There was a damp-sage smell in the air, stuff wetted by the fog, and even here down in the barranca the earth had been dampened a little, so that laying the blanket didn't rouse the dust. But Davie brushed the blanket with his hands and straightened the corners meticulously. Then he moved the peaches and toast onto the blanket and rummaged in the laundry basket for the can opener. He wasn't going to look at that paper. He wasn't going to touch it, or read it, or anything.

He ate two peach halves and half a piece of toast. Then he wiped his fingers on his jeans and crawled over to the bush and yanked the paper free, tearing it.

> Hello, Davie
>
> No more phone calls, okay?
>
> I think I'll need the keys about three nights from now. Friday. And I'll need them for a couple of hours, no more. Nothing hard about that now, is there?
>
> It gives you plenty of time, too.
>
> Maybe the best way would be for you to lay the keys on the top rail of the gate, the gate that you open to come up here. The back gate. At ten o'clock at night. Or as near to ten as you can make it, Friday.
>
> I'll be waiting, but you mustn't hang around or try to see me. That would be very, very bad for your sister.
>
> If there's any reason you can't do this on Friday, family plans or anything, tear off a bottom corner of this note and hang it back where it was. Be sure it's a corner small enough so there's no part of this message on it.
>
> Now—the last and very important thing. Burn this paper in your little stone stove and leave the ashes just as they are. I can tell by the ashes whether you've done this last, most important thing.
>
> MR. KEYS

Davie read the thing twice. The signature—the typed name at the bottom—was not funny. It was a kind of joke that was an insult, Davie knew.

He was looking for the matches in the laundry basket, turning over the pans and canned stuff, when he heard a crashing and crackling below from the mouth of the barranca. Then came hoof-beats and the snorting of the horse. He thought at once of Suzie. But the rage, the fury at her innocence and her not-caringness, didn't come. He'd grown up a little, he realized with new insight; at least he'd grown up enough so that he didn't blame Suzie for what might happen to her. For being a girl with a body that could be hurt—

He stood up, at the same time folding the paper without thinking about it and stuffing it into the back pocket of the jeans.

The person on the horse wasn't Suzie; it was Mr. Warren himself. The big old gray horse picked and swayed his way up the barranca, and the man's tall figure towered in the hazy light. Mr. Warren was a lean, sunburned man, all sinew and leathery skin, about fifty, who looked like a cowboy to Davie. There were a lot of wrinkles around his eyes, and he had a hawk's nose. He wore a wide-brimmed hat, jeans, a faded shirt. His legs fitted around the gelding as if they'd been molded there. He had on worn Spanish boots, the kind with a lot of decoration worked into the leather. No spurs. He wouldn't let a spur touch the gelding. He rode with one gloved hand on the pommel, the reins tucked under his thumb, and the other working a twig between his teeth. It was hard to remember, seeing Mr. Warren, that his family had owned this whole valley and hillside, and still owned all this range of hills, miles and miles of it with perhaps oil down below, and had only recently sold off parts of the valley, where blocks of big homes were beginning to appear among the miles of orange groves.

It was hard to think of Mr. Warren as a millionaire, which he was, according to Davie's dad.

"Well, there, hiya," Mr. Warren said, pulling up the horse. He loosened a toe from a stirrup and rubbed his leg against the edge of the saddle as if to relieve an itch or a cramp.

"You keep a mighty neat camp here," he went on, looking everything over. "I like your stone fireplace. Shows you've got sense and don't build fires out where brush could catch. Brush is dry as old bones right now, been so long since we had rain. Ever sleep up here?"

"No, not yet," Davie said. He was well aware that he was trespassing here in the barranca; his dad had outlined the boundaries when they had moved up here a long time ago. But Mr. Warren had ridden this way before—in fact, he had come by when Davie was first fixing the little camp—and he made it plain that Davie was welcome. "I might, before it starts to get real cold at night."

"You do that," Mr. Warren told him. "I used to sleep out when I was about your age. Had an old sleeping bag. Had a short-legged pony then, a pinto. He did guard duty. I'd stake him out, and then all through the night, when I'd wake up for a minute, the way you do when things are strange, I'd hear him chewing and scuffling around and yanking on the rope. Then I wasn't afraid."

Davie wondered how Mr. Warren had known he would be afraid. He'd thought of sleeping up here many times but thought he might get scared in the middle of the night and have to sneak back to the house, and then Suzie would say a few things to tease.

Mr. Warren looked up the rising cleft of the barranca. "Ever see any possums around? Ever see Old Jack?"

"The big jack with part of his ear gone?"

"That's the one. I heard some shooting—last year, it was. A punk kid up here with a twenty-two. I took his gun and run him off. He was real sore about it."

"Was it somebody who lived up here?"

"Nope. Never saw him before. But the next time I caught a glimpse of Old Jack, part of his ear was off. No sense in using a nice old rabbit like Jack for target practice. You want target practice, get you some beer cans." Mr. Warren probed with the twig. "Well, might as well mosey. I like to keep an eye on things."

"Can I ride your horse someday, Mr. Warren?"

Mr. Warren seemed surprised. "Why, sure—that's what we talked about, didn't we? And you've earned a ride times over. Here, you get up. Just hold the reins easy, no tightness, no pulling, and he'll take you on up the barranca. Don't worry, he never bucks or acts up much. Oh, he might give a few crow hops if he sees a lizard. But that won't throw you."

All the time Mr. Warren was giving directions he was swinging a leg over, letting himself down out of the saddle. Davie's heart was thumping, and his throat felt dry with excitement. He gripped the pommel and, with Mr. Warren boosting him, found himself high, high up on what seemed a mountain of horseflesh. "G-gosh," he said, "I didn't know he'd be this tall—"

Mr. Warren laughed. "You'll get used to it. Now just go on up the barranca slow and easy, and pretty soon I'll give a whistle and he'll turn around and come back. Knows I've got a sugar cube." Mr. Warren patted the gray gelding on the rump, and the horse looked back and made a blowing, inquisitive noise through his big nose. Mr. Warren gave a sharp slap, and the gelding moved on up the narrow, brush-crowded trail.

It seemed to Davie a towering, skittish, heart-stopping way to travel. He hung onto the pommel with sweating hands, not forgetting to leave the reins loose. He wanted to look around, see how things appeared from this skyscraper angle, but found his attention riveted on the horse and where he was putting his feet and whether he was sticking to the trail and not suddenly going off to climb the cliffs that shut them in. There were unfamiliar noises, creakings and rattlings from the saddle, from the bit in the gray's mouth. Davie gripped with his knees until his legs ached.

Suddenly a bolt of pride brought color to his face. He was actually riding; he was on a horse, making it go, or at least it was *going*. Nobody had to tell him now how it felt to be on a horse; he knew. He knew how it felt to be miles up in the air and having to hang on, and though Mr. Warren hadn't shortened the stirrups for this short ride, by stretching on one side, he could get a toe in one stirrup and see how *that* felt, too.

The gray horse came out on a level patch where the brush had thinned. The sun was burning the last of the fog away, and on the sandy floor of the barranca Davie could see his shadow, his and the horse's together, and he waved a greeting. Then Mr. Warren whistled, far away it seemed, and the gelding's ears twitched as if something had tickled them. Deliberately but with a show of interest, too, the gray turned and headed back down the barranca.

Mr. Warren helped Davie down and then fished a sugar cube out of his shirt pocket and held it out on his palm for the gelding. "How was that?" he asked.

"It was wonderful. I mean, I sure liked it a lot," Davie said, wanting to be sure that Mr. Warren understood that he had remained calm and collected and in no danger of making a nuisance of himself by losing his balance and falling off and getting hurt. "He's sure easy to ride. I didn't have a bit of trouble. I never knew a horse could be as easy to ride as he is."

"Yep, the old boy is gentle and sensible, all right. Sensible is what counts. In people, as well as horses. Now, you, Davie— you're a sensible boy. You fixed your little fireplace so's no fire gets away from you. We wouldn't want the barranca burned out, that's for sure. So *sensible* means to watch matches and fires. Really, sensible just means doing what's expected of you. By your parents and other grown-ups. You do what's expected of you, Davie, and you'll get along fine."

"Yes, sir," Davie answered, looking at the big gray horse and wondering when he was going to get to ride him again.

Mr. Warren was back in the saddle in one angular hike of his long body. "Just keep doing what's expected," he repeated.

"Thanks a lot for letting me ride him."

"You're welcome." Mr. Warren pulled the glove back on his hand, and then he pushed his heels into the horse's flanks and moved off up the barranca, swaying and creaking, and finally out of sight.

Davie hurriedly put all his stuff back neatly into the basket. Carrying what was left of the toast and the can of peaches, he headed for home. He had to tell someone right away about the beautiful, scary, and important thing that had happened to him this morning.

Suzie, working on her closet, listened with such an air of indifference that he went looking for somebody else and wound up knocking on his grandmother's door. He could hear the vacuum cleaner running in there. When she came to the door, she was wearing an apron and had an old-fashioned dustcap on her head.

"Oh," she said, and smiled. "Come in. I'll turn off the vacuum. I'm about through anyway. Here, take this chair."

She seemed more cheerful, bustling, lighthearted than he could recall for a long while, almost the way she had been before Cootie had died. She wheeled the vacuum into a closet, took off the apron and cap, and got out the cookie jar.

Davie told her about riding the horse.

"Yes," she said, "that's always a great day for a youngster. I remember as if it was yesterday—we were visiting some people who had a country place. It was somewhere near Riverside. The man had an old black horse he plowed the orange groves with, a huge thing, and that day he let us take turns riding while he led the horse around the yard. And I felt as if I were a mile straight up in the air, and there was no saddle, just a blanket, and the horse's back felt as flat as a floor. There was nothing to hold to but the mane, and it seemed as slick as a piece of wire. I must have been"—she paused for a moment—"about eight years old. And I never forgot."

They ate the cookies companionably.

"When Mr. Warren whistled, the horse turned right around."

"Well trained," she said.

"Mr. Warren had a cube of sugar in his shirt pocket."

She smiled a little. "Yes, that helps."

"Would it hurt a horse—I mean, his teeth maybe—if you gave him too much sugar?"

"He could get colic. But it would take a lot. A sugar cube now and then keeps them happy. Or an apple."

Davie was making plans; he'd ask Mr. Warren to let him clean up in the stable, and he'd take some sugar and an apple, and the horse would learn to do things for him the way it did for Mr. Warren.

"Davie, you've got a hole in the knee of those pants. Take them off and let me stitch it up for you."

He looked down. There was a hole. The pants were almost new, too. His mother hardly noticed any more whether there were holes or not, so maybe he'd better get the pants mended while he could. He stood up and unsnapped the top above the zipper and then hesitated.

His grandmother got out of her chair and walked toward her bedroom. "Just hand them in through the door. My sewing machine's in the other room." She went through, leaving the door open a little. Davie unzipped and stepped out of the jeans. He had to take his shoes off, too, and he walked in his socks and his underpants to the door and held the pants through.

He went back to his chair, munched another cookie, and thought about Mr. Warren's horse. Maybe when Suzie was in a better mood, she'd give him some pointers. She could ride well, so well that Mr. Warren trusted her to go out alone with his horse. She could give him some lessons, and then Mr. Warren would let him go off anywhere he wanted, maybe for a whole morning, just riding across the hills out of sight of any houses or people at all, the way it had been in the days of the pioneers and the Indians.

He heard the sewing machine in the other room.

Maybe if he and Suzie got together and begged hard enough, their dad would get them a horse of their own. There was room for a corral and a shed out back, far enough from the house if you put them in the east corner. It wouldn't matter if the corral was small because he and Suzie would see that the horse got plenty of exercise outside.

He remembered then some discussion a long time ago; the pool had been put on the slope to the south of the house so that if anyone wanted to keep a horse, there would be room on the north side, toward the hills, the natural place to ride.

His grandmother's hand emerged through the partially opened door holding his pants. "Here you are, Davie. All fixed."

He put his pants and shoes on again quickly. His grandmother came out of the bedroom and sort of picked up a thing or two as if she were not thinking of what she was doing, and then she gave him a queer look. He thought that her mood had changed, too. She didn't have the bright-eyed humor anymore. He wondered, as he headed for the door, what had changed her so suddenly.

7

Vicky and Jeff walked toward the door of the restaurant, his hand tucked against the inner side of her elbow, warm, possessive. She waited while he paid the cashier; he took a bill from his wallet and put it on the counter with the deliberate way she knew so well, and the cashier flashed him a glance and a smile that didn't include Vicky. But Vicky was used to that, too. Women admired Jeff, and he seemed totally unaware of it, and of them, as if they didn't really exist for him.

Outside, he guided her toward the car in the parking lot. "You know Davie well enough, I guess, so that if something more happened you'd recognize the symptoms?"

"Yes, I'm sure I would, especially now."

"Since this thing—this plot or whatever it seems to be—is apparently in the waiting stage, the getting-ready stage, why not just keep quiet for a few days and see what happens?"

"There were the threats against Suzie," she reminded him. "If anything happened to her—"

"Oh, I doubt that there'll be anything from this mysterious caller except talk," Jeff answered. He opened the door, and she slid into the big leather seat. Jeff went around to the other side. "Kids imagine things, read things in that aren't there. Why didn't this man on the phone ask for your father or mother and really stir things up? He's not serious. It's a bluff, maybe even a kind of tasteless joke. Your grandmother's right, you know. Davie should just laugh and hang up."

"He's too scared to do it, I guess."

"Don't let it scare you, too."

She wanted to believe, to be reassured. She put her hand on Jeff's shoulder and leaned her cheek against it for a moment. "I'd better talk to him again today. He tried to keep out of sight this morning. He's sorry that he told me as much as he did."

"Sure he is. You know how kids are. By this morning he was over his scare." Jeff turned the key in the switch, and Vicky pulled away and fastened her seat belt. Jeff gripped the gear lever; they headed for the street. "Don't let Davie be the butt of a freak looking for kicks. Tell him to slam the receiver. And that'll be the end. You wait and see, I'm right."

They were pulling out of the fringes of town now and up the long straight street, bordered by old pepper trees and big old houses, that led to the cuplike valley which their homes overlooked. Jeff's people had been here longer than Vicky's; his father had bought the land from the Warrens more than ten years ago, and their house had been one of the first, across the valley from the Stoddard place and on a much gentler rise, with no hills behind them.

Jeff was the only child. When he had been small, his mother had been a semi-invalid, in and out of nursing homes. An aunt of his father's had run the house; she had died about the time Jeff's parents had moved up here. His father's business interests had always kept him on the move, most of the time between the coast and Chicago. When Jeff's mother's health had gradually improved, she had dabbled in art and sculpture. Her own gifts proving minor, she turned to collecting the works of others, to joining art societies and to helping at exhibits.

The car gathered speed smoothly. "Are you taking me back home?" Vicky asked.

"No. I want to talk some more. Not about Davie's spook. About us." He glanced over at Vicky. "You have been doing the thinking you promised to do—"

"Yes," she said softly, her eyes on the long avenue of trees.

"And what, then?"

"I still don't know."

"Your mother and dad putting on any pressure?"

"No, or at least not with words. When Mother thinks about it, when I try to talk to her about it, she seems upset. But it's briefly and not often. You know, ever since Cootie died, she's been on this thing with the house. The changes, the decorating."

"I know. What about your dad?"

"Dad's tired. His mind always seems to be somewhere else. I know he wants me to go to college, get a degree, especially now that junior college is out of the way. It's unfinished business. And he thinks twenty is too young to get married. But I guess his job takes too much out of him. He hasn't talked to me at all." For a moment she thought of telling Jeff about the overheard conversation with Mr. Ralston and then decided against it. It was something she hadn't been supposed to hear.

"And you, Vicky. You must have some inkling."

She turned to look at him. "I love you very much."

"It isn't money"—he stepped on the brake for a moment because of a dip in the road, then slowed, turned aside into the shade of a small group of eucalyptus trees, stopped. He took Vicky's left hand in his—"because we'll have plenty, I'm going to find a way to get around that trust Aunt Donna left. I'm going to talk to old Bowman this week. There has to be something I can do. A way to get hold of a chunk of it, a real bankroll—"

Vicky wasn't an attorney's child for nothing. "If Mr. Bowman drew up your aunt's will—"

"My dad's aunt. She practically raised me."

"Your dad's aunt then. If Mr. Bowman drew up her will, it won't be easy to break. And you should think, Jeff, you'll be doing something she didn't choose and perhaps wouldn't like. People have a right to leave money, property, anything they own, the way they want to. And maybe to your dad's aunt there were good reasons—"

He had released his seat belt and now leaned over her, to shut her lips with a kiss. She tried to pull free for a moment, to finish; she believed in what she was saying and wanted Jeff to see the truth of it. But he held her, and then she took fire from the kiss, her senses almost swimming. She surrendered, her arms around him.

When he let her go, he said mockingly, "Save the lawyer talk, darling. I know your dad must have brainwashed you long since. I'm glad the will was made and done long before he went into business with Bowman and I can't blame him for it. Not that Bowman would have let him handle it—Aunt Donna was a kind of pet of Bowman's, and in fact, I wouldn't be surprised if they'd been lovers once. Nights under the moon, scented with orange blossoms . . . forbidden passions and all of that. She was cute when she was young. I saw a picture of her."

Vicky had to smile. "You're always making up scandalous things about the most respectable people—"

"I saw old Bowman's picture once, too, somewhere, and he wasn't so bad, along about forty or so. If you want me to ask him about the affair, I'll do it when I go in to demand my fifty thousand."

"We don't need anything like that!"

"Of course we do. We'll have a honeymoon and I've got to finish school. You're too cute to need a degree, but that doesn't apply to me. I can't hypnotize people with my looks."

They were close, leaning together, and again Vicky was filled with the wonderful feeling of shelter and protection, the sense of Jeff standing between her and the ugly things of the world. "Do I hypnotize you, darling?"

His tone was suddenly serious. "I don't know of any other way to describe it. You are my only reality, Vicky. You're the only one who isn't a shadow. A paper doll. Something to blow away in the wind. I was all in a fog when I found you—"

This time she pulled his mouth against her own. Of course, they'd be married. Who needed the University of Arizona, and being all those miles from Jeff, and living in a sorority house, and keeping your love life nourished with hasty phone calls and meager letters from a busy man at Cal Tech? Who needed silent desert days, and hot books, and droning English professors stuffed with Shakespeare? And loneliness?

It seemed to Vicky that she was drowning in Jeff's kiss and that inside her was a great fiery pulse aching to be quenched, driving her, as implacable as a roaring blaze.

He drew his mouth free for a moment. His eyes seemed stunned, unfocused. "When, Vicky, when? My God—"

"Soon. Soon."

In the kitchen Davie poured a glass of orange juice and made another piece of toast. Eating, leaning against the kitchen counter, he was suddenly aware of the crackle of paper in his back pants pocket.

He licked his fingers and reached, and in the same moment he remembered and jerked his hand away as if he had almost touched something hot. In all the excitement of riding the gray gelding, he had not done what he was supposed to do. There were no ashes up there in the little stone fireplace, and if the man had already come to look, he knew that Davie hadn't followed directions.

Davie jerked open a kitchen drawer, found a matchbook, and rushed out. The sun was bright now and cast his shadow ahead of him as he ran for the gate. Dust rose from his pounding footsteps. The barranca breathed down its sun-warmed smell of dried sage and dust and mysterious distances. He got scratched because he was in such a hurry, weeds dragging at him, but then, finally, he was at the little clearing under the bank. He opened the paper to read it once more—*Friday . . . The back gate . . . and you mustn't hang around or try to see me*—and then he put it carefully into the improvised stove and watched it curl and blacken into ashes.

It was done, all according to directions, just as the man had wanted.

Now what he had to do was to find out where his dad kept his keys. Squatting there in the sunlight with the last of the faint smoke drifting and disappearing, Davie decided that he would wait out beside the driveway when it was time for his dad to come home. He'd stick with his dad all the way into the house and watch what he did and whether he put his keys in some secret place or whether they were just in his pocket, or what.

Davie wouldn't let himself think about what he was going to do, the right or wrong of it. The man didn't want inside the house, he had decided. If he had wanted that, he'd have had Davie open the door at night. He wanted the keys, and they must open something, but so long as it wasn't the house and the man didn't want inside to do those things to Suzie, Davie wasn't going to figure it out any further. What the man must be after belonged in that grown-up world of lawsuits and judges and money and courts and property that his dad dealt with. And probably even if the man, or his dad, tried to explain what it was, he wouldn't understand it. He had listened to his dad many a time, and none of it about the law had made any sense.

Davie sat on the bench by the pool from four o'clock on, just to be sure he didn't miss his dad. Suzie came out a little after four, in her blue bikini, and dived in. When she came up, she watched him for a minute and then asked what he was doing just sitting there like that, and he told her that his friend Joe might come over and he was waiting for him. Suzie dived some more and swam around on the bottom of the pool like a submerged seal. She was very brown and active, and her face had a hot vitality in it as if she were ready for anything. She made swift, clean strokes when she swam.

If I told her, Davie wondered, *would she believe it? Does she know that girls can be treated like that?*

The thought of telling Suzie what the man had said about her on the phone made Davie feel warm and sickish. He got up and moved, so that he sat where there was a breeze. He didn't watch

Suzie in the water, but he couldn't shut out the sound of her vigorous monkeyshines.

She climbed out dripping and pulled off her cap. "Tell me about riding the horse," she commanded unexpectedly.

Davie was surprised. "I already told you."

"I was busy. How far did he let you go?"

"I went up the barranca a way." He remembered what he had wanted to ask Suzie. "Do you think Dad would let us have a horse?"

A fly settled on her long brown leg, and she slapped at it with her cap. "If we nagged and nagged, maybe. There's room for one. I could teach you to ride."

"Would you?"

"Sure. Someday. You could have been riding already; some kids learn when they're real little. I saw some once at the riding stable, and they weren't much more than six or seven."

"Mr. Warren gave the horse a sugar cube. Do you ever do that?"

"Sometimes, if I think to take sugar along when I'm leaving here."

"Grandma says too much sugar could give a horse colic. What does Mr. Warren call that horse?"

"The horse's name is Sarge, but all Mr. Warren ever calls him is Hey, You. I think Mrs. Warren named the horse, before she left Mr. Warren and got a divorce."

"Mr. Warren's been married?"

"Sure. And had two kids, only his wife took them, and they live in Paris or someplace. She got a lot of money out of Mr. Warren. It's called alimony, that kind of money. Mr. Bowman got the divorce for her, and Mr. Warren didn't fight it. He just let her and the kids go. I don't think he could be such a hot father, just letting the kids go like that, but Dad says there wasn't anything he could do, so maybe it's all right. And maybe if the kids were still there, Mr. Warren would be busy teaching them to ride and I'd never get on that horse of his. Everything has its good side," she finished philosophically.

Davie thought miserably: *There's no good side to this thing I'm in. There's no good side about stealing your dad's keys.*

After a moment he asked, "When should we ask Dad about getting a horse?"

She thought about it, twisting a leaf between her toes. "Maybe at dinner. You let me do it. I was reading a thing the other day, about psychology, when to ask people things, like favors. And the article said that for a woman, asking her husband, to do it while he was eating a good meal."

Suzie was always digging up bits like this, how to handle other people, the tactful and best time to do things.

"So it could apply to us, see? We'll wait, and I know that Grandma is going to get dinner tonight. I heard Mom tell her before she left to go shopping, put in the roast at four thirty. And the potatoes later. And you know, Dad likes roast beef and baked potatoes."

It could work, Davie thought.

Suzie went on inside to change back into her clothes, and he looked at the water and thought about going in, too, but then there was this important thing—he had to wait for his dad and watch every minute to find out about those keys.

At a quarter of five his dad's car swung in from the street and climbed the sloping drive in front of the house. His dad got out, and reached into the car for his briefcase. He carried the briefcase as if it were heavy, and Davie ran up and said quickly, "Here, Dad, let me carry it."

His dad nodded and handed over the briefcase and then reached back into the car again and brought out the keys. For a minute Davie had a great choking thump of success and felt his face flush and his arms go weak, but then he saw that these were just the car keys. There were two of them, and he remembered one worked the switch to turn on the motor and the other opened the car trunk. He already *knew* this. Why had he forgotten? There were always just the two keys on their small chain. And his dad always dropped them into his right coat pocket. Always.

His dad touched him on the shoulder and looked at him and smiled. "What have you done all day?" He sounded as if he really wanted to know, and Davie thought about riding the horse, and almost spilled it out, but then kept quiet because this might give away what he and Suzie were going to ask at dinner.

"Oh . . . not much," he said. He lugged the heavy brief-case and followed his dad to the front door.

His dad tried the knob, but the door was locked. His dad started to go on down the walk toward the pool, the big double glass doors there, but then he seemed to change his mind. He reached into his pants pocket and dug out some keys—five or six keys this time, and they were in a worn black leather case. His dad selected a key and opened the front door and went inside. Davie followed.

His dad didn't put these keys back into his pocket. He headed for the bedroom, and while Davie watched, he went straight to the big dresser and opened the top right-hand drawer, a small one, and dropped the keys in it. Then he began to take off his coat and loosen his tie.

"You can just put the briefcase down, Davie. Or no, wait, sup-pose you take it to the den. I'm going to have to work in there."

His dad went into the bathroom, opening his cuffs and rolling up his shirt sleeves. Davie heard water running.

He went over to the drawer and opened it just a little. The keys were in there, along with a cuff-link case and some ironed handkerchiefs and a cigarette lighter his dad didn't use anymore.

A little breath of air stole out of the drawer bearing the clean laundered smell of the handkerchiefs. The keys caught the light with a gleam of metal; he counted them, and there were six, all different sizes. One was the house key, but what were the others?

He heard his dad shut off the water in the basin. He would be coming out in a minute. Davie shut the drawer and left the room.

He felt almost dizzy with excitement and dread, a strange, empty kind of fear that dried his mouth and made his feet heavy and awkward so that he stumbled in the hall.

8

On Friday it was hot, scorching, and then some dark thunderclouds gathered over the mountains far to the east, and there was a smell of rain and wet earth. Davie, raking leaves beside the pool, lifted his head and thought with a rush of relief: *If it rains, he won't want the keys. If it rains, he won't come.*

A few big drops lashed out of the wind to spatter on the decking. The leaves he'd gathered into a pile spiraled off the top, whirled, plunged into the pool. There were more big drops; they made a sound like eggs being cracked. Davie stood entranced, hoping.

It was going to turn out all right after all.

The last few days had been discouraging ones. Suzie had asked about the horse at dinner that night, and his dad had said he'd think it over, and then nothing more had been said, and Suzie had retreated from the idea of nagging until later, when nothing else had worked, a last resort. Meanwhile, Vicky had been watching him. Yesterday after breakfast she had met him outside, and there were just the two of them, and she had said, "Any more phone calls, Davie?" And he had answered truthfully that there hadn't been any.

Now it would rain, and the man wouldn't come for the keys.

I can put them out there on the gate just to be sure, Davie told himself. *There can't be any harm in that. Because he won't be coming to get them, in the rain.*

The eucalyptus trees whipped back and forth, shedding more leaves. His dad had debated about cutting them down when the pool had been built. They dropped long streamers of shaggy bark, as well as leaves and pods; they were the wrong kind of tree to keep near a pool. But Davie had heard his dad say, finally, to

Grandma: "They're over fifty years old, Mother—I just can't have them destroyed. We'll rake."

Davie ran a hand across his hair, exploring, and his hair was wet. It really was raining.

The clouds were rolling overhead now, not as black as they looked to the east, but dimming the sun and lowering the temperature. A wind sucked its way up out of the valley, bringing the smell of the orange trees and plowed earth. Davie propped the rake against the nearest tree and ran for the house.

The big Family Area was dark and empty. He tried to remember where everyone was. That morning his mother had stopped by the breakfast nook where he and Suzie and Vicky had been eating, and she'd said, "I'll be downtown most of the day. Make your own lunches out of what there is in the refrigerator."

Vicky had glanced up as if something in what her mother had said were a kind of betrayal. "You promised to listen to me today, Mother. You said that we could talk."

His mother's face had got hard and impatient. "Well, let's put it off until after dinner."

She began to tell Vicky what to do about dinner, but Vicky broke in. "After dinner it will be something else, another excuse. You'll have a headache and be lying down. Or you'll need to hang pictures. Or the new throw rugs won't match what you've already bought and you'll have to compose a letter to the decorator—a nice friendly letter because you can't treat him the way you treat us."

Anger had flared in his mother's eyes. "Vicky, you'd better not say anything more—"

"Just this, Mother. You had three other children beside Cootie. Don't they count? Does his dying make them worthless, unwanted?"

His mother was white now, and her eyes looked unexpectedly big and afraid. "I won't talk to a daughter such as you," she stammered. "Now or ever. Keep away from me."

"It's the truth," Vicky cried toward their mother's vanishing back. "It's true. You hate us because we're still alive."

Davie had never heard Vicky talk like this before. It stunned him. He thought his mother might take it up with their father that night, and he hoped that she wouldn't jump his dad as soon as he got in and perhaps make his dad forget the routine about putting the keys into that certain drawer.

As soon as their mother was out of sight, Vicky got up from the breakfast table and went to her room. Suzie had gone on eating, but slowly and thoughtfully, as if she were remembering what Vicky had said. Davie had wanted to ask, "It isn't true, is it?" because he wanted to be sure that his mother wasn't the way Vicky had said; she didn't want to be rid of them because she couldn't have Cootie, too. That was just too awful to believe.

Instead, he had asked, "Do you think we'll ever get a horse?"

"Oh, sure," she answered, to his surprise. "Someday. We'll talk to Dad again. And this stuff that Vicky said to Mom, we'll use that, only in another way. I'll have to figure out just how to say it. He needs to see that we're neglected, that Mom ignores us, doesn't care whether we're around or not—"

"You mean, it *is* true?"

She looked at him as if he were a baby. "Of course it's true. Don't you ever stop to think— No, I guess you don't. A boy wouldn't."

"We do just as much thinking as you do," he said indignantly.

"Well, then, don't you ever wonder why Mom never has any time for us? Why she's always buying and buying stuff for the house and scrooching the new cruddy furniture around so it might impress somebody? Only nobody comes, I mean, people like she wants—"

"It's all because of Cootie?"

"Sure. And don't you know that our mother had a nervous breakdown after Cootie died? And maybe she pushed Grandma down the stairs so her leg broke and crippled her? And maybe she'll drown you and me and Vicky out in the pool some midnight?"

He had felt battered, scared to death, and angry beyond any anger he had ever known. "It's a lie! You're lying! You're making it up!"

And Suzie had looked at him with that expression of kindness she could wear when she wanted to, and she'd said, "Yes, little brother, it's a lie. And I'm a mean old sister to tell you these ugly things."

He had watched her to search out any change of expression, any hint that it hadn't been a lie at all, but she went on eating her poached egg and toast. And when her eyes met his again, she smiled.

He remembered something he'd heard, or read, a stray fact. "Is it true that people who have things like . . . uh . . . nervous breakdowns can"—she was watching him, now, a look of caution about her—"that later on they can kill somebody, or do something else bad, and nobody does anything about it?"

"I think they shut them up," Suzie had answered.

"That's all?"

"Well, it seems . . . it's something like they're sick," Suzie explained.

"And if this was true, this thing you told me about Mom, if she'd had a nervous breakdown, and made Grandma get hurt, and tried to hurt somebody else too—it would just be she's sick?"

Suzie nodded, still watching him as if he might be in danger of slipping over some line, perhaps.

"But it's not true," he added.

Again she reassured him. "It's not true, so forget it."

Now, standing in the empty quiet kitchen, he remembered the comfort of that moment, of knowing that the bad things couldn't be true and that their mother was all right. Because somehow if there were something wrong with your mother, especially if there were something wrong with her head, with the way she thought and acted, then you'd just want to die.

Their mother was downtown, and Vicky was in her room—or maybe she had gone out with Jeff. Suzie should be around somewhere.

He looked for her in her room. There was a pile of school clothes laid out on the bed as if she had been sorting them when something had drawn her away. A little radio played on the nightstand by the bed. Vicky's bedroom was also empty. He looked in at the big bedroom, his parents' room, and studied the dresser there in the shadows, the four banks of drawers with their brass pulls, the door to the dressing room open and showing a pale glow from the mirror, and it seemed to him that the room held the secret of what he meant to do there. There was something offended and disapproving in the air of the room, as if the bad act had already been committed.

He shuddered with guilt. Then he told himself that what he was going to do was so much better than letting the terrible things happen to Suzie that he was justified. And he didn't have a choice.

He was turning to go back to the kitchen when he heard the soft tap of a typewriter from the den. He listened, wondering. His dad couldn't be home; there couldn't be an interruption of the routine about the keys on this most desperate of days. He stole down the little hall that led to the den and opened the door a crack. Vicky was there at the desk, using his dad's typewriter.

She looked around at him. "Oh, hello, Davie. Want something?"

"No. I heard the typewriter."

She nodded and sat looking at the paper in the machine and nibbled her lips a little.

"Are you writing to the University of Arizona?" he blurted.

She gave him a surprised glance. "Yes."

"And you're going to marry Jeff?"

"Yes."

He hung there in the doorway, not knowing what else to say. The thoughts that charged through his mind were inexpressible —they were made of loneliness, the loneliness of losing his sister, of having her marry and move away and not be a part of them anymore but to begin to be a different family entirely. He thought suddenly: *What will Mom do with Vicky's room?* And the idea of the room being stripped, empty, was almost as frightening as what might happen to Suzie.

Vicky was smiling at him. "You look as if you might even miss me a little."

"Yes," he managed to get out, "I guess I'll miss you a lot."

"You'll still have Suzie. And she's more your age."

"Sure." He wanted to say, "But we need *you,* too," and couldn't say it. His throat was working in some funny way, unmanageable and dry.

"Everyone grows up and leaves home someday. Mom and Dad did. And so will Suzie, and so will you."

"Will you move far away from here?" he asked.

"No. And you'll see me every once in a while, so you won't forget all about me."

He didn't believe it. Jeff Norbert would keep her at home somewhere. When they went out anywhere, it would be to the beach, or dancing, or to an affair fixed up by his college. Jeff wouldn't want Vicky coming back to see her family. Not very much, anyway. To Davie's surprise, he found his opinion of Jeff altering swiftly.

"You ought to stay," he said. "We're going to get a horse. Suzie says Dad will get us one before too long, if we keep asking. You could ride every day. I could show you how to get to the Indian burial ground."

She seemed interested. "You've been there?"

"No, not yet. But I saw it once from a long way off. I know how to find it again."

"Isn't it just mounds, dirt? And weeds?"

"Somebody digs up there. Maybe it's Mr. Warren."

"You saw somebody digging?"

"No, but I saw a shovel stuck in the dirt, the handle sticking up. Couldn't you tell Jeff you have to wait until we get the horse?"

"I don't think he'd understand," she said, not smiling.

"Are you sorry about not going to the University of Arizona?"

"Yes. In a way. But we all have to make a choice at times. If I could be two people, if I could marry Jeff and at the same time go to the University and be single and have all the fun, it would be wonderful. But I can't."

"Does Mom know?"

"I guess she does. She won't let me talk to her about it, though."

"Is it because she's kind of sick?"

Vicky's glance was sharp. "Who told you she was sick?"

He thought: *I can't get Suzie in Dutch.* "It was something I read in the paper, a column or something. How people do things they can't help."

Vicky sighed. "She can't help it. That's the truth. And I shouldn't have popped off at breakfast the way I did." She looked almost unhappily at the letter in the machine. "We should all be very patient with her."

He wanted to ask, "Will Mom get over it?" But he was afraid to hear Vicky's answer. A great lash of wind threw a lot of rain against the window; the drops sounded almost like little hammers, and even in here he could feel the drive and pressure of the tumult outside. He thought with a feeling of release: *It's going to be a real storm, and the man won't come for the keys after all.* And that would be the end of it, the end of the phone calls and of being afraid all of the time.

The door behind him, which he had left half-shut, opened all at once, and Suzie was there. He turned with a start, and Vicky cried, "What on earth happened to you?"

Suzie was damp, all over, her hair wild and windblown, and all down one side of her face and throat was a smear of mud. Her hands were muddy, too, as if she'd tried to wipe some of the mess off with them.

"You fell in the mud," Davie said.

She looked at him with hot, indignant eyes. "There isn't any mud, or anyway not yet. There hasn't been enough rain. This is some ratty kid's idea of a joke." Her voice trembled and broke.

She put up a hand to touch the side of her head. The drops on her face weren't rain at all, he realized; they were tears.

"What happened?" Vicky said, frowning, getting up from the desk.

Suzie broke down and sobbed for a little while, and Vicky cradled her, mud and all, and stroked her head. Finally, Suzie said, "I went over to Mr. Warren's to see if I could ride maybe, and then the wind came up like it did, and I knew he wouldn't want me to take the horse out because with all the weeds and things whipping around, he might spook. So I started home. And there where all that old lantana is growing—you know, there's a barranca, only it's a little one—"

"Yes, I know," Vicky said.

"Something made a lot of—of crackling and crunching, and I stopped to look, and then this big ball of mud just flew out and hit me. And the kid ran. I could hear him running . . ." Behind the tears, sheer rage burned in Suzie's eyes. She bit her mouth to stop its shaking. "I would have chased him, but that lantana is full of thorns. And it's high and thick."

"Let's hope he got a few scratches for himself," Vicky said to comfort her. "And come on, I'll wash your hair for you, and you can shower and change, and you'll be better than new."

Suzie caught hold of Vicky and pressed her head against Vicky's chest. "I wish I knew who it was! I wish I knew!"

"So do I," Vicky said quietly. "Come on, now."

"And why?" Suzie wailed. "Why? Why? I haven't done anything to anybody!"

"There aren't any little kids very close by either," Vicky said. "So maybe it was—" All at once she looked at Davie and frowned. "Are there any new kids here in the neighborhood?"

He said stiffly, "No. And the ones I know, the ones my age, wouldn't throw a chunk of mud at my sister."

Vicky took Suzie away to the bathroom to wash up, and he was all alone. The room seemed funny and lonely now that they were gone, and the wind made a noise at the windows like someone tearing a piece of cloth, and he thought of that big chunk of wet mud that had sailed out of the brush to hit Suzie.

It hadn't been any kid.

It was the man on the phone, the man that wanted his dad's keys tonight, and the chunk of mud had been a reminder—things could happen to Suzie a million times worse, dirtier things and things she couldn't wash off under a shower.

He went over to the desk and sat in the chair, staring at Vicky's letter without seeing it. He felt cold and alone, scared. He saw all at once he should have told somebody right away, when the creep made that first phone call. Only he hadn't been able to figure out the one he should tell. And nobody had seemed to want to listen.

He wanted to tell somebody now, but it was too late.

He had to get those keys and go through with it after all.

9

In her rooms at the top of the stairs, Mrs. Stoddard stood looking out her window. At this level she could see the whipping tops of the eucalyptus trees and the water of the pool that shivered under the wind. The clouds were rolling, dark, thunderous.

"It's going to be perfect for him," she whispered to herself. "The storm couldn't have come at a better time for him."

It would grow dark early, and the noise of stirring brush and spattering rain would cover *his* sounds. She pictured him, ugly and sneaking, for some reason all twisted and dwarflike, a gnome out of hell, though she knew, reasonably, that he must be just a man. Just an ordinary man who had some strange hold over Davie and would force Davie to do what he wanted. Right now it was keys, and later it would be something else. He posed some threat to Suzie—the note she had read, the note in Davie's pants pocket, had mentioned Davie's sister. The exact wording of the note was gradually fading, but she remembered that the day was Friday and the time was ten o'clock. And the keys were to be left on the back gate.

When she had taken Davie's pants to mend them and had found the note, her first instinct was to demand that Davie tell her all about it, but then she had recalled his other visit and the air of nervousness he'd had, the difficulty in expressing himself. She had decided that Davie would probably not tell her the truth, or not all of it, and this thing had to be nipped right now, cut off sharp, the man exposed and punished.

Her son, Thomas, might be thought the logical one, by some, to step forward in defense of his family. She had considered telling him of the danger and had then rejected the idea. He had enough to worry about. *She* would confront and unmask this threat, this abomination. At the moment of decision a great flood of confidence and self-satisfaction rushed through her, sweeping away all doubt about what she meant to do.

She would repay her son for years of shelter and support. She would be giving back a little in return for all that he had done and, most of all, for his understanding and forgiveness at the time of Cootie's death.

The thought came, too, that once she had succeeded, the evil driven away, there might be a return of warmth and closeness in the attitude of the family; she might become a part of them again. The time since Cootie had died had been a lonely one, filled with a sense of isolation and self-blame.

Her daughter-in-law, who had been an enemy with accusing eyes, might even soften!

She had made her preparations. Clothes had to be chosen, black garments that would blend with the night. Soft-soled shoes that wouldn't crunch on gravel. A dark scarf for her whitening head. A flashlight, a powerful one, and a police whistle.

She had found or had shopped for these things, and they all were in a carton now in the bottom of her closet. She had been afraid that if anyone had seen them, her secret might come out. No one had come here, though. With the things packed in the box and nothing to do but to wait for Friday, she had drawn a big breath of relief, and then for a reason she didn't understand, she had cried. The sense of aloneness, of so much depending on what she did, had been so strong that she had almost told Thomas after all.

But she hadn't. And when the tears had dried, the feeling of self-confidence had returned. She would cope, and she would succeed.

Somehow she hadn't pictured a wild, stormy night. She had imagined the dark and the silence and the stealthy sound of a man's coming, but not wind and rain and the crackle of trees and brush.

Twice during the day she had gone to the carton and checked everything in it, especially the big flashlight. The beam was strong, filling the closet with light, throwing into sudden relief her hanging clothes and the bar from which they hung and the underside of the painted shelf above.

At noon she made tea on her little electric plate. She was too nervous to eat. The warmth of the tea calmed her a little, so that she was able to lie down and sleep for a short time. At times she heard the children below, going in or out of the house, but no one came near her. She would have to appear at dinner, or Thomas would wonder and check up on her. This must be a perfectly ordinary day, she thought—until the very end, when she would save them all.

Everyone was already at the table when she went down for dinner. For a change, her daughter-in-law wasn't standing on one foot with a cup of coffee but was sitting next to Thomas and handing dishes of food to Davie and Suzie. Vicky was the quietest, picking at what was on her plate, and Mrs. Stoddard saw the pallor and the look of unhappiness and decided that the girl wasn't going to the university after all—she was going to marry her young man. She was being driven to marry him because of her mother's thorny air of distraction and ill temper.

Sitting down in her chair next to Suzie, Mrs. Stoddard looked around at the rest of them. Her heart was heavy with sympathy for Vicky, who was so obviously miserable, but this was no time for blame. She loved all of them, and in spite of their indifference to her, this night would certainly change everything. She even found herself trying to see things from her daughter-in-law's point of view. Perhaps Margaret was so miserable that she actually didn't know what she was doing to the rest of the family. She couldn't understand that in her grief over Cootie she was destroying the love of her other children.

"Good evening, Mother," said Thomas from the other end of the table.

"Good evening, son."

Margaret handed dishes to Suzie without glancing toward her mother-in-law. Her mouth was tight, pinched; her eyes seemed filled with anger. Perhaps she had had words with Thomas. Perhaps he was, at long last, protesting the way she acted, her silly infatuation with spending and rearranging the house, her indifference to the children.

As if surmising his mother's thoughts, Thomas said, "We have had a discussion tonight, Mother. Vicky and Margaret and I. Some things have happened which have tried all of us, and we have become, not a family any longer, but a collection of strangers. I think you have suffered from this change perhaps more than any of us. The children, after all, have youthful optimism and short memories—they wake up every morning without the weight of what has gone before."

Vicky gave her father a hurt, puzzled look.

"I am not talking about you, Vicky," he put in. "Though I had hoped that your plans for going to Arizona, the excitement of getting ready and the whole idea of the big change, would distract you and help you forget what is going on here at home."

"How could I forget for a minute? It's like being ground to death between stones," Vicky said clearly.

Her mother jerked her hands off the table and clenched them in her lap. Her eyes burned, fixed on her plate. She looked like an animal at bay.

My poor son, Mrs. Stoddard thought, *you are far too late with this woman. And far too gentle.* And then, with a touch of fear, she wondered if her daughter-in-law could be so ill, so removed from reality, that she represented a real danger to her children.

Thomas was looking at his wife, frowning, not in anger, but with an expression of worry. "Margaret, can't we make the effort to become a family again? To show love and respect for each other? I bring this up now, at mealtime, not to spoil appetites or rouse anger, but because this time of day, when we are together at table, should be most happy. There should be a feeling of interest in each other, sharing the affairs of the day when we have been separated—"

She lifted her eyes. Something about her made Mrs. Stoddard think of a snake—and she was instantly ashamed of the comparison.

"You make me sick," Margaret Stoddard told her husband. "Yes, you do. You *all* "—she stared at each one venomously in turn—"all make me sick."

Thomas drew in a deep breath and shut his eyes for a moment. All the color drained from his face, and he looked years older than his real age, his mother thought. She was becoming frightened by this scene. Thomas shouldn't have begun it in front of the children.

"Couldn't we talk about it later?" she offered timidly, and saw the rush of relief in the eyes of Suzie and Davie. But Vicky wasn't with them; she was answering her mother's look with one of contempt and loathing.

"You aren't a mother to us," Vicky told Margaret. "You haven't been one for a long time. You run all day through the shops, looking for silly knickknacks and trash, while we cook and feed ourselves and try to manage our clothes—you won't even replace the cleaning woman who quit, you won't even take time for that, because you've got to show us how little we matter. And I guess you want everybody to go on feeling sorry for you because you lost Cootie. Well, I'm sorry Cootie died, but I'm not sorry for you. Not anymore. I just hate you."

Vicky stood up and carefully folded her napkin beside her plate and walked away. The light over the table shone in Margaret's white face and stricken eyes. For a moment she was dazed, silent. Then she roused, and her gaze flicked from one to another, from her husband to Suzie to Davie, and finally settled on her mother-in-law. Mrs. Stoddard felt the flame of hatred, as if something physically hot and violent had licked out at her.

"You hideous old woman," Margaret said in a slow, grinding tone, "what are you doing here at my table? You brought death here. Why don't you have the decency to go?"

Thomas was saying, "Margaret, shut up!"

But she went on, "Why aren't you dead, too? Why aren't you under the ground with dirt in your face, along with my little boy?"

"You apologize to Mother, or I'll—"

"My little boy whom you killed?" Margaret finished, and stood up. She looked at the table as if for something to throw, and Mrs. Stoddard's instinct was to duck for cover, but if this had been Margaret's idea, it was forgotten. She gave Thomas a bitter stare and turned away.

"Margaret! Wait. You can't just—"

"Shut up," she told him over her shoulder.

Thomas looked at his mother, and she saw, much moved, that there were tears in his eyes. The children sat with heads bent, picking at their food, embarrassed and miserable. A great feeling of compassion for the three of them, for Vicky, too, rushed through Mrs. Stoddard. It was up to her to smooth things—and after all, once this night was over, things were going to be quite different indeed. She had the power to save their world for them against unimaginable danger.

"Mother, I can't tell you how I hate this . . . this—"

"Don't worry about it, son. It's much better that such feelings not be allowed to fester, that they be brought out into the open. I don't think either Margaret or Vicky will hold these feelings permanently. And probably the time that they *would* have held them has been shortened by this explosion."

Actually she didn't believe it, not quite—Margaret would always blame her and hate her for Cootie's death. And Vicky's estrangement would be deepened by her marriage and leaving home. If things didn't improve, there would be further and more bitter eruptions. But she was glad now to see that her son's attitude was less shocked and concerned; he was relieved that she had taken the scene as she had—or as he supposed she had. Probably Thomas had some sort of business worry on his mind, and this was why he had made the attempt to improve matters by bringing Margaret up short. He had wanted peace in at least one area of his life.

"Margaret will apologize."

"No. I don't want it, and you mustn't demand it of her."

He was silent then. He had lost all appetite, was simply waiting for her and the children to finish the meal. He looked wretched and lonely there at the head of the table, the lines in his face deepened by the glow of the overhead light. His world was being destroyed by his wife's erratic reaction to grief.

My poor son, Mrs. Stoddard thought, trying to choke down a few bites of food so that she could decently leave the table. *If you only knew what's really going on, this strange thing with Davie— but I'm glad you don't. You will only know of it when the danger is over, when I've caught this criminal and exposed him.*

Mentally she ticked over the things hidden in her closet, the things she would need in just a few hours. This mental rechecking had become a habit during the past few days. Each item must be just right—the black garments and the scarf for concealment, the rubber-soled shoes for quietness, the light for the exposure of the criminal, and the whistle for summoning help.

The scene was crystal clear in her mind, out there by the back gate—a man, big and burly and dressed roughly, a low depraved type, caught in the beam of the flashlight, standing there helpless as the family, summoned by her whistle, gathered in shocked astonishment behind her. What should she say first? "Thomas, this man came to rob you—" Or maybe, "Thomas, this man forced Davie to steal your keys, and there they are on the back gate where he had expected to find them—" No. Too long-winded. Short and crisp would be better. "Thomas, search this thief."

For a moment another idea intruded—the man might not stand still, might not wait to be accused. He might just run away. He might even just disappear permanently.

Once I've seen his face, though, she told herself, *he won't dare try any more of his tricks.*

He could even be someone we know!

She felt a flush mount to her cheeks. It would be terribly embarrassing to catch someone who was familiar to them. When she thought of this possibility, the scene in her mind turned all askew. She was shaken and uncertain, and the man, some faceless friend, was beginning to bluster. With an effort, she brushed this thought aside.

We ought to have a dog, she thought suddenly. *A big strong German shepherd, something like that.*

There had been a dog several years past, and he had died of distemper when little more than a puppy, and the children's grief had been so heartbreaking to Thomas that he had never replaced the pet.

But I could certainly use a big dog tonight.

Too late now.

At nine thirty she was all ready. She had on the old black dress and sweater, her hair tied in the navy blue scarf, the rubber-soled shoes on her feet. She watched the little clock on her bedside stand, and exactly at one minute past nine thirty she picked up the big flashlight and the whistle. The flashlight was silver-colored, and she had encased it in an old black sock of Thomas', cutting out the toe for the light to shine through.

She saw with surprise that her hands were shaking. Was she really so nervous, without even knowing it?

Just keyed up, she told herself fiercely.

But for an unwilling moment she was afraid—terribly afraid—of going out there in the dark. The feeling passed. The shaking in her hands didn't stop, and there seemed to be cold spots in her lungs and around her heart, and she kept wanting to swallow.

Nothing's wrong with my courage, though.

She stole from the room, down the stairs to the lower level. The kitchen had been tidied up, dishes put in the dishwasher, lights turned off except for the small night-light which cast big vague shadows out into the passageway. She went to the rear door, opened it, and went out. The night was cool and windy, full of the smell of damp left by the rain. When her eyes had adjusted to the dark, she picked her way through the trees and shrubs to the back fence and along that to the gate. The white fence was visible, dimly, reflecting the light from the sky, such as there was in spite of the high black clouds.

She found a spot amid some shrubs and crouched down to wait.

Time passed with an interminable slowness. She grew stiff and chilled, her limbs aching, her eyes beginning to burn from the strain of staring into the dark. Davie wasn't coming, after all—

But then, there he was, all at once, slipping up like a wraith toward the fence. She heard the faint metallic jangle of the keys. A sudden anger filled her, and she wanted to say, "You bad boy, aren't you ashamed to be doing such an evil thing?" And when Davie had slipped away again, the idea came to her to just take the keys and go back into the house and tell the whole thing to Thomas.

Of course. This was the logical thing to do. Having the keys would be irrefutable proof, and Davie couldn't lie about what he had done, couldn't deny the danger. He would have to explain the affair to his father, from beginning to end.

She stood up, tottered from a cramp in her leg, then controlled the spasm and walked to the gate. It occurred to her that she hadn't been out here, in this part of the yard, more than a dozen times, if that many, and how suddenly she felt the closeness of the wild country, the tangled brush and the damp earth of the hills. She shivered. Then she reached for the top bar of the gate.

There was a sound nearby, a rustle and then something almost like a human voice, a muttered word or two; she half turned. She sensed some rushing thing, hitting downward, aimed her way. Her grip on the big flashlight tightened in fear, and the beam sprang on, shockingly brilliant in all that dark.

The thing struck her and stunned her, and she fell to her knees, and the big light cartwheeled from her flaccid hand and shone its beam into a face—a face hanging there suspended in the midst of the crackling pain that filled her head.

She tried to say, "How could you?" but the words wouldn't come.

10

Thomas Stoddard lay awake in the dark, staring toward the ceiling.

He was alone in the big bed. Margaret was in the den, on the couch there, or he supposed that she was. *If she's awake,* he told himself, *and she's not, she's asleep, dead to everything—but if she is awake and thinking of that scene tonight, it's with pity for herself and no regret for the mess she's made of our lives.*

She's played the martyr ever since Cootie died, and she's made my life and my mother's life a hell, and Vicky and Suzie and Davie are nothing to her but annoyances.

And I've stood by and let it go on, the crazy compulsive shopping and house changing and the neglect of human beings—

And so when did I resign as head of this outfit?

When did I become this weak-kneed simpleton?

He was filled with such bitter outrage at himself, such hatred for

Margaret, that he wanted to get up, go to the kitchen for some coffee, and sit up smoking and loathing himself, but he couldn't, he couldn't afford the loss of rest and the drain of energy because the work at the office was heavier all the time, more important, more mind-filling, and he had to try to sleep and rise tomorrow to face the job again.

End of a father. End of a husband.

When did I become this thing that thinks only of money, of security? Just when did I make the bargain that ended my being a man?

Did the change begin when we moved here? We had a good ordinary house on a good ordinary street in town, and then Margaret heard about these lots out here on the flank of the hill, and we bought and built—so the kids could have a horse, as I recall—and it seemed we became like kings looking out over our valley, we became little Caesars, each in a hollow crown, and each alone and split from the others, not right away maybe, but all too soon, and don't tell me we would have reacted to Cootie's death as we have, if we'd stayed in that other home. That home had warmth and lovingness in it among its other good qualities.

This house killed Cootie, this house that Margaret is so fanatically determined to make perfect.

I've got to get up and have some coffee and smoke.

He was propped on an elbow, one foot poked forth from under the covers, when he heard a sound from a distance, from some other part of the house. He couldn't define the noise; it wasn't loud. It could have been a door banging under the pressure of the wind—the wind was still up, plucking and whistling around the cornices and the windows—only, of course, any outside door had to be locked. He was sure of that. They weren't so innocent or so far from town that they'd sleep behind unlocked doors.

He got out of bed and felt around for his robe.

He stood there in the dark, knotting the belt of the robe, listening for a repetition of the sound. After a moment he went out into the corridor and turned toward the other end of the house.

It seemed to him that even indoors the air had a fresh, rainy odor, and then he thought: *There is a door open.*

There was a night-light in the kitchen. He touched the switch there, and the big fixture in the ceiling sprang into brilliant life. Yes, the noise must be that of a door, hitting a wall. It couldn't be anything else. He went on toward the rear entry, turning on lights as he went.

His mother lay across the sill, on her face, and it was her hand that was making the door bang. Her outstretched fingers could just touch the bottom of the door to give it a push.

Thomas Stoddard looked at her, it seemed to him, for at least a full minute, waiting for the shock to register, waiting to be able to scream. Finally, he tore his eyes off her to look beyond; the light spread out into the yard, the trees and shrubbery touched with strange new greens, unnaturally alive, and beyond that he could even see the fence, far away at the rim of visibility, white as wax against the blackness. He leaned against the wall and fought against being sick.

His mother had stopped moving.

He got control of himself and knelt hurriedly beside her, and all the time a hammer was going inside his brain: *Call a doctor, call a doctor.* He put a hand on her bloodied shoulder, the cloth of her dress sticky and dull red, a red that came off on his hand, shockingly bright; he wiped his hand on his robe.

Don't touch her head.

Oh, God, don't touch that.

Mustn't even move anyone like this.

He went back to the telephone, in the kitchen, and got hold of a telephone operator and told her that there was an emergency—they needed a doctor and an ambulance in a hurry; somebody was dying. And yes, they had a family doctor, but he never made house calls. No, never. But yes, he might be willing to meet somebody at a hospital, if it happened to be the hours he usually went to the hospital, but probably not otherwise. And anyway, this wasn't going to wait—a woman's brains and her blood were all over her, and somebody had to get here quick.

Then, at all the impersonality and obfuscation and delay, he started to yell, and he called the telephone operator names he hadn't used for years, not since he'd played football in college, and he told the woman that if his mother died, he was going to see that she was punished—yes, personally!

The operator remained cool and patient; she needed information, and he had to stop yelling to give it.

Then he simply dropped the receiver on the small desk, not thinking that somebody might need to call back, and went to the open door again and knelt by his mother.

If this were I, he thought, *and my mother were in my place, she'd have my head on her lap, cradling the whole wounded mess, and she wouldn't feel revulsion and sickness—she'd be raging and strong.* But he couldn't touch her. He was cold all over, and shaking. He began to notice things he hadn't seen before, like the kind of clothes she was wearing, an old black dress and a pair of poorly dyed tennis shoes and, lying half under her, a black sweater. Out there on the ground scuffed with dirt was something else, black or almost—it looked like a scarf.

She was holding one hand tight as if there might be something in it, and when he pried open her fingers, a whistle fell out.

What in hell had she been up to?

He looked out into the yard, thinking that it must have happened out there. The strange greenery, the white fence, the dark beyond, made a scene of menace.

Some sound made him turn quickly, and there was Davie, big-eyed, obviously stiff with fright, and Thomas barely got him to the kitchen sink before the small body convulsed and Davie was sick all over everything. After the sickness passed, he lay inert for a moment or two, propped on the rim of the sink, gasping. Thomas ran water, took paper towels off the roller, and cleaned up.

"You, go back to your room and stay in it."

"What's wrong with Grandma?"

"None of your damned business."

"Was she outdoors? Did she get hurt outdoors, in the yard, do you think?"

"I think." Thomas took Davie by the shoulders, the wet shoulders of his pajamas; he was propelling him toward the hall when Davie suddenly squirmed out of his grip and rushed back to the entry. "Dammit, Davie, you come here!"

Davie was trying to lift his grandmother's head, but gently, and he was crying; he was begging his grandmother's forgiveness for something. Thomas took hold of the child's hands and firmly lifted them away from the bloodied shape on the floor.

"In your room. Didn't you hear me?"

"It's all my fault!"

"Of course it isn't."

"But it is! It is! It was the keys, he wanted the keys, and she must have gone out there, and he hit her!"

I'm dreaming this, Thomas thought with a burst of relief and shut his eyes for an instant to give the nightmare time to dissolve. *I must be dreaming a thing that makes as little sense as this.* And with his eyes shut he waited for the sensation of waking. It didn't come, but what Davie had said began to whirl through his mind like an icy wind.

He looked down at his son. Davie was white and drawn, and he seemed smaller, shrunken in on himself, and terribly afraid.

"What was that you said?"

Davie shivered. "The keys. Your keys. He wanted them."

"Who?"

"I don't know. The man on the phone, the one who said something awful might happen to Suzie."

"I can't believe it, but you'd better tell me about it."

Standing there in the entry with his mother's body on the floor beside them, Thomas listened, still not believing, while Davie told him about the phone calls and the note on the bush and the final arrangements about tonight. They were still standing there and Davie was confessing about stealing his keys when the siren whirled up the hill to stop in front of the house.

The two men who had come with the ambulance examined Mrs. Stoddard swiftly. One stayed with her while the other went out to use the radio phone and to bring a stretcher on wheels. They were very serious young men, and when they looked at Thomas, he knew that he mustn't believe that his mother had a chance to live.

The detective's name was Caldwell. Thomas didn't know if he was a city detective or was attached to some county sheriff's division. Caldwell was a slim man about six feet tall, somewhere past forty, with a tanned face. His gray eyes had the flattest and most uncommunicative stare that Thomas had ever seen.

Thomas had dressed, throwing on his clothes in the bedroom, with Margaret standing in the doorway, her face swollen as if from crying, wearing a new robe, dark blue, that he had never seen before. There had been some kind of conversation between them; he thought that he had told her some of the stuff Davie had told him, but actually he couldn't remember. The time since he had found his mother on the doorsill was a confused, tormented dislocation.

He knew, though, somehow, that Vicky was dressing now to go with him to the hospital, while Margaret was to stay here with Davie and Suzie. There seemed to be something else, some detail he had to tell her, to warn her about, only now he couldn't recall it.

Caldwell had a slow, careful way about him. He sized Thomas up with a long look, not minding that Thomas impatiently watched him doing it, and then he examined the place where Mrs. Stoddard had fallen and looked out into the yard from the back door, and then he asked Thomas to come with him and went into the Family Area. He sat down in a chair that faced the blank television set and indicated a nearby chair for Thomas.

But Thomas didn't sit down. "I have to go to the hospital right away."

I have to be there when she dies, he thought. *I can't let my mother die alone. I've neglected her, I've left her open to Margaret's meanness, and now I can't—*

"I won't keep you long, Mr. Stoddard. I know that you have to be at the hospital. But time—here as well as in that surgery—time, as they say, is of the essence. We have to know, in order to do our job. We're getting men up here and we are lucky—it's night and there won't be an instant mob of nosy people."

Thomas sat down on the edge of the chair. "Please be quick, then." For a moment his senses dimmed, and he felt dizzy, as if from exhaustion and tension.

The detective seemed to be aware of every change, of every

effort at covering up. The flat stare made Stoddard think of a cat. "Why did you get up just when you did? You said that you were in bed—what made you decide to come and investigate?"

"A sound. I wasn't asleep. We'd had an—there was a disagreement at dinner, it didn't amount to anything, but I was lying awake, thinking. And then there was a noise like a door hitting the wall."

"A repeated noise?"

"Yes."

"And you knew that any outside door should be shut?"

"And locked. Of course."

"You also said that someone unknown had demanded that your son deliver your keys, leave them at the back gate. Now, are your keys actually missing?"

"Yes, they are."

"You've checked to be sure?"

Thomas rubbed a hand across his head. The room looked off-center, crooked, and his head hurt. He *had* looked for the keys, but now he couldn't recall the moment; he couldn't remember opening the drawer and not seeing the keys in there. "I must have."

"And your son has confessed to taking the keys out and leaving them as he was told to do?"

"He believes that there was a threat against his sister, that this man was going to do something to her if he didn't obey him."

"May I talk to your son when you have gone?"

"Yes, surely."

"Do you think he'll tell me the truth?"

"Davie's a completely honest boy. I'm sure that he would have told someone the whole story days ago if—" He stopped; he couldn't say, *"if any of us had been willing to listen."* He knew that Caldwell must be measuring and interpreting his hesitation. "I'm sure," he finished lamely.

Caldwell waited a moment and then said, "Are you sure that you weren't kept awake by some sound from outside? An argument? Blows?"

"The wind," Stoddard said. "It whines all around the house;

it must be sucked up here from the floor of the valley. When there's any wind at all, we get it here. And that's all that I could hear."

"You mentioned a disagreement at dinner, Mr. Stoddard, and that it didn't amount to much. Have there been any serious arguments, any serious breaks, in your family relationship?"

"What do you mean?" Thomas stammered.

Caldwell just waited; he knew that Thomas understood what he had said.

"We—we had a very bad thing happen here," Thomas got out finally. "My youngest son was killed. He ran his tricycle full tilt into the glass doors. . . . They're over there behind those draperies; only now they're safety glass—"

"I remember it," Caldwell said quietly.

The weariness, the sense of exhaustion were crushing now. "The tragedy changed everything."

"Your mother was blamed for it?"

"Oh, no." Too quick, he knew, too much on the defense, a lie. He had to be calm, quiet; he had to match Caldwell's slow patience; only he couldn't—there was this pounding knowledge that he had to get to the hospital before his mother died.

I have to tell her, he thought, *I have to make her hear and believe—I never blamed her for what happened to Cootie.*

Caldwell was saying quietly, "You and your wife were together tonight, I believe. I understood that you share a bedroom."

He started to say, "Yes, of course," and get up to go; only the words didn't come, and he knew that Caldwell had seen the sudden fear and astonishment in his eyes.

He *had* to say, "Yes, we share a bedroom." That was all that was required; it was all Caldwell wanted to hear, that Margaret and he had been together. And he couldn't get the lie out. Vicky was in the doorway that led into the kitchen, silhouetted there against the brighter light, pulling on gloves, beautiful and slender, his child, and she must have heard Caldwell's question, and she, too, must be waiting for his answer.

And the answer wouldn't come.

Margaret had been in the den—*or had she?*

11

Stoddard rose to his feet and faced Vicky across Caldwell's seated figure; he tried to throw off the tiredness, the fear and confusion—and then he heard his own voice saying, "Yes, it's true, we share a bedroom at the other end of the house. You may look in there if you wish. I keep my keys in a small top drawer of the bureau."

Vicky smiled at him. Her eyes were red-rimmed; she'd been crying, but now she wanted to seem cheerful to him, a bulwark in his grief, and Thomas was deeply grateful, and he thought: *We needn't be split up as a family, and we needn't be strangers living here together. She's my daughter, and I love her so much I'd die for her.*

She came forward. She nodded to the detective as if understanding who he must be. She slipped a hand through her father's arm. "Come on, Dad. Let's go and see about Grandma. She needs us."

A terrible pain seized him, and it was as if everything were being wrenched around inside him, and the thought of his mother alone in the hospital was like a knife in his brain.

Oh, God, don't let her die before I can get there.

Vicky drove him to the hospital. There were glaringly white corridors, silent, empty, and lots of lights, and a smell he could never forget, a smell neither of living nor of dying but of some sterile state between. And he himself felt suspended in that state, embalmed, caught in a vacuum, while he and Vicky waited in a room with rattan couches and a lot of smoking stands and two innocuous paintings of birds over sunshiny cornfields.

It seemed hours before anyone came to tell them anything. His eyes burned and his mouth felt dry from smoking, and Vicky was just sitting there, white and tired—he had long since explained all that he knew about what had happened to Davie and had discovered to his numbed surprise that Vicky and his mother had already been aware of some of it.

The one who came finally was a young doctor in a white doctor's coat, tall, lean as if with plenty of exercise—didn't doctors play golf together every Wednesday? Stoddard wondered irrelevantly—who sat down with them and asked if they wanted anything, coffee or food. It seemed that there were some drink- and food-dispensing machines in some corridor nearby. Vicky accepted the offer of some coffee, and Stoddard wondered if she just wanted to delay hearing what they had to hear. The young doctor went away and came back with a plastic cup of coffee, and Vicky sipped at it while he said what had to be said.

His mother wasn't dead after all. There had been some emergency repairs but not much, because the thing to do, it seemed, was to wait and see how much repair needed to be done. Or could be done. It was all brain work and diagnosis took time. And then the doctor explained that though Mrs. Stoddard was still alive, it might be a long time, if ever, before she knew anyone or was able to do simple things for herself. She had been savagely battered, and it was a miracle that she was still living.

"My mother always had a will to live," Thomas told the doctor. "Even in adverse times, even under cruel conditions—like those she's had to endure recently." He broke off, unable to go on, and the doctor looked sympathetic but didn't ask what he meant, for which Stoddard was grateful. Vicky knew what he meant, and that was enough.

She took his hands in hers. She was still wearing the gloves. Under the glove on her left hand, third finger, he felt the metallic hardness of a ring she wore. He circled her hand with his fingers, pressed lightly. The stone was a big one. Jeff had given her an engagement ring sometime during the past few days, and all his dreams for her, the university, the growth as a single woman, a career, didn't mean anything now.

If she leaves now, he thought, *if she hurries off to get married and to start living with Jeff, we've lost her.*

And then he thought with strange new insight: *This is the kind of time when you lose people. You either lose them, and they never come back, or you find them again forever.*

Yes, in this kind of time . . .

Joseph Caldwell had been out in the backyard, supervising a couple of men who were studying the ground around the back gate under floodlights. The decision had been made to stake off the area and to wait for daylight, though there didn't seem to be much chance of getting good prints—the light, gravelly soil had been thoroughly pocked by rain and yet had not absorbed enough moisture actually to make mud, which would have been an advantage. Even now the wind was stirring a smell of dust, and by morning the whole backside of the property could be dried and blowing. Not, as he reminded himself, that there seemed anything important to blow away. There were bloodstains, a few, and the marks of Mrs. Stoddard's dragging herself to the house. But then, they already knew that this had happened.

There was no sign of a flashlight, though it would seem that Mrs. Stoddard should have supplied herself with one. Caldwell was going inside again to use the phone. He wanted to be sure that a police cruiser had been sent to Stoddard's office and that somebody would be staked out there, in case the office had been the target of the man who had wanted Stoddard's keys. The theory seemed most likely; if the man had wanted to get into the house, he could have asked Davie to leave a door open.

There was another nagging idea. If the object of getting the keys, getting inside the office, had been to snatch something real quick, the quarry could have come and gone by now, by acting quickly, by breaking a few speed laws which probably wouldn't deter him.

I'd better talk to the kid, Caldwell thought.

And to Stoddard's wife, though she isn't supposed to have known anything about it all.

Mrs. Stoddard didn't appear, but the kid was in the big room that Caldwell already knew was called the Family Area. Davie was sitting in a big overstuffed chair, with his knees up under his chin. Caldwell thought he looked scared. He watched Caldwell come across the room toward him.

"Hello, Davie. Your dad said that we could talk."

"Hello, sir," Davie said politely. "Have you heard anything about my grandma?"

"I guess your sister will call when there's anything definite. Do you want to tell me about those phone calls? When they began, and who it might be, and any other ideas you might have."

Davie sat silent, as if thinking, and then replied, "I never did think it was any kind of a joke. I always knew he was serious." He looked at Caldwell to see how these opinions were being accepted. "I knew he would hurt somebody if he wanted to; only I thought it would be Suzie because she was the one he talked about."

"What would he do to Suzie?"

A look of strain came into the boy's face, and he answered, "I can't tell you."

"Pretty awful?"

"Yes, sir."

"Well, suppose you start at the beginning and tell me what you remember. Maybe later you'll remember other things, odds and ends that suddenly occur to you, and when this happens, I want you to write down these things so you won't forget to tell me about them—this is if I'm not around right then."

"I understand, Mr. Caldwell." He hesitated with a sudden air of shyness. "Are you a detective?"

"Yes. Didn't your father explain before he left?"

"I just wanted to make sure."

"What do you want to know about being a detective?" Caldwell said kindly.

"Did you ever . . . well, did you ever have to use a gun and shoot somebody?"

"Yes."

"Did you kill him?"

"Yes." Caldwell thought: *Don't ask how many.*

Davie didn't ask. He began to talk about the telephone calls, carefully skirting the threats to his sister and finally leading up to the last message, the note that had hung on the bush in the barranca. "I knew it was wrong to do what he wanted, to get the keys for him. But I—in the end I didn't know what else to do."

"Didn't you think about telling your father and mother?"

There was a brief flash of surprise, as if one of these might be the last person Davie would consider telling his troubles to. Which? Caldwell asked, "Didn't you even warn Suzie?"

"I wanted to, bad enough." Davie told him about the mud throwing. "When she came in all muddy like that, I knew it had been him—he wanted me to see her that way; he wanted me to understand what kind of things could happen to her. So it seemed as if it was just up to me to get the keys."

"Now, when you were in the barranca—getting back to that—wasn't there a chance you'd see him there? He might have been watching to make sure you'd burn that letter."

"There was just Mr. Warren." A sudden look of understanding, of inner revelation, spread over Davie's face. "I've just thought of something. I rode the horse, and then I forgot to burn the note right away, and it was in my pants when I came to the house. My grandma saw a hole in my pants and took them to sew the hole up—and that must be when she found out. I mean, she must have read the note—and that's why she was out there tonight. I couldn't understand—"

Caldwell waited patiently to let the boy accustom himself to the new ideas, think them through fully, get the bigger picture.

"She must have had some kind of hint, though," he prompted finally, "to have caught on that quickly."

"Well, I did try to tell her about the phone calls, but she thought I meant somebody must be reminding us of Cootie. In case we were beginning to forget."

Caldwell had a pretty good idea of what the scene must have been—the scared kid trying to talk to his grandmother about this sudden and unbelievable awfulness, and the old lady too wrapped up in that other horror to hear him. And thinking of old Mrs. Stoddard, Caldwell saw that she must have felt isolated and rejected here; it wouldn't be hard to withdraw from contact with the family, shut away as she was at the top of those stairs. And with the family oblivious . . .

"Well, let's get back to what you found in the barranca. How long after you saw the note, and read it, did Mr. Warren come along?"

Davie shook his head. "Not long, I guess. I don't remember

exactly. I felt kind of sick. I would have burned the note, but then I heard the horse coming."

"How far is Warren's place from here?"

"Well, there are four houses in between, and then Mr. Warren's place is so much bigger. The grounds around it are, is what I mean. He used to own all this land up here, everything."

"He still owns the hills, is that right?"

"Yes, he kept the hills. My dad says there is supposed to be oil under them."

"I wonder why he doesn't drill for it, then."

Davie seemed puzzled. "Maybe he has enough money already. Or maybe if he sold the oil, he would have to give some of the money to his wife."

Caldwell's eyebrows went up. "And he wouldn't like that?"

"They're divorced. It's called alimony. My sister Suzie told me, Mrs. Caldwell took the two kids and went to Paris. Mr. Bowman —he's the man my dad works for—he got the divorce for them."

Caldwell was silent, letting a few new ideas hatch and try their wings. Davie muffled a yawn. At last Caldwell said, "Did Mr. Warren say anything about your fireplace, or what you'd been burning, or anything along that line?"

Davie shook his head. "Mr. Warren always seems pleased about my camp, that it's neat, and mostly we talked about an old jackrabbit that I've seen in the barranca. Mr. Warren knows about him."

"Mr. Warren didn't mention the fireplace? Not at all?"

Davie frowned and scratched his chin. "I don't know. Maybe he did. I hadn't been burning anything, though. It was later, after I'd gone to the house and Grandma had sewed my pants, it was after that when I went back to the barranca to burn the note. So *he* could see the ashes."

"This voice on the phone—" Caldwell could see that the kid was getting tired, was keeping his eyes open with a terrific effort and only out of politeness, out of obedience to his father. He was, Caldwell thought, a pretty doggone nice little kid, one he wouldn't have minded having himself. If he'd ever got married, of course. "Did it ever seem familiar to you at all, this voice?"

Davie's sleepy eyes widened. "Yeah. Sure. Gee, why didn't I

remember that? One time, I think it was the second time he called
—It's kind of mixed up in my mind, the two calls."

"Sure, I understand."

"Well, all at once it seemed that I knew him. It just popped into
my mind, and it seemed as if the next minute I'd know a name.
His name. And I said something like, 'Hey, I *know* you!' If I'd
been smart, if I'd stopped to think, I wouldn't have said that. I'd
have listened harder and sort of let my mind . . . uh . . . you
know—"

"Yes."

"Only, I wasn't smart," Davie winced at his own stupidity. "I
was kind of excited. And when I said what I did, he got real mean.
He told me if I went on thinking about who he was, the bad
things would sure enough happen to my sister."

"Did this man on the phone sound like an old man or a young
man?"

Davie looked at the ceiling and chewed his lip. "I can't quite
decide. Most of the time, I figured, he wasn't talking in his real
voice. He was trying to hide what he really sounded like."

"You know, Davie, our memory is a queer thing. We can try
and try to recall something without any luck. We push and push,
and nothing happens. And then one day, when we're not trying
at all, when we're thinking of something else entirely, what we
were trying to remember just pops into our mind. And that could
happen to you. Easy. The name you almost thought of could
just"—Caldwell snapped his fingers—"like that."

Davie brightened in spite of his tiredness. "Really? Could it?"

"I'm betting that it does."

"*When* it does—" Davie's face flushed with anger.

"When it does, you tell me. No heroics. If you should let this
man know that you've recognized his voice at last, both you and
your sister—your whole family, in fact—could be in real danger.
And very bad things could happen to all of you, because he might
decide that he had to shut all your mouths."

Davie moved uncomfortably, and Caldwell decided that the
things which had been threatened over the phone had been pretty
terrible.

"If you remember who this man could be," Caldwell went on,

"you come and tell me. Nobody else. You don't breathe a whisper to *anybody*. Promise?"

"Yes." But it was said grudgingly, Caldwell noted.

"Now, shall we go and have a look at your grandmother's rooms? I don't expect to find any evidence there, any clues. I think that she went out tonight to try to catch your blackmailer—"

Davie looked puzzled, and Caldwell put in: "Yes, blackmailer. That's what he is, Davie. Blackmailers don't always ask for money. But I guess the word I really want is extortioner. A blackmailer promises not to tell, and an extortioner promises not to hurt—if he gets what he asks for. So shall we go to your grandma's rooms?"

Davie led the way, and they went together up the stairs to the overcrowded sitting room and bedroom. Caldwell turned on the lights as they went and took a careful look around. His idea was that Mrs. Stoddard should have had a light with her, logically a big one, and that perhaps in the excitement of that final exit she'd forgotten it, left it here.

He sent Davie away to bed and continued the search. He re-examined all the places she might have laid the light down at the last minute before going and then went into the closets and found out that Mrs. Stoddard was a woman who kept a million souvenirs of the past, of the time when she'd had a husband and when Thomas Stoddard had been a kid.

But of any flashlight, there was no sign at all. Nor had there been out there around the gate.

Well, maybe they'd find it in the morning, thrown under a bush, out of sight.

Or maybe something else had happened to it.

Caldwell hoped that this latter idea could be true.

12

It was a little past midnight when Margaret Stoddard came out to the kitchen to see Caldwell. She was wearing a blue dress, her hair was neat, and she didn't look as if she'd been to bed at all. She asked Caldwell if he intended to stay at the house all night, and when he said that he did, she offered him successively coffee, food, and bedding. He told her that he might have some coffee later on. Right now he wanted to think and to make a few notes.

"Are we in danger, do you think?" she asked, very composed and as if the thought of possible danger weren't something she really believed in.

"I don't know." Actually Caldwell thought the possibility quite good. The extortioner would either have raided Stoddard's office or not, depending on how quickly he had moved after getting those keys and whether his errand with them hadn't been too lengthy. With the job either balked or out of the way, he would now have time to think. And perhaps he would be thinking about Davie Stoddard and how much the kid would remember and what sudden ideas might occur to him.

It had to be the office, the law firm. There wasn't anything else.

Someone needed to see something or grab something or destroy something. What had been grabbed or destroyed should be found missing, a telltale gap. If the aim had been to see, to examine, to learn something kept in confidence, then they might have a harder time.

"If you want anything," Margaret Stoddard told him, "don't be afraid to help yourself. Or to come and get me. I don't expect to sleep tonight." She turned a little, and the light from the kitchen slid across her face, and Caldwell saw where powder had been used to conceal the signs of tears. Not recent tears, he thought. Not, perhaps, for the old lady.

"Perhaps you could give me this information, Mrs. Stoddard. It's a small detail. Did your mother-in-law own a flashlight?"

She seemed surprised. "Why . . . really, I just don't know."

"If she had bought one recently, where do you think she might have got it?"

"In town, of course. Perhaps a hardware store. Again, I just wouldn't know."

"Does she own a car of her own? Could she get to town without any of the family along?"

Margaret Stoddard shook her head. "When she needed anything, she either asked one of us to buy it for her or she rode into town with Vicky. I don't think that she had been to town recently. She didn't go out much anymore, since she—she was hurt in a fall."

"I see. I'll talk to your daughter about it then."

Margaret said good night and left for the bedroom wing of the house. Caldwell smoked and did some thinking, sitting in the Family Area with just one lamp on across the room. After a time he stretched out on the couch and shut his eyes.

Don't, he thought, *go pinning any hopes on that flashlight.*

It's out there under a bush.

He slept, lightly, and the house was silent except for the dying whine of the wind.

It was four thirty when Caldwell awoke. His gray eyes opened, and for several seconds he lay unmoving as if orienting himself in the strangeness of the house. It was a big house and he felt its space and its quietness. It was a house that seemed on first examination to be full of comfort and warmth, but Caldwell had learned long ago that such houses could contain the most abject human wretchedness and so had not been surprised at what he had observed about the Stoddards.

He got up and went to a lavatory which he had noticed near the back entry. He washed his face in cold water, used a pocket comb on his hair, and then, feeling refreshed, he went for a soundless walk through the corridor that led to the bedrooms.

He would have heard any noise of Thomas Stoddard's return or that of his daughter, so this must mean that they were still at the hospital and that perhaps the grandmother wasn't in too good a shape.

The bedroom doors were shut, and behind them he felt the stillness of sleep, all except the one at the end, where a light showed. Mrs. Stoddard must be in there; he wondered what she was doing. Beyond this last bedroom was a short dead-end hall and another door, and he looked in there. It was a businessman's den or home office, with family overflow in the way of books and games. He noted the couch. A folded blanket and a pillow in a white slip were propped on the arm of the couch as if ready for use or as if folded for putting away.

He went on to the front entry, examining the living room with its air of formal elegance and lack of use, and then back to the kitchen. He warmed coffee in the percolator, drank it standing beside the sink, and then rinsed out the cup he had used and put it back into the cupboard. He let himself out, unlocking the rear door where Mrs. Stoddard had fallen. It was still dark out here, no sign of the sky's getting lighter, but Caldwell did not turn on the outside light. He waited beside the wall of the house until his eyes had adjusted to the dark. Then, walking almost soundlessly, he went all the way around the house. When he came to shrubbery growing close to the wall, he investigated until he was sure that nobody was concealed in it. When he reached the rear of the house again, he followed the dimly visible path that led out to the back gate. The gate and fence, painted white, showed up clearly in the night.

He leaned against the gate. As soon as it was daylight, the other officers would be back to check whatever trail the attacker had left. It would be a miracle if they found anything. Anybody with the quality of shrewdness this character had shown wouldn't have left a trail that they could follow.

He must have gone off spotted with blood. They might find a few drops of Mrs. Stoddard's blood—with unbelievable luck, close to a good tireprint out on the road.

I'm snatching at straws.

He returned to the house and telephoned headquarters in town. He learned that Stoddard had gone to the office, had been met there by members of the City Detective Bureau, along with Bowman, who owned the law firm. They were still going over records, looking for any evidence that the place had been entered and something examined or taken away, but so far there was no sign of anything wrong.

Meanwhile, the hospital wanted Thomas Stoddard to get back there. His mother had taken a turn for the worse.

The same young doctor met them. He didn't ask them to sit down, or to brace themselves, or to forgive his optimism of a few hours ago. He told Thomas Stoddard that he should come with him quickly, because his mother had at the most only minutes of life left, and his silence toward Vicky left it up to her whether she wanted to be at the scene, too. And Vicky came along.

Thomas Stoddard thought at first, seeing his mother, that they had mixed up their patients and were showing him the wrong woman. This woman had a hugely swollen face, black with bruises, a mouth like cut liver, under an enormous turban of bandages. Nothing resembled the features that he had known all his life, the comfortable likeness of his mother. He looked helplessly at the nurse and at the detective. The nurse seemed sorry and composed. The detective looked grouchy. Vicky touched her father's hand. "Dad, say good-bye. She might hear you."

Well, Vicky had more sense than he did. She knew her grandmother when she saw her.

"Mother . . ."

His voice sounded ridiculous to him, a silly croak. He bent and put his lips against the bruised hot forehead under the bandages that smelled of antiseptic. This was good-bye, and he didn't feel sorrow or grief; he had instead just a stunned fear, a terror of the day that he had to get through, and he saw that for all this while since Cootie had died, he had meant to find a way, a sure way, to let his mother know that he didn't blame her for Cootie's death, that he still loved her just as much as ever, only now time was going, it was too late, and he had never made the effort, and he felt afraid because he was going to have to live with this negligence, this lack in himself, forever, and beginning with the day that was dawning outside right now.

"Oh, God," he cried brokenly.

He bent, arched above the bed in agony, and then Vicky was holding him, turning him, as if she had become the parent and he the child, and through his brimming tears he saw the doctor giving a significant look at the nurse. There was a brief throaty rattle. His mother was dead. His mother had lived the last part of her life alone, he saw, shut off from their mercy and understanding, completely rejected by Margaret, an outcast.

"I'm to blame for it all," he said, shattered by insight into his mother's loneliness.

"No, you're not," Vicky said firmly. "If anyone is to blame, it's Davie—and he's just twelve and a half. You can't expect him to think like an adult or to be brave like an adult. Dad, let's go home. You need rest."

He looked at the doctor, still with some hope, but the young doctor was now, in the kindest and most solemn way, pulling up the sheet to cover the broken face, and he didn't return Thomas Stoddard's glance.

The one who seemed suddenly full of interest and purpose was the detective. He nodded toward the sheeted body as if some phase of the affair had just ended, or had just begun, and turned quickly to leave the room.

It occurred to Thomas then that the police had a murder case on their hands, and he felt afraid, strangely—afraid for himself and for Margaret and for their children. This was going to be a million times worse than the horror that had taken possession when Cootie had died. All their lives would be swept by a cold wind, a searching and chilling draft that would seek out every cranny and pocket, that would turn over every word and every thought betrayed. *I just can't live through it,* he thought, his heart thudding painfully. *I want to die.* And all at once he knew how people felt just before they killed themselves. *If you need to bad enough,* he told himself, *you can do it. I never could see before just how they nerved themselves, but it doesn't involve nerve or will at all—it's just running, getting away from the intolerable.*

Vicky had led him out into the hall. A couple of young nurses paused in their conversation to look them over curiously, and he tried to appear composed. Vicky gave him her handkerchief, and he wiped his eyes with it, breathing in the magnolia smell of her sachet.

"I ought to get back to the office," he said.

"No, you're going home. Mr. Bowman can answer any questions for the police. He probably knows more about everything there than you do, anyway."

"We should telephone the house first, tell your mother to get Suzie and Davie up—"

"Why? Let them sleep. Most especially, let Davie sleep as long as possible because this particular day will be hell for him. Come on, Dad."

She drove, and he sat with his eyes shut, willing himself to relax and to put off the shock, the full impact of death. Actually it wasn't too hard to shun the thought of his mother for the time being. His mind shied away from the scene in the hospital room; the memory of the young doctor carefully pulling up the sheet to cover his mother's face was something he couldn't endure; it made him feel as if he were breaking apart inside.

The country had the peculiar light, the grayness of dawn, and trees and fields and orange groves looked damp and remote, and the sky had the loneliest look of all, clear and without color, empty.

Thomas stared out the car window for a moment and then closed his eyes again. "That detective spoke to you as we were leaving the hospital. What did he say?"

She kept her eyes on the road ahead. They were climbing into the valley; a few patches of fog blew apart as the car rushed through them. "He said that in a murder case there has to be an autopsy, and that there will be one on Grandma."

"He was coming out of a telephone booth there in the hall."

"Yes. Of course, he'd phone in right away. Grandma's dying makes a big difference."

"Don't you think that we—that we could have been kinder to her after Cootie died?" He almost whispered the words, hating to ask her to think about her brother and what had happened that day in the twilight. "Do you believe what she told us? That there was someone else outside, in the yard? That Cootie made a dash to see who it was?"

She was silent for a minute or so. "As for being kinder to her— I don't feel that any of us were unkind, except Mother. And looking back, Mother must have had things on her mind, unhappy things that we didn't know anything about, even before Cootie died, or she wouldn't have acted as she did. And as she has, ever since." Vicky swung the car into the side road that led up to the flank of the hills. There was a faint tint of pink to the sky now, and the trees looked greener, more alive. "But as for there being someone in the yard, a mysterious stranger . . . I just don't know. I used to wonder if Grandma actually believed it herself."

"But she told the story to everyone."

"For a while. And then she stopped."

"I think your mother did something, is why she stopped."

Now Vicky's face turned fully toward him, white with sudden shock, her eyes filling with tears. "She couldn't have—"

"Perhaps not. But Margaret got so mean and so hysterical about that time. It was understandable. She just lashed out at everyone."

"But she wouldn't make Grandma shut up about something that was *true!*"

"Wouldn't she?"

Vicky let the car slide toward the edge of the road and stopped on the shoulder. And now she too was whispering. "It couldn't be that tonight . . . that Mother had anything to do with—but no, she was with you."

"I lied about that."

"What?"

"I lied to Caldwell. I told him that Margaret . . . oh, I didn't really say that she was with me, I just said, yes, that we shared a bedroom, and if she keeps her mouth shut, she's safe. I didn't tell him that my wife was punishing me tonight, as she often did, by sleeping on the couch in the den."

"Mother was in the den? Not with you?"

"Not with me."

Vicky's face seemed to recede, to grow foggy, through his tired eyes; he suddenly wanted desperately to lie down and sleep. The desire to black out was like a tide, a rising lethargy that threatened to swallow him. "I'm just about beat, I guess. I feel as if I can't talk to anybody, face anybody, that I have to sleep."

"We could just stay here for a while and you could nap."

"No," he said, "we'll go on home. Caldwell will be there, and I'll have to answer his questions."

"Will you tell him the truth about where Mother was tonight?"

"Maybe. Eventually. I don't know."

"Anyway, Dad, the one who killed Grandma has to be the man who phoned Davie, who made those threats to get hold of your keys. There really isn't any reason to suspect Mother."

"Suppose the man was waiting, and saw Mother . . . and saw your mother slipping out there, following Davie, checking up? And suppose the man just kept still, and the encounter was between Margaret and Mother? And when the attack was over, he just helped himself to the keys? Would anything be any different?"

"Dad, you're tired beyond enduring. Mother couldn't have killed Grandma. I won't believe it."

He slumped dejectedly. "I hope I can keep my wits together while I talk to Caldwell."

"You won't have to," Vicky said firmly. "I'll do the talking when we get home."

13

When they reached the house, there were several cars in the street, one of them a black-and-white police cruiser. Thomas Stoddard had a brief moment of hoping that Caldwell would be involved in what was going on, obviously an official investigation and probably out at the rear gate, where his mother had been attacked. But no, as they entered the house through the big double glass doors from the pool area, there was Caldwell, plainly waiting to greet them.

He knew about Mrs. Stoddard's death, and his first remarks were perfunctorily sympathetic. Well, give him credit, Thomas thought; at least he was saying something about their loss, and if he sounded rather perfunctory, it could be because he'd had as little sleep as Thomas himself.

"Where are the other officers?" Vicky asked.

"Out at the back," Caldwell told her. "I'm afraid we're not having much luck. The weather was against us. There are a few things I need to—"

"Would you mind if my father went to his bedroom and had some rest?" she asked. She sounded young and polite, the proper tone to use on an older policeman, and Thomas almost smiled in spite of his exhaustion.

On his part, Caldwell had decided on his first glimpse of Stoddard that the man should be allowed some relief. He wasn't going to stand up to much more. It was true that under such tensions and such almost unendurable tiredness, sometimes facts came out which might otherwise have remained concealed. But this was a family situation, Caldwell reminded himself, and by using Thomas Stoddard without pity, the police might well lose more than they could gain.

They needed the cooperation of every single member of this family.

"Certainly. Do go and get some rest, Mr. Stoddard."

"I'll be glad to talk to you."

She was pulling off her gloves, and Caldwell didn't miss the gleam of the big diamond. *Engaged,* he thought; and then he wondered if there had been anything in the home situation which had inclined the girl toward getting married and leaving. Well, probably, he decided. It couldn't have been much fun around here since the little boy had died. Thomas Stoddard as yet hadn't moved, and he too looked at the ring, but with an air, Caldwell thought, as if he'd been hoping it wasn't there.

"Well . . . I'll go and lie down for a little while," Stoddard said.

"Yes, Dad, you do that." Vicky slipped off her coat and flung it on a chair beside the television set. Then she sat down. Caldwell offered her a cigarette, and she shook her head and told him she didn't smoke, but in a minute or so she was going to have a cup of coffee.

"How about now?"

"No, let's talk—you ask some questions, and if I can't think of the answers now, maybe they'll come to me over the coffee. I guess you want to know first of all if I heard anything of what must have gone on outdoors last night. And I'll have to say, I didn't. I was in my room with the radio on, trying to organize my —my clothes. I've made a change of plans for the rest of the year, and some of the things I bought are going to have to be returned, and these were what I was deciding about."

"It was windy, too," he reminded.

"I guess it was. I didn't notice. The first I heard, I think, was the ambulance siren. I remember I dropped whatever I was holding when I heard it, and then almost at the same moment, someone was crying in the hall—that was Davie, and Dad was making him go back into his room. I didn't hear anything at all from the rear of the house, that part of the yard out by the gate, nothing."

She was a very beautiful young lady, Caldwell thought. She didn't look much like either of her parents. Her eyes had an honest, sensitive expression, and Caldwell decided that she would take a lot before she would rebel, and he hoped in that moment that she was getting a good man.

"Your grandmother hadn't mentioned anything she had planned for last night?"

"No. We had talked about Davie's problem—what we knew of it, that he had received some phone calls that had upset him. But we didn't come to any decision, just to wait and see what happened next—a bad idea I can see now. We should have gone to Dad."

"Apparently your grandmother kept her plans to herself."

"I don't understand how she knew what was going to happen—"

Caldwell explained about the note, forgotten in Davie's pants pocket, and his grandmother's taking the pants to mend them. "That's when she got the picture. That must be when she began planning what she meant to do. She collected some old clothes, dyed some tennis shoes, somehow got a scarf to cover her hair—"

"I gave her that," Vicky said suddenly. "She came to me a few days ago and asked if I had some old scarf I didn't want anymore."

"Did she ask you for a flashlight?"

"No."

"And you didn't get one of them for her when you went shopping?"

"Shopping . . ." She repeated the word as if finding a new meaning in it. "You know, she did ask me to take her to town the other day. Day before yesterday, it must have been. She wanted something at a hardware store. She didn't say what."

"And you drove her to town?"

"Yes. And we stopped at Baker's—we've traded there for years. She might have charged whatever she bought. If it was a flashlight."

"Even if she paid cash, would they know her there, remember her?"

"Oh . . . probably." Vicky Stoddard seemed to gather her nerve or her courage to ask: "If you think she must have had a flashlight—was she beaten with it, do you think?"

"I don't know."

"And why"—her eyes were suddenly brimming in her white face—"why was she beaten like that? Why did he have to—"

She was on the verge of breaking down, and Caldwell hurried to put in an answer, to keep it on a commonplace level as much as possible. "I think she surprised somebody. The unexpected danger, the fright out of nowhere, can bring an instant and more violent reaction than would normally be the case. She caught somebody there who hadn't thought he'd be caught. And the sudden jolt made him vicious, I mean, perhaps more vicious than he would usually be."

She wiped away the tears with the back of her hand, and the big diamond gleamed in the dimness.

"How about that coffee now?" Caldwell asked. "Your mother made a fresh pot not too long ago, and it's still hot."

"All right."

"Just sit still. I've learned my way around your kitchen."

"Thank you," she said, trying to sound as if she weren't ready to cry.

Caldwell went into the kitchen and got down a couple of cups. He forgot saucers for a moment—in his bachelor apartment he never used them. Then he remembered, and put the cups into saucers, and laid a spoon into the saucers, too. "Cream? Sugar?" he called over his shoulder.

"Both, please." She sounded muffled, all alone, desolate.

Give me a hood with a broken skull in an alley any day, Caldwell told the percolator soundlessly. *Give me orphan narco pushers. Give me unmarried bank robbers with slow trigger fingers. But give me no more grandmothers.*

He brought the coffee into the family room, spoiling the effect by jiggling some of the coffee out of the cups.

"Thank you," she repeated, and sipped at the steaming cup.

"There's another thing," he told her after a minute. "From the hospital. The nurse and the officer who were with your grandmother say that she spoke a couple of words. She didn't seem to be conscious, exactly, but the words were pretty distinct."

"What were they?"

"If you're wondering why they didn't mention this to you and your father while you were there—"

"I understand," Vicky said. "It was police business."

"Yes. Well, the words she said were, 'Reflection. It was the reflection.' I've been trying to think of what she might have meant, in connection with what happened out there last night, and I don't seem to get anything." He waited, watching how she obviously turned her mind to it, trying to figure a meaning for him, waiting for her eyes to light up and her lips to open, but nothing happened. She drank some more coffee, and finally, she glanced up at him and shook her head.

A uniformed officer came in through the entry and on to the kitchen. He stood there, and Caldwell got up and said, "Find anything?"

The other just shrugged. His boots had damp-dirt smudges on them; a weedy twig was caught in the elbow of his whipcord jacket.

"Did you go up the barranca?"

"Yeah. Nothing there . . . well, there were a few hoofprints. We went over to Warren's, and his horse was gone. It lets itself out and roams around." He glanced at the percolator, and Caldwell told him to help himself. "There weren't any blood spots except just around the gate. It rained just enough to spoil any shoemarks. It looks as if we've drawn a blank so far, but of course, we aren't giving up. We'll find the horse and look him over."

"That's a long shot," Caldwell said softly.

"Sure. But who knows?"

"There must have been a car pulled in somewhere off the street. Look for a spot where a car might be concealed or even half-hidden—low trees, brush, anything that might make a screen."

"We've done that, too."

Caldwell took his cup into the kitchen and washed it, dried it, and put it away. He excused himself to Miss Stoddard, leaving her to think or to go have some sleep if she wanted to. He went out to the back gate. Under the morning light it looked perfectly ordinary. It was made of one-by-fours and painted white, with a flat top rail where those keys must have rested. Beyond were the hills with the barranca cutting down through, the crests of old palms showing up high against the misty sky, the fronds like ragged fans. He saw hoofprints leading up into the barranca, but they didn't look new and had been pitted by the rain.

"What a night he had. What a perfect night," Caldwell said under his breath. He heard someone crossing the gravelly yard behind him and turned and recognized a reporter whom he knew, a local man who represented one of the big Los Angeles papers. The reporter waved a gloved hand. He had a big camera with a flash attachment.

"Is this where it happened?"

"This is it."

The reporter glanced back toward the house. "I was out here before. The time the little kid died, you remember."

"Did you talk to the grandmother then?"

The reporter hung the camera strap on his shoulder, took off his gloves, and fished for cigarettes. "Oh, sure. I got hold of her at the beginning, while she was still willing to talk. It was kind of pathetic in a way. She told me later that I hadn't quoted her right, hadn't put it just the way she had wanted it in the paper, and I tried to explain the mystery of rewrite and what an editor can do to your stuff if he feels like it, but she was hurt, and I guess she went on blaming me. But she wouldn't talk any more about the mysterious stranger—if there ever had been one."

"What did you think at the time?" Caldwell asked. "Did you think there really had been somebody out here?"

"Hell, I don't know." The reporter blew smoke out into the air, and it drifted away in the sunlight.

"Would a little kid on a tricycle make a dash for a stranger? Forgetting a glass door? Or would he be more likely to tear out to meet somebody he knew?"

"Like his mother and father?" the reporter said slyly. "Could be."

"I don't think anything like that happened," Caldwell answered with a touch of stiffness.

The reporter shrugged. "Well, what can you give me about the old lady? Think she tangled with a prowler? Or is it more complicated than that?"

Caldwell would have liked to keep the newspapers gagged, but he decided that too many people knew the truth and that somebody was going to talk eventually. "Give us a break for a couple of days," he said. "Somebody was threatening the family, threatening to harm one of the daughters, unless the kid, Davie Stoddard, delivered the keys his dad carried, brought them out here and left them—"

The reporter nodded without any show of surprise so that Caldwell decided that he had already got part of the story elsewhere. "And the keys are gone?"

"Yes, they're gone."

"The old lady put up a battle for them?"

"She wasn't supposed to be in on it at all," Caldwell explained, "but she found out what was going on and took steps. She jumped somebody who hadn't expected company. If you want to help us, you can play up the idea of a prowler right now."

The reporter looked down at the cigarette in his fingers.

"Who'll we be fooling? The guy who konked her? I don't think. He knows you know everything about him except who he is, and that maybe the kid knows that, too. Weren't there some phone calls?"

"You seem to have just about everything," Caldwell said with irony. "But—as I said—if you want to help a little . . ."

"What did he want with the keys?" the other man asked, ignoring Caldwell's remarks. "To get into the house? Or what?"

"You can figure that out."

"The law offices, then."

Caldwell reflected that when he'd been very young, he had figured out that no man could be a doctor, a lawyer, or a Catholic priest for any time at all without hearing everything it was possible to hear. But he had long ago added cops and reporters to the list. Along with hearing everything came a protective immunity to shock, surprise, or insult. Even, perhaps, to involvement. Or perhaps the immunity to involvement came first. It was something to think about when he had some free time, which wasn't now.

"Do you think he got into the office?" the reporter wondered as he threw away the cigarette and unlimbered the camera for a shot at the gate. Caldwell was facing the house and saw the second newsman as he rounded the corner. The reporter, hearing footsteps, looked over his shoulder and said, "Hi, Joe."

Caldwell answered the reporter's question to himself. No, he didn't believe now that the extortioner had got into the offices. He must have gone somewhere to do the necessary job of cleaning himself from the old lady's blood. By the time the chore had been done the man's wits and caution and sense of self-preservation would have had time to assert themselves, and he would have kept as far from those law offices as it was possible to get.

The two newsmen were exchanging personal chatter, and Caldwell left them and went back to the house.

To his surprise, Thomas Stoddard was in the kitchen pouring himself a cup of coffee. He looked exhausted and used up, with graying beard beginning to show on his face. He wore a pair of pants that to Caldwell seemed like the ones he might do yard chores in. He had on a blue shirt, not fresh, and was barefooted. He glanced at Caldwell with what seemed to be apology. "I tried to sleep, and then I began to think about all of the things that must be done. The most important . . . new locks, both here and at the office. I've got to telephone a locksmith, and get hold of Bowman—" He took a sip of the coffee, and Caldwell could see how his hand shook.

"Yes, that's a good idea," Caldwell said.

"I know you want to talk to me," Stoddard hurried on, "and so, why not now?"

"You look pretty worn-out."

"No, I'm all right. I want to get it over with. I don't want to lie in the bedroom awake, going over and over what's in my mind, and try to answer the questions you have to ask . . . I mean, try to recall exactly what is the truth. I've got to tell you first of all, and I know this is what you want to ask . . . and yes, I can think offhand of about two dozen people who might like to get at papers in our office. Or maybe even more. Maybe fifty. Maybe, if I stopped to really think about it, more than a hundred. Only, I don't see how you can go to all of them and demand an accounting of their movements last night, or ask if they have alibis, or anything like that, because the questions in themselves would be a kind of accusation—"

"You let me worry about that," Caldwell said quietly.

"But you want the names, anyone I can think of?"

"Yes, I want the names."

Stoddard put down the cup and seemed to make an effort to shake himself together, a kind of tightening up, though Caldwell sensed that his tired senses were beyond reviving except with much sleep and rest. "Let's go into the living room. I don't want to sit in there." He gestured toward the Family Area. "If I had my way, I'd never see the room again. Nor the house."

Caldwell wondered, as he followed Stoddard, if the wish extended to any of the people here and, if so, whom?

14

In the big elegant room, Thomas Stoddard parted the draperies a little, looked out at the slope in front of the house and then around inside, and Caldwell thought that his expression was one of bitter regret. Stoddard pointed out a couple of formal chairs, silver brocade, and Caldwell sat down. He thought that the room seemed a little monotonous in its light pastel colors, but that perhaps when it was to be used—for entertaining, for example—it could probably be brightened by flowers and might be attractive.

He stretched his legs. Stoddard sat down and rubbed a hand across his eyes. Caldwell said, "To start with, there's no use firing a shotgun when a rifle will do the job. The man we want knew a lot more about your family and your home than anyone you would have met only at the office. He was no casual contact. He'd been here. He had noticed the closeness between your two younger children, and he had sized up Davie with some care—you might almost say, leisure. He knew how to bring pressure to bear and just when to increase it. He knew of Davie's camp in the barranca. He was bold enough to hide close to your home to throw mud on Suzie. In other words, if he'd been seen leaving the area, he wouldn't have been noticed as an outsider, someone who didn't belong. Doesn't all this clear a lot of names from your thoughts?"

Stoddard had been following him intently. "Yes, I guess it does. If it's the truth. What would prevent someone who needed a look at our office files from coming up here to size up the house and my family? We live on a public street. Hikers use the hills behind the place. Riders, too—the hills are really Warren's property, but he's broad-minded and wouldn't run anyone off unless he made an obvious nuisance of himself."

"Have anyone in mind?" Caldwell asked.

Stoddard shrugged tiredly. "No. And I guess that really I agree with you. It must be someone I know, someone the family knows. I hate to admit it."

"Trying to force Davie to give him your keys is one thing, Mr. Stoddard. Killing your mother is quite another."

"I can see that, too."

"Will this make it harder for you to suggest names for investigation?"

Stoddard nodded. "Of course it will. I don't want to accuse anyone of murder, even of the murder of my mother. It's too serious a thing."

"Well, we have to start somewhere," Caldwell said, "and so—suppose we start with Warren himself. He knew about the camp in the barranca; he's friends with your children because of the horse. What's the state of his divorce settlement?"

To Caldwell's disgust, Stoddard, tired as he was, bristled right up. "I couldn't tell you that. Such information would have to come from Mr. Bowman."

"Bowman keeps the Warren file to himself?"

"Yes. You see, Mr. Bowman had a law office for years here, without a partner or any assistants. He ran everything himself except for Miss Church. Miss Church retired last year; she must have been close to eighty—"

"Taking her secrets with her," Caldwell put in grimly.

"What I'm saying," Stoddard went on, "is that some clients are still Mr. Bowman's private responsibility."

Caldwell shrugged. "Well, your common sense will tell you that we won't respect any such boundaries. Anyone who had business with your office is suspect—I guess I should say, is possibly suspect. Do you mean to tell me that you have no idea whatever about Warren's current affairs?"

Stoddard flushed, and his exhausted eyes seemed filled with guilt. "I guess I can tell you that Warren wants his wife to settle for a lump sum. A very generous amount, actually. Mr. Bowman is trying to work it out."

"Wouldn't Warren be kept fully informed about everything as the negotiations went along?"

"I can't see why he wouldn't," Stoddard said.

"Then why would he need to see any documents in your office? Or to remove any, if that was the idea behind all this?"

"I can't imagine why he would need to do either of those things."

Caldwell spent a moment in thought. "Do you know why Warren wants to settle this amount on his wife? I presume it's to shut off any future increase in payments—"

Stoddard, lifting a hand jerkily, broke in. "That's the usual motive, but whether it is Warren's, I can't say."

"He's sold off a lot of his land up here," Caldwell pointed out. "I suppose, about as much as he wants to, here on the lower part of the hills and in the valley. He's marking time now. There must be something more, further development of some kind, and he's hesitating."

"How can you say what he's doing?" Stoddard said impatiently. "He certainly can't be hurting for money, even with what he sends to his ex-wife in Europe. Maybe he's not hesitating, he's finished."

Caldwell tried to look as if he might believe it. He changed tack a little. "Warren inherited all this, didn't he? From his old man, I think I heard somewhere."

"His father came here from England as a young man; it must be almost fifty years ago. He bought all of it, the valley and the hills, for almost nothing. It was desert. Nobody knew there was water just waiting to be drilled for. Old man Warren experimented with this and that—this is what I've heard from Mr. Bowman. The old man had grandiose ideas about re-creating a bit of England, a country layout copied after the property of some earl or other back home. He almost went broke and almost lost everything, and it was Warren himself, not much more than a kid, who finally got him to settle down and put in orange groves and start making money. The old man left Warren the land, but that was about all. It was Warren's foresight and ambition that made all the difference."

Caldwell's eyes were averted before Stoddard could see the cynical understanding that the detective felt. Caldwell told himself that a man in Warren's position would find it ten times harder to give up a share of his wealth to a divorced wife than one who'd had it all handed to him like a cake on a platter.

And no wonder Warren was known as the Lone Ranger here-abouts. He must ride that ridge of hills and think of the oil waiting to be drilled like a thirst-driven pilgrim above an underground river. The earth no longer kept its secrets, like the water Warren's father had found in the cup-shaped valley. They exploded bombs in the ground and studied the sound waves in their computers and knew exactly what was where and how to get it. Warren knew what he had. The question was: How badly did he want to keep his ex-wife from sharing in it?

We want to remember, Caldwell said to himself, *that our bugger here didn't start with the idea of killing anybody. He started out with the need to get at some keys and an idea of scaring a kid enough so that the kid would get them for him. He got spooked last night and killed the old lady, but that doesn't change the simplicity of the thing in the beginning. So maybe Warren did just want to go over that file in Bowman's office and make sure that Bowman was carrying on a correspondence with the wife which was what he wanted. Lawyers have been known to handle things differently from what clients instruct them. The legal mind can be a pretty tricky machine.*

"How have your contacts with Warren turned out? No trouble, I take it," he said finally.

"We've never had the least misunderstanding," Stoddard replied firmly. "Mr. Warren has been generous to the children in letting them ride the horse. Well, he's let Suzie ride, and he's let Davie do chores and be around the horse with the prospect of riding eventually."

"Wouldn't Davie know Warren's voice?" Caldwell asked. "Too well, really, to be fooled on the phone?"

"I don't know."

"Mr. Stoddard, you look pretty well used up. Why not try to rest again, and I'll talk to you later on? I have a couple of errands to take care of right now, anyway."

Stoddard hesitated for a moment as if wondering if he could rest if he went in and lay down again. He nodded at last. "I can give it a try."

He stood up, and after a moment he offered Caldwell his hand.

"Thanks for what you're doing. I know it has to be done."

They shook hands. Caldwell said, "Just before death came, Mr. Stoddard, your mother spoke a few words. Only the nurse and the detective were there to hear them. She said something about a reflection. 'It was the reflection.' Does that mean anything to you?"

Obediently Stoddard appeared to try to think. "No, I guess it doesn't."

"Well, then, I'll be going. Temporarily."

He had decided to take care of talking to the clerks at Baker's Hardware himself.

From the open door of his car in the driveway, Caldwell looked back at the house. It was beautiful and big, he told himself, and spoke dramatically of success. The man who had planned the house, the architect, had tried to form the lives of the people living in it. He had molded the house around the Stoddard family like a machine to organize their behavior. And how much had the unknown architect had to do with the events of last night? Perhaps more than anyone realized, Caldwell decided.

Stoddard was sick of the place, which was understandable.

The house had isolated the old lady at the top of her stairs and had provided a den adjacent to their bedroom for Stoddard's wife to retreat to when she was angry. Caldwell had made up his mind that the bedding in the den meant that Mrs. Stoddard had been there.

He would talk to the wife later, and no doubt the truth would come out.

He started the motor, turned the car toward the street. The valley was marked by patches of pale sunlight, and the breeze had the freshness of wet earth washed by the rain. Across the valley on a ridge lower than this one were other big homes, and they too looked washed and shining. The valley itself had lost some of its orange groves, and here and there were blocks of houses, not as large as those that faced each other on the ridges. *But quite decent and livable,* Caldwell told himself, *and quite beyond the paycheck of a police detective.*

"You knew all about the paycheck when you went into it," he said half-aloud, guiding the car down through the lane lined by pepper trees and eucalyptus. "You were so smug about being on the side of the law."

He grinned. It occurred to him that he still was.

Davie washed and dressed and straightened his room, went to the kitchen and made toast and cocoa and ate and drank that, and then waited. The house had a terrible, secret-keeping stillness. He didn't see the detective around anywhere. There were no men out in the backyard.

He went back to the bedroom wing of the house and listened. He thought he could hear his parents talking in their bedroom, very softly. He remembered the bitter, ugly scene at dinner last night, his mother's telling his grandmother that she wished she were dead, and he wondered if his mother were sorry now and might be telling his father she hadn't meant it. You weren't supposed to think or to say bad things about dead people, and Grandmother was dead, and so those bad things had to be taken back. A brief remembrance of how his grandmother had looked, lying on the floor beside the back entry, flicked through his mind, but he quickly shut it out. It was too awful to remember.

He wondered where Vicky and Suzie were. He thought about knocking on their doors, but something kept him from doing it.

He looked into the den, but no one was there, and it was full of shadows.

He returned to the kitchen and went restlessly on through and on outside to the pool. The wind had blown a lot of trash into the water, scraps of brush and leaves and streamers of bark off the eucalyptus trees and some dead blooms of oleander. The decking was splotched with wet places in which dead leaves were stuck. He thought about getting the rake and tidying up, a surprise for his dad, and then happened to glance out toward the street and saw a couple of cars there, men lounging beside them smoking. He had no idea who the men were, whether plainclothes detectives or newspaper reporters or the advance guard of curiosity seekers, but he took no chances. He hurried indoors.

He wished that someone would come whom he could talk to.

He could go back to the den and choose a book and read there. That ought to be all right. Or he could stay in his room and touch up some of his old airplane models.

Somebody ought to come soon and explain what he should do.

He wandered to the back entry and stepped out. No one was there, either, though he thought the police might be. It all looked so familiar and ordinary that it was hard to remember what had happened there just last night. It seemed dreamlike. But then, suddenly, what had happened to his grandmother swept through him with a shock, the impact of what had actually been done to her, the beating and how she must have crawled for help, dragging along on the ground like an injured animal. Bleeding. In the dirt. And it couldn't have been much more than a minute or two after he had laid those keys on the top bar of the gate and had rushed back to the house with a big sigh of relief.

He shook with a fierce hatred of himself. He hadn't even had the guts to wait, to watch. He might have saved her, yelled a warning, done *something*.

Early that morning his dad had opened his bedroom door for a minute, had wakened him by whispering his name, and had told him that his grandmother was dead. Fogged by sleep, he had wondered afterward if he had dreamed it, but now he knew it had really happened. She was gone. She had tried to save them from the creep and it had cost her life.

He wanted to go back in the house, now, and then he thought with a rush of hope that maybe his dad would sell the house and they would move away. Surely his dad wouldn't want to live here anymore, not after what had happened to Cootie, and now this thing with Grandma. They could move back into town. He didn't remember much about living in town, except that your friends were closer and so was school. You didn't have to ride a school bus; you walked. And after school you could stay and fool around on the playground equipment.

Stubborn dislike for himself kept him out there staring toward the fence. *Chicken,* he told himself. *You couldn't wait even a minute last night. Let's see how you stand it by daylight.*

He forced himself to walk out to the gate, though his heart thumped and there was a thickness when he tried to swallow.

But then all at once he couldn't bear to wait there, right on the spot where she must have stood last night, and he pushed open the gate, half-blinded by angry tears, and went on toward the barranca.

It was drying, with a musty smell of dead brush and pockets of dankness. He pushed his way through, following the dim track marked here and there by old hoofprints.

I might as well bring the stuff down from the camp, he thought. *I won't want to go up here anymore. Probably Mr. Caldwell doesn't want any of us to go off all alone, away from everyone else. He didn't say so, but probably he wouldn't like it.*

The camp seemed small and dismal. The old pots had water in them, and the blanket was wet. It all looked silly and childish suddenly. It was a place where he had played, pretended, like a little kid. He felt far too old for it now.

He began to roll the damp blanket tighter, and all the time something else was there, waiting for him to look at it, demanding to be seen. He kept his eyes away from it as long as he could and then looked, and it was what he knew it was, a square of white paper stuck on the same bush as before.

He didn't want to look close enough to read, but he had to do that too, at last. The letters had been scratched on with a burned stick. They were dim, and in places the stick had gone through the paper and left holes, but the message couldn't be mistaken. There was no way, sick as he felt, to pretend that he didn't know what the letters said.

Too Bad
for
Your
Sister

15

Thomas Stoddard felt a slow drag toward wakefulness. He fought back angrily, clinging to shadows, burrowing his face into the pillows. There was something waiting that he couldn't cope with, couldn't endure, and he wouldn't try now; he wouldn't wake and see it. He tried to shut out the sense of the room, the knowledge of where he was. But in the end it was useless. He was awake. He lifted his head and looked around him. The room was dim. Margaret was on the lounge on the other side of the room, huddled there with her eyes hidden in her hands.

There was no sound. If she was crying—and of course she wasn't—she was doing it very quietly.

He tried to fight off the feeling of despair, but his mind wandered, and he found himself remembering his mother; her body would be at the morgue now. They did autopsies on people who died violently. Someone had told him so at the hospital, or perhaps he'd already known it. When the autopsy was done, they'd send the pieces to the funeral home. Had he told them which one? Had Vicky?

Did it matter?

His mother had spent her life, or most of its adult part, rearing him and loving him, with the last few years under Margaret's ugly thumb, separated from the rest of them by those stairs, by the length of the house really. Hadn't Margaret told the architect to put in those stairs, to make the little suite for his mother on a different level from the rest of the house? He couldn't remember now. It seemed to have occurred in another lifetime or on another planet.

Why blame Margaret? his inner voice demanded. *Everything that she did had your implied consent. You could have acted like a man, like the head of the family. A woman like Margaret, an adult neurotic child, will go as far as she can, but a man could have stopped her. A real man.*

He got out of bed and stole soundlessly, swiftly, toward the figure on the chaise. He felt his hands shake; his lips drew back against his teeth in a feral expression. He stood over her for a moment; she didn't move. He put down his right hand in a gesture that was almost a caress; the hand hovered over her, and then his fingers slid into her hair, tightened, pulled hard. He jerked her head up.

Her face had no expression in it, no reaction to the pain of his hard grip in her hair, no fear. It was a pale mask in which her eyes glowed. He slid his left hand across her windpipe and pressed in slowly on each side of her throat, and still there was nothing but a kind of watchfulness.

"I ought to tear your goddamn head off," he heard himself saying, and scarcely knew his own voice. "You killed my mother. Slut. Whore."

He thought she wasn't going to say anything, but then she answered, "Will that make things better for you? Will it pay everything back? Go ahead."

He wanted to take her head between his fists and by some superhuman effort crush it to jelly. He even, for a moment, knew how it would feel to do it. There would be a resistance, the bone and the covering of fine muscles and skin and hair taut and strong between his hands, the round shape of it, the knowingness of the brain inside and the senses, the eyes still watching and the ears listening, breath being sucked into the lungs, and then with the pressure increasing he would feel the first distortion, the first giving way, and perhaps there would be a sound, the creak of bones, and the toughness would be there still, the hardness under the fabric of hair and skin, but now it would be going out of shape, and she would be dying.

"Go ahead," she said again. "You want to. So do it."

"I wish I could," he got out. "I just wish I could." It seemed that the head he held in his imagination had broken suddenly and that the shredded ends of the pieces of skull were sticking into his hands. It was a strange sensation; he still gripped her hair with his right hand and his left was at her throat, but the truth was that his palms stung with those broken bones and blood was running down his wrists, her blood. He felt sick. He felt older than God, drained, tottering.

She put up one of her hands all at once and stroked his fingers that clutched her throat. "Thomas," she whispered.

He jerked both hands away and moved back toward the bed. He sat down after a moment, facing her, and looked around for his shoes and socks.

She spoke with a practical tone, businesslike, ignoring what had just passed between them. "We have to talk, Thomas. That's why I came in here and waited until you woke up. We have to plan some kind of . . . of unity, of being organized. This could be worse than it was when—" She stopped talking, and a moment passed while he thought she might be listening to something outside the room. "It could be worse than it was the other time. There could be the same kind of people up here, all that trash that came to stare. It's because of the neighborhood, and the way the papers wrote it up when . . . that other time, the things your mother said—"

Waves of black rage pounded through his temples; he dropped the shoe he had picked up. "You rotten whore, don't you blame anything on my dead mother."

A gray pallor came into her face. She kept her voice low, placating. "We have to be prepared. We have to be ready for it."

"Is that all her death means to you?" He shifted on the bed, and she retreated on the lounge as if getting ready to defend herself. "Her dying as she did just means some idle trash might run up here to look us over? We'll have to endure being gawked at? Is this what counts? Our minor embarrassment and loss of privacy?"

She looked watchful and afraid, and for a spinning moment he wondered if she could somehow have shared that nightmare in which he had broken her skull. "Nothing I say can change what happened to her. No regret, no hope that I could go back and do things differently—"

"As if you felt that way," he whispered.

"It wouldn't change anything if I did. She's dead. We have to go on living. We have a home. We have children."

He began to laugh. He couldn't help it. She put her hands over her ears.

All at once he felt tired, finished. He put on his socks, shoes, and went into the bathroom to wash. When he came out, she was still sitting there on the edge of the chaise cushion, still watchful and as far as he could see completely in control of herself. That's what was so ugly, he thought, her air of business as usual. Of keeping up appearances.

"You didn't see my mother," he said quietly.

Her lips framed what might have been a silent no.

"She wasn't nice to look at, those last hours she lived."

A speculative expression entered Margaret's eyes as if she were trying to figure out what he might say next.

"I intend to give every cooperation to the police," he went on. "I want them to catch her killer. There is no real punishment anymore, so even when the murderer is caught, he'll probably spend a short time in prison and be paroled—but anyway, you can get ready to answer some questions because I'm going to tell Caldwell that we weren't together last night. You weren't here with me, and I don't really know where you were."

For the first time she seemed truly shaken and incredulous. She said a few stammered words and then fell silent again.

"If your crowds come—the crowds you seem so worried about —maybe they'll take some special interest in *you.*"

"You couldn't do it!"

"I'm going to do it right now. And—about your not being in here—I want that arrangement made permanent. You can take over the den or one of the other bedrooms. I don't care. I just never want you in here again. After this thing is all settled, after they know who was after Davie for those keys and killed my mother, then we'll get a divorce."

She tried to gather herself; she made an obvious effort not to show the shock and dismay. "I don't think that even your mother would have wanted that."

"She's not here to say so. Get your clothes . . . get everything that's yours . . . out of this room and the bathroom. And those damned paper flowers . . . Good God, take them the first of all."

He walked past her, opened the door, slammed it behind him. He stopped in the hall, drew several deep breaths, and felt the shaking gradually settle out of him. There had been some near thing in there, something he didn't want to think about too closely. He had better watch himself around Margaret after this. It might be wisest to have somebody around, some third party, Vicky or someone, when he talked to her.

Nothing had happened in the bedroom just now. But something had been damned well on the verge of happening.

He started toward the other end of the house, and then it occurred to him: The one who'd killed his mother must not have meant anything to happen either, and the rush of rage and hate had come up, bursting, towering and irresistible, exactly like the feelings he had had sitting there on the edge of the bed.

He hesitated, frowning, and then determinedly brushed it from his mind. He wanted to check upon the children, Davie especially. Davie must not blame himself for what had happened to his grandmother. He had to be consoled. Thomas Stoddard went to the kitchen and on into the Family Area, looked out at the pool, met the cool stare of a reporter or detective who was sitting on a poolside bench, retreated back through the kitchen to the rear entry. Davie was out there, bringing back what must be his camping stuff from the barranca.

Thomas held the door for Davie to pass in. "Hello, son."

Davie didn't look up. There was dampness on his face, sweat maybe. "Hello, Dad."

"You've cleared out the camp?"

"I figured Mr. Caldwell wouldn't want me spending much time up there by myself."

"That's a sensible idea," Thomas agreed. "Is Caldwell around here somewhere?"

"I don't think so. I think he went away."

"Where are you going to put your camping stuff?" It was kind of junky-looking, Thomas thought, the broken basket with the odds and ends of pots and stuff. He really didn't want it in the house.

Davie looked down at his burden as if seeing it for the first time. He hesitated. There was a look of strain, of deep worry, in his face. "Well, I guess I had an idea about putting it in my room. But I really don't have space in the closet."

"Well, how about letting me boost it up to a high shelf in the garage? It'll be okay there, and if you ever have a notion of wanting it again—"

"I won't ever want it again," Davie said quickly and firmly.

For a moment Thomas wondered if anything might have happened in the barranca to frighten Davie and then decided in the next instant that Davie would have told him about any such thing at once, and what this appearance of anxiety and fear was all about was an aftereffect of last night's disaster. Davie had made up his mind to clear out his childish retreat and, in doing it, had come face to face with the finality of change that tragedy must bring. He was simply growing up.

Thomas patted his son's shoulder. "Here, let me carry all that. You can open the garage door."

Davie let him take the basket. Their hands touched in the transfer, and Davie's face lifted all at once, his eyes fixed on Thomas', and there was the feeling that he was going to say something, that he had something important to tell.

Or was it a longing for comfort and affection?

Lugging the camping stuff back toward the rear door, Thomas felt a sense of guilt and grief. Why on earth had he let his kids practically grow up without knowing anything about them? Two girls and a boy—and they were strangers. In the face of their need for him, their father, he was voiceless and inept, a stumbling fool.

Davie opened the garage door, a narrow house-sized entry, and they went together into the dim, gasoline-smelling interior. Shelves had been built across the wall next to the yard. Thomas lifted the basket to the level of his head and pushed it into a vacant spot and then noticed that it was next to a stroller that had belonged to Cootie and found when he turned that Davie was staring at the stroller with a look of shock.

Thomas tried to speak normally. "Lots of stuff here we ought to get rid of. It's silly to keep it all."

The two family cars sat shining in the dusky light, but Vicky's small car was gone.

"What about Grandma's things?" Davie asked.

"You mean, all the stuff in her apartment? Well, it'll have to stay put for a while. There's no hurry."

"But what *will* become of it?" Davie's tone was anxious and insistent. "You won't . . . it won't go anywhere like a—a secondhand store, or a junkyard—"

Thomas took his son by the arm and led him back out into the sunlight. That moment when both of them had recognized the stroller had been something he didn't want to share with Davie again. And now he didn't know what to tell Davie about his grandmother's things. How do you explain to a child that when a life ends, the things that mattered in that life lose their value, that they must be discarded to make room for what belongs to the living?

"There's no hurry," he repeated, at a loss.

"Well, I mean . . . someday," Davie said. "I guess I'd just forgot about all the things Cootie used to have. He had a tricycle and a whole lot of toys and even picture books, and now they aren't around anywhere; I just realized I haven't seen anything of his for a long time. So that's why"—he choked up, and his voice died to a whisper before he regained control—"why I wondered about the things Grandma had. She had so much."

"She had everything that used to fit in her house, just about," Thomas said. "When she moved here with us, I tried to get her to discard it all, those big pieces of furniture and all the crockery and silver and linens, and she wouldn't do it."

"But you won't throw it away."

"No, son, we won't throw it away."

A time would come when Davie would understand the inexorable progress and finality of everything human and its end. But it was natural that now he wanted to be reassured that his grandmother's place in this house, her niche, was not to be obliterated carelessly and hastily. She was still a part of them, still belonged to them, and the proof was that her things should remain.

A fleeting thought crossed his mind as they walked toward the rear entry of the house, wondering where Vicky might have gone. She should have told someone before leaving, explained where they could reach her. He had supposed that after the long hours of last night, she would still be in bed.

"I wonder where Vicky is," he said aloud.

"Maybe she's over at Jeff's place," Davie answered.

Thomas frowned. "She told you she was going there?"

"No. But I think she talked to him on the phone a while ago." Davie showed the look of strain, of worry, that Thomas had noticed before. "I—I came to the house, I mean I ran down here and I went to the kitchen and she was there, talking on the phone, and then after I'd waited a few minutes I went back up the barranca for my camping stuff. It was—it was just a kind of extra trip I made, or something."

The awkwardness, the feeling of difficulty that Davie seemed to have about talking on the subject roused Thomas' curiosity for a minute. He started to ask Davie why he should have run down to the house before going back to the barranca for the basket, why the extra trip had been necessary, and then decided that Davie had had enough of quizzing that day.

"Let's fix an early lunch," he said instead. "Let's see what's in the refrigerator."

Davie didn't look interested, and the expression of worry didn't go away.

They went in through the back entry to the kitchen, and Thomas stood there looking at the neat, spacious interior, everything clean and in order, a room made for the comfort and convenience of a family, what should be a food-smelling room, a room rich with something being baked, and he was swept by a raw grief and sense of loss. The place was stone-cold, and if it smelled of anything, it was of antiseptic cleanser and floor wax, and it was as sterile and as mocking of life as must be the morgue in which his mother lay.

16

Vicky left her small car in the driveway and walked quickly toward the front of the house. It was a broad white house with a pillared porch and red tiled steps. On each side of the walk leading to the steps were mixed blue lantanas and pink geraniums, low and creeping growths now past their best bloom and smelling to Vicky of autumn, of ashy blossoms and dead leaves, with weedy grass infesting the outer edges, because a lot of the time Mrs. Norbert was away and the gardener wasn't very efficient, when he came at all.

Jeff must have been watching for her. He opened the door before she could ring. He was barefooted, damp-haired, and he wore the glasses he used to read, big spectacles that distorted her view of his eyes. He had on an old blue summer shirt and denim pants. When Vicky came in, he enfolded her with his arms and held her close, not trying to kiss her. She felt the calmness, the strength and warmth, and shut her eyes gratefully. After a moment he reached past her to close the door.

She pulled free and went on through the entry, a little uncertainly.

"I'm here alone," Jeff said. "Dad's in New York, and Mother's in San Francisco whipping an art show into shape. Some goon who makes crockery totem poles or something." His tone was grave, and Vicky thought: *He's not trying to share my grief or to pretend that nothing has happened. He's waiting to see how I feel.* She tried to smile at him. He touched her elbow. "Let's go on back to my digs. We might get caught in the cobwebs if we stay in here."

This part of the Norbert house had always made Vicky think of a monastery. There was a shadowy emptiness and quiet; heavy furniture that never seemed to be moved, dark tables and chairs that reminded her of monks laboriously smoothing and fitting oak together with wooden pegs. Her steps echoed uncannily. In the rooms she passed, the floors shone with light from unseen windows, but there was too a sense of everything undisturbed, timeless. *It's the dust,* Vicky thought, *that makes it seem so alone.* Mrs. Norbert was seldom home long enough to bring in and supervise household cleaning help, and when she was away, Jeff refused to be bothered.

Jeff had two rooms connected by an archway, on the northeast corner of the house, and this was a different world. He had plastered the walls with posters, drawings, experiments in perspective done in ink, color splashings, ads, souvenirs, and bookshelves. There was a look of life here, of humor and daring. The windows were open wide, letting in sun and air and an occasional bee. His bed and the chairs were cluttered with stray books. The desk was a mess.

He followed Vicky into the room, shut the door, and then stood there looking at her in a way that seemed almost puzzled.

"I'm just sick inside, Jeff," she stammered. "And I keep thinking of the way she had to live there with us, like a . . . some stranger we didn't quite want." She stopped because she knew she was going to cry.

He took off the glasses, slowly, carefully, and rubbed the back of his hand across his eyes. "Of course, you feel like that. Anyone would; I mean, it's just the natural thing. We all—everyone—remember all the things we didn't do, and we see the one who is dead in a way we never did before. It's because of the finality, darling. Knowing it's all over, beyond touch, beyond being changed. How could you not be moved by that?" He came close and put up a hand to stroke her hair. "I love you, Vicky. And I couldn't love anyone who wouldn't feel as you do."

She caught his hand and pressed it to her cheek. "Oh, Jeff, I love you too! So much, so terribly much! And this sudden awful thing mustn't change things—"

"How could it? It has nothing to do with us."

"I guess I expected you to tell me not to dwell on Grandma. Not to give way to what I feel."

"I'd have to be crazy to say that."

He led her to the bed, and they sat there, together, and she told him all about the events of the night just past. He held her hand and sat bent forward as if listening closely. "How is Davie taking it?"

"I haven't talked to him yet. I know Dad went in and spoke to him last night just before we left for the hospital. He must know that she is dead. And he mustn't blame himself."

"I guess I'd better tell you," Jeff said slowly. "I was over at your place earlier this morning."

It was Vicky's turn to be puzzled.

"A police car came by, real early, and the officer got out and rang the bell until I answered. He wanted to know whether I'd seen anything over there on that opposite ridge, any strange cars, any people acting queerly, sneaking around, and I told him the distance was too far for that. I mean, too far to make out if a car was strange or any details of a person's actions. You see the houses plain enough, and that's about it."

She nodded, remembering her view of Jeff's house from across the valley.

"By then, of course, I was demanding to know what had happened, and I got it out of him. Then he wanted to know if any strangers had been hanging around over here, using binoculars or anything like that, and I told him that if I'd ever seen anyone spying on your place, I'd have jumped him, because I knew you and your family, and in fact, you and I are going to get married. Then of course, he acted like he'd struck gold."

She tightened her hand on his.

"So then I had to convince him that you and I weren't having a lovers' quarrel and that the engagement was perfectly solid and that I liked your family, and no, your grandmother had never shown any disapproval toward me, and that I didn't really know her too well, just to speak to, a pleasant older lady—"

"How ridiculous!"

"No, it was all right; he was doing his job. And not doing it badly. He wasn't obnoxious in any way. I also told him that you had spoken to me about some queer telephone calls Davie had been getting. And that the two of us had decided that the calls didn't amount to much. We didn't do what we should have, which would have been to raise so much hell that Davie would have spilled it all and we might have prevented what happened last night."

"But you said that you'd been at our house today."

"When the cop left. I was wide-awake by then; I couldn't wait around here; I had to try to see you."

"But you didn't after all—"

"The damnedest thing . . . And I still don't know why it threw me off the way it did. Why it changed everything. I drove to your place. I left my car in the street. Not too close, there were cops parked in front of your house, and I wasn't going to mingle—I'd had enough cop for the time being." He grinned suddenly as if at his own inexplicable quirk. "I didn't go up the driveway, either. I cut through that vacant land between you and the neighbors. Got thoroughly full of stickers, too. Foxtails in my socks, you could say. I had the idea I'd go around to the back and rap on your window. I didn't want to see anybody but you."

"This was still very early?"

"I don't know what time it was. There was a kind of mist in the air, a clammy feeling, so it was still early, yes. There is a lot of tangled brush in those lots, lantana and scrub palms and sage and what not, and it was all wet, dripping with dew or fog. I tried to walk quietly and get close enough to size up the back of the house without being seen. I didn't want to run into the detectives, if there were any. But instead of the police, I saw Warren."

She frowned. "Mr. Warren?"

"Yes. And I got the impression he'd been doing what I was doing, only coming from another direction. He'd gotten close enough to see something, too, because he was standing absolutely still, looking toward your place. In fact, he was so damned still for a while it was kind of hard to believe he was a person. He had on old clothes, faded stuff that blended in with the dead brush."

"What did he say?"

"Not a damned word. I don't think he saw me. He was standing there as still as a statue. The way he looked, something about all that stillness, stopped me in my tracks, too. I waited. It seemed to me I didn't even breathe."

"That's all he did? Just watched?"

"It seemed forever that he just stood there. But then all at once he turned and went back toward his own place. He just faded into the brush. When he came back, he was leading his horse. He cut up one of those smaller barrancas, but I wondered—"

It seemed to Vicky that into the warm, sunny, open room something strange and cold had drifted. She pulled her collar up around her neck.

"I wondered if he wasn't really headed for that big barranca that leads up from your place."

"Why did you think that?"

"I don't know."

"That's all that happened?"

"It wasn't really what happened." Jeff was frowning. "It was the way he looked, the way he acted."

"You know Mr. Warren pretty well. Why didn't you just speak to him? Ask him if he'd heard about my grandmother?"

"He'd heard about her, all right."

"Well, you don't *know* that."

"I know it. Don't ask me how I know it. But that's why Warren was there, as still as a spook."

"So what did you do next?"

"I wish I'd followed him, but I didn't." Jeff flung himself back to lie stretched across the bed, looking at the ceiling. He took off the glasses, laid an arm across his face. "What I did—I went up to the spot where Warren had stood, and there I had a good view of the whole back of your place, the house and the yard, the fence, the opening of the barranca. There were two men out there, standing, talking, and one of them had a big camera and looked ready to take anybody's picture who stumbled into the scene, so I just faded. I went back to the car and drove home and gave you some time and then called you."

She turned and stretched out beside him, propped on her elbows. The big ring flashed in the light; she touched it and brushed the shining stone with her fingers. "Well, Mr. Warren must have seen what you saw. And he wouldn't care to be snapped by a reporter, perhaps, any more than you did."

"Less, I guess. He's a funny old coot in some ways. I mean, sitting there on all that dough, the king of the mountain. And the mountain bulging with oil. And he doesn't seem to go anywhere much or find much to do in the way of fun."

"We can't all be alike, Jeff. What would be fun to you might not be fun to him at all."

"He could own a boat, for one thing. With his money he could afford an oceangoing tub and sail the South Seas if he felt like it."

"So he doesn't feel like it. He has his horse and he rides a lot. He's been good about letting Suzie ride, and he's promised Davie that he could, too. You know, we should have a horse of our own. I remember that Dad and Mother talked about it when we first moved up here. We were going to have a horse of our own; there was room for a stall out there and a shed for tack. Only the horse never got bought, nor the rooms built."

There was a short space of silence, during which it seemed to Vicky that she could really see the stall and the tack room, that they existed there in the corner of the big back area which had been set aside for them. And the horse. An eager but gentle palomino, who would put his head over the corral fence to whicker for apples, with eyes like brown velvet jewels.

She sighed, knowing that it hadn't been and would never be.

Jeff said, "You don't really care, do you? Aren't you past the stage of being horse-struck like kids around twelve, fourteen?"

"It's not me," she said. "It's Davie and Suzie who should have had the horse. And it's Davie and Suzie who've been hurt the most by the things that have happened, the way my mother has acted, the split between Mother and Dad that existed everywhere but on the surface. I was, after all, almost an adult. I was old enough to understand that I would soon be free. Dad didn't see it, but I couldn't join in his game of keeping me a little girl. I don't just mean college, that part about staying in school. There were other things."

"You are quite grown-up, yes, indeed," Jeff said with a hint of mockery. He reached for her, pulled her closer, so that her face was just above his and her view of his eyes filled everything, and she almost forgot her grief and her regrets.

He cupped her chin between his hands. "And you belong to me."

"Yes, I belong to you."

"We're all alone here."

"I'm aware of that."

"And you have some old-fashioned notions, too."

"I'm a red-blooded woman," she told him, "and how old-fashioned my notions are remains to be seen."

"You want to be tested?"

"Not right now."

"I think you've fallen way behind the times."

"It could be. If you believe the books and the movies—"

"Why shouldn't you believe them? They reflect life. I mean, real life. What we have up here on our little Olympus is something else. Suburbia diluted. Peopled by paper dolls. It's hard to see any of it as real, or important, or having anything to do with the two of us. It could be, I hope, that when the valley fills up with a lustier kind of people, when all those new houses are populated, maybe a kind of life-stirring miasma will blow up here off them, and maybe my mother will stay home once in a while and quit smelling of turpentine and quit yapping about art long enough for my father actually to get into bed with her again."

"Jeff . . ." She tried not to laugh. She didn't want to laugh; the grief and the regrets were too close, too raw, to be forgotten so soon. "As you said to me, do you really care?"

"I try to care. I can see that at least your parents reacted to each other. They're realer than my parents. My old man doesn't even know what's happened to him. He thinks it's normal to have a woman who's wrapped up in other people's funny frenzies, who thinks of him and me as necessary impediments to her real interests. He thinks he's *supposed* to keep flying back and forth across the country fooling around with money. He thinks that's all there is." Jeff laughed a little. "I should add, if he thinks or feels at all."

"Maybe what your parents have is what they want," she said with sudden insight. "Maybe it's comfortable for them. And I wouldn't downgrade it. It could be they're insulated against the kind of thing that happened between my mother and father."

"Insulated," he said. "That's the word. Packed away in sawdust like dolls. It won't ever happen to us, Vicky. You're my reality; you exist; you fill my world." He pulled her closer until their lips met.

Vicky closed her eyes and surrendered to his arms. Here in this sunny room, fresh with the smell of trees, warm with love—this was the place, and the time, to be consoled, cherished, made whole again. Jeff would replace the sorrow with a whole new world of belonging. She was his now; she was no longer part of her family. She felt Jeff move from under her, lifting her gently aside, letting her down on the bed with their positions reversed, so that now he bent above her. He kissed her again.

"Vicky . . . couldn't it be now?"

"Yes. Yes." And she thought truly it could be, and she was swept along. To a certain point. Then the necessary mechanics became more than she could endure, and she pushed Jeff away. "Wait. I don't know—"

He was roused, trembling, insistent. "We can't stop now."

"Wait." She sat up, hastily buttoning her blouse. He tried to hold her hands, pull her toward him; he reached inside to touch her again, and for an instant she almost yielded. Then some wretchedness she couldn't control shuddered through her, froze her with its ice. Jeff took his hand away, and she finished with the buttons, tears running down her face.

17

Davie stood in the dimness at the far end of the room and watched the pool area through a small opening in the draperies. It had seemed for a while that the day might stay sunny and clear, but now the clouds were back, and the bench on which his dad sat with Mr. Caldwell was in a big puddle of shadow. The water rippled a little with a shivering motion, and some eucalyptus leaves sped out, turning like sailplanes before they dropped to make more ripples still. His dad looked mad and unhappy, and Mr. Caldwell had a pipe out and was filling it from a pocket pouch while he listened.

Davie knew what his dad must be telling Mr. Caldwell because his mother had explained it to him in the kitchen a short while ago.

She was dressed the way she was when she went to town, a suit and nylons and high heels, but she wasn't really going to town because of her hair and the way her face looked. She was dressed up for some reason to stay home. She poured coffee for herself—Davie was making bread and jam—and her hands shook. She didn't look at Davie while she talked to him.

"Your father is going to crucify me now, Davie; he's going to get back at me because I grieved for Cootie and he thinks I neglected him and the rest of you, and I insulted his mother, and in some way I don't comprehend I'm the reason his mother had to die. He's going to throw me to the police."

The tone was kind of broken; only there was a coldness there, too, and Davie didn't believe what she had said about his dad until now, until he saw his dad out there talking to Mr. Caldwell, telling Mr. Caldwell something that made Mr. Caldwell want to stop and fill his pipe while he got used to it.

"I'm not asking for your loyalty," his mother had gone on. "Not

yours and not Suzie's and God knows not Vicky's. Perhaps what
he says is true and I don't deserve any loyalty, any defense whatever. I did all that I did out of perversity and meanness, out of
hatred. I hate you all—he says. So I don't ask anyone to stand up
for me."

Davie had moved away from her because she made him feel so
uncomfortable and he couldn't understand what she really wanted
him to do. Was he supposed to fight off the cops? What with? And
besides, it was illegal. A cop went where he wanted and took
away whomever he chose. So what could he do? She ought to talk
to his dad and try to get his dad not to turn her in for whatever it
was—Davie didn't believe, either, that she could really have killed
his grandmother. Wouldn't the cops know that? He had gone into
the family room, and his mother had stood on one foot and sipped
her coffee, her eyes almost shut and her un-made-up face gray and
withered. He had eaten his bread and jam, wiped his fingers on
his pants, watched television for about twenty minutes or so. And
now his dad was out there by the pool with Mr. Caldwell. Talking.
Doing just what his mother had said he would do.

There were others out there, not as near the house. A couple of
uniformed officers were putting sawhorses out by the road, signs
tacked to them. He couldn't read the signs from here, but the other
time they'd said NO PARKING. Beyond the cops a man who was
short and hairy, dressed in a blue T-shirt and old khaki shorts, was
taking a picture of the house with his camera. A kid with hair like
shredded wheat clung to one of his legs, sucked candy on a stick,
made faces at some fly or gnat that must be bothering him.

He was the kind of kid a fly would love, Davie thought.

Davie's mother had gone, probably back to her bedroom or the
den. The house was silent. Vicky was away somewhere, but Suzie
ought to be around. He had to talk to her. Davie's mouth dried up
when he tried to think of things to say. A warning. Cool, though,
offhand. You had to handle Suzie just right. You had to be careful.
How could he manage, "Look, Suzie, you've got to watch yourself, what you're doing, where you go, every minute," without
making her more curious, or cross, or not believing, so that she
would do something really crazy?

Suzie was the kind of girl you couldn't figure out. You never knew how she'd take things. When you expected her to get mad or be the meanest, she'd turn around and be nice as pie, the way she was that day after the first phone call, when she'd come down the barranca on Mr. Warren's horse. He had pounded her leg, hard, wanting to hurt her. But she hadn't been angry in return. How could you understand a girl like that?

Well, of course, he really ought to talk to Mr. Caldwell. This new note up there on that bush meant that the man who had telephoned wasn't giving up. Everything had gone wrong; he had the keys, but the cops would be waiting and watching for him to use them, and he'd killed somebody, too. He knew he was in the soup. So what was left?

What was left was, he was going to hurt Suzie.

He was going to do some of the things he'd talked about on the phone.

Davie shut his eyes, turned from the curtains, feeling sick.

He should have told his dad about the note when he'd brought that camping stuff down out of the barranca. Or even earlier, when he'd raced out of the barranca with scaredness hammering at his heels and had met Vicky.

Why couldn't he just tell them? What stopped him, dried his mouth, made him sick inside?

He sat down on a couch, stretched out his legs, put his head back against the cushion.

Get yourself together, said an inner voice. *You ain't a little bitty kid anymore; you ain't out there with haystack hair and a sucker, batting at a fly. You're big, almost grown up, old enough to have some sense.*

He knew, though, what dried his mouth and made it impossible to speak. What did it were the talks on the phone, the things the man had said might happen to Suzie, the sick, nasty, hideous things he'd said he—or somebody—could do.

Well, then, said his inner voice of good sense, *what you need is somebody you can tell all that stuff to, get it off your chest.*

What I want, he thought in disgust, *is to have somebody tell me that nothing like any of those things could possibly happen. There's no way anybody could do those things to a girl.*

Only I bet there is.

He thought: *If school had started, I could go to that counselor, that Mr. Stedman. You never stumped him. You never even surprised him. He'd heard it all.*

Well, Mr. Stedman might be back in town by now. He might be listed in the phone book. School was about ready to open; he should have returned from wherever teachers and counselors go in the summertime.

So—get up and look in the phone book. Try his number.

If he's back from vacation, he might be willing to listen and give some advice. At least, you could practice telling to him what you're going to have to tell to somebody else sooner or later.

Davie got off the couch and went to his mother's desk, took the phone book from a drawer and opened it, leafing through until he found the page with the Stedmans. There were just five listed. The first was Annabelle Stedman, then came B. W. Stedman, Frank Stedman, Wilona Stedman, and Y. Stedman. It occurred to Davie that he didn't know Mr. Stedman's first name.

He tried them all, dogged in his search. Annabelle Stedman's mother answered and said that her daughter was at work, and no, there was no Mr. Stedman connected with either one of them in any way. Her husband was dead, she was a widow, and her daughter hadn't married yet. And also no, she was not related to or acquainted with any Mr. Stedman who was a school counselor. B. W. Stedman was a cement contractor, according to his wife, who sounded young and harassed. There were kids squalling in the background, and a dog barked. No one they knew worked as a school counselor, either. Frank Stedman didn't answer the phone. Wilona Stedman's voice quavered with age, and she thought for a time that Davie was calling about adjustments on her gas bill. But yes, she did have a relative who worked for the schools. He was a landscape gardener, and he was employed by the Pasadena School District. He also collected old pipes, if that would help. At home. Pipes you smoked, not pipes in the ground to water things. He had enough of that at school.

Davie stifled a kind of panic he felt coming over him. One more to go. Y. Stedman. Davie said a soundless prayer, begging that this could be his Mr. Stedman. He'd know the voice in a minute. There'd been that hassle at school about sneaking smokes in the lavatories. Davie hadn't smoked, but he knew plenty of kids who did. Mr. Stedman had questioned him but hadn't asked, or even hinted, that he squeal on anybody. And when Cootie had died, Mr. Stedman had had him in for a couple of talks. Not about Cootie, exactly, and no probing or quizzing, not asking him to lay bare any emotions. Just talk. It had helped somehow, and he hadn't realized it until much later.

But then, below Y. Stedman's name, he saw an added line, and it read ACCOUNTANT, TAX SERVICES, and he knew that he had come to the end of this hope.

Mr. Stedman must have a telephone.

Unlisted. Hadn't one of the kids at school said once the counselors all had unlisted numbers so they couldn't be bugged at home, nobody could bother them after they shut up the offices at school?

Davie was turning from the phone, and there was Suzie, all at once. She had on a tan shirt and short brown pants. Her feet were bare. Her eyes were red and swollen, and he knew then that she must have been in her room, all this time, crying about Grandma.

"Hello," she said. "Is Mom around?"

"Somewhere. She was in here a little while ago."

"Is she—is she all right?"

Davie thought about telling Suzie what his mother had said and how she had looked when she'd drunk that coffee, but finally he just replied, "She's kind of upset, of course."

"Where's Dad?"

"Out by the pool. Talking to Mr. Caldwell."

"Have they caught the one who did it?"

"No, I don't think they have."

"They never will, either," Suzie intoned darkly, opening the refrigerator.

"What makes you say that?"

She took out the milk and the butter and put them on the sink. "Because it may not even be a *person* at all. It's a jinx. The house is cursed. It was built under a hex, something evil. A cloud. Can't you feel it sometimes? I kind of thought about it a little when Cootie died. After all, why should he have ridden that tricycle through the glass doors? Grandma was in here with him. He had that whole Family Area to tear around in. It was just queer. Entirely unexplainable."

She had put a small skillet on the range, lit the gas flame, and was putting a pat of butter into the pan, getting ready to cook an egg.

"I thought you'd been reading up on psychology. Not superstition."

"Sometimes the two overlap in a mysterious way," she said, giving him that I'm-so-much-older look.

"I don't believe it."

"You've heard of witch doctors, haven't you?"

"Sure. And so? Who hasn't? They beat drums and dose you with dried frogs' feet."

"Not always. Sometimes they have uncanny powers, based on real sound knowledge." She plopped in the egg, tossed the shell into the bin under the sink, stirred the egg to scramble it. "Put in a piece of toast for me real quick. I forgot."

He got bread and made the toast. "So what has a witch doctor—"

"This land, all of it, the valley, the hills, everything, belonged to the Indians."

"Oh, for the love of—"

"It did!"

"Well, so did all of it, for Pete's sake, from the Pacific to the Atlantic!" Davie buttered her toast without even thinking about it. This was the craziest—

"How do we know what was here?" she demanded. "They had their holy places, their cemeteries—"

"The burial ground is away off up there." He motioned with the knife with which he was buttering the toast.

"Well, *something* might have been here," she retorted, giving him one of those dark looks that made him want to hoot.

And still, even while wanting to make fun of her, he felt a funny chill, as if something with cold little legs had crossed his neck. "Jeez, you've got it bad today; you're gone. Gone."

"Nevertheless," she said, lowering her voice and standing there looking at him from under her hair, spooky, "the house is haunted, and there's something ominous here. I can feel it. I think Grandma felt it, too. She said something once."

He felt like a sap because he had to ask. But he had to. "What?"

"She said that this house was built for unutterable woe."

"Bull!" he cried, forgetting in his confusion that he was not allowed to use the word. His dad had forbidden it.

"Wasn't it? Look at what's happened."

"You're crazy!"

"You are." She took her breakfast and went into the dining area. He stood there in the kitchen, uncertain. Suzie sat down, arranged the plate with the scrambled egg and toast, the glass of milk, eating utensils. She was deliberately precise and exact in arranging what she had brought, not looking back at Davie, apparently not even thinking about him or their conversation. She unfolded a paper napkin with exaggerated care.

Davie thought: *She made that up about what Grandma said. Grandma never used goofy words like "unutterable woe." Suzie got it out of a book.* But knowing this didn't seem to change the advantage Suzie had. She was sure of herself, and he was not.

What he ought to do was to leave her here, not say another word, and go on out to the pool and tell Mr. Caldwell about that note in the barranca. Then Mr. Caldwell would come in here and give her some warnings that would take her off her high horse. Davie could even see it, himself walking across the deck and Mr. Caldwell and his dad falling silent, watching him, and then the words that would ring out in the silence, Mr. Caldwell's air of patience changing to excitement, his dad rising in anger—

"I'm going to think of something to do," Suzie said from the dining area.

"Like what?"

"I don't know yet. I'm going to ask Vicky to take me to the library. I'll find something."

"Yeah, I can see you, asking Miss Murphy how to lift a hex."

"Miss Murphy," she pointed out cruelly, "is the *children's* librarian. And I haven't been in there for years."

"Davie," said his father's voice, "will you go see if your mother can talk to Mr. Caldwell now?"

Davie turned, startled. His dad was just inside the glass doors, a dark outline against the light from behind.

"Mr. Caldwell can talk to her in the den. I imagine that's where she is right now. Go and check, will you?"

Davie hung there, unwilling. He was suddenly afraid of what his mother might expect him to do. Defend her against Mr. Caldwell? Help her barricade the den? In all this strangeness, he was lost. He went over to the refrigerator and took out a big bottle of juice.

"Davie, didn't you hear me?"

"Uh . . . yes, sir."

"Go find your mother, and if she's in the den and will see Mr. Caldwell, let him in. He'll be at the front door. Now get going." His dad had crossed to the dining area. Suzie took a bite of toast, half turned around, looking over her shoulder at her dad. "I have a few things to say to you, Suzie. To start with, you aren't to go anywhere at all without my permission. Anywhere includes the ground right outside. You aren't to go out a door without my knowing it. You aren't to answer the phone. You aren't to stand in a window where you can be recognized from outside. And you don't open the door to any visitors."

Suzie made a sputtering protest with a mouth full of toast.

"Did you hear me, Suzie?"

"Yes, Dad."

Davie went off to the hallway that led to the other part of the house. His dad had certainly laid down the law. But would Suzie obey? He wished he knew.

18

The hall felt shut in, airless. There were no sounds from any of the bedrooms. Davie tapped at the den door, then opened it a little. His mother was in there, all right. She was on the couch, still wearing the suit and the high-heeled pumps. She was all curled up, huddled at the end of the couch, her eyes shut, her face pressed into a bed pillow and a folded blanket. Her hair looked worse than ever, tangled and fallen over her forehead; Davie wished she'd brush it. She made him think of a curled animal, something hurt and trying to hide, and sudden tears stung his eyes.

"Mom . . ."

She didn't open her eyes. "Yes, Davie."

"Dad wants to know if you'll talk to Mr. Caldwell."

She didn't answer right away. "Do I have to?"

"I don't know. Should I tell him you won't?" Then what came next, he wondered? Battering down doors? But his mother was sitting up now, pulling down her skirt, pushing back the fallen hair. He noticed the deep lines at the corners of her mouth, how sunken her eyes looked, and how when she touched the pillow and blanket as if to straighten them, her hand was thin and frail.

"Davie—no, I'll see him. But a minute first. Some things I want to say. You're awfully young to have to understand. But no one else will listen. I have to tell *you.*"

She folded her hands on her lap and waited as if expecting him to answer.

"Sure, Mom. I'm listening."

"There's been a lot said about the time I have spent on this house. Ugly, twisted talk that had no relation to the truth. I'm supposed to have—" She stopped talking; she was looking at the window. Davie looked, too. He remembered the day she had brought home the new draperies for the den. The old ones had looked okay to Davie. These were deep orange with seaweed shapes in brown. When his mother went on, her voice was quieter; it had lost its determined note. "No, I'm not going to defend myself. Not now. Not to any of you."

She made it sound, somehow, as if she were at bay, as if the rest of them were strangers.

She squared her shoulders inside the jacket, stood up, brushed at her skirt. "If Mr. Caldwell wants to talk to me, you may bring him here."

"Mom—"

"Yes."

"Would you fix your hair a little?"

Her face twitched. She put up a hand, brushed back the locks over one ear.

"I mean, in front of a mirror," he said apologetically.

She turned on him eyes that seemed suddenly to burn. "Can't you—can't any of you—ever see anything *right* about me?"

He stood there ashamed, helpless. He wanted her to straighten her hair and put on some powder and lipstick because the way she looked now was a kind of defenselessness all in itself, a giving away of something he couldn't even express. A not-caring. And as fair as Mr. Caldwell seemed to be on the surface, Davie didn't want his mother not caring with him.

"I'm sorry," he got out finally.

But again, after a minute or so, her mood changed. She ran her fingers through her hair at the neck and looked thoughtful. "I shouldn't have snapped at you. You're right. I should make myself presentable. I'll go bring my things from the other bathroom and put them in this little bathroom here—I might as well tell you, Davie, this will be my room from now on. I won't be sharing the big room with your father." In spite of the stricken way she talked, she tried to smile at him. As she went out, she touched his shoulders with a hand on each, a brief grip, not quite a caress. It was the first time, in a long while, that Davie could recall her touching him.

He turned back and walked to the front entry. He opened the big front door, and there was Mr. Caldwell, smoking his pipe, and beside him was someone else. Mr. Ralston. He was puffing on a cigar. He wore his usual sort of stiff black suit. A white shirt and a subdued blue necktie. When he saw Davie, his face crinkled up the way it did when he smiled. He wasn't wearing a hat, and his bald head shone.

"Hello, Davie. I was just passing the time with Mr. Caldwell here. Old acquaintances, we are. I know it's maybe not the best time in the world to come calling—but is your dad free? Would you ask him if he feels like seeing me for a few minutes?"

"Sure." Davie opened the door wider, and the two men entered the house, Mr. Caldwell carefully knocking out his pipe into some shrubbery first. Davie looked at the detective. "My mother will be in the den in a little while. Will you wait for her, please?"

Caldwell nodded, said good-bye to Mr. Ralston, and walked on in the direction of the den. The den was also the place where Davie's dad had always talked to Mr. Ralston, and for a moment Davie was at a loss. Mr. Ralston must have understood, for he gave Davie the Santa Claus crinkles and said, "No need to take me anywhere, I'll wait right here. And if your dad isn't up to talking to me, it's fine. Just give him my sympathy."

Davie turned to start off, but then there was his dad coming from the other part of the house; he seemed to be headed for the den, and Davie started to tell him that if he was looking for his mother, she'd gone to get stuff from the bathroom to fix her hair. But there was no chance and no need. Davie's dad stopped when he saw Mr. Ralston, then came on more slowly.

Ralston discarded his cigar into one of the planters that lined the flagstone entry. He stepped forward, shook Thomas Stoddard's hand. "Tom . . . I know there's nothing I can say—terrible tragedy. I know this wasn't the time to come, either, but I was up here to see Warren and felt I ought to stop for a minute."

Thomas Stoddard hesitated for a second or so and then said, "Of course, it was good of you to come."

"If there's anything at all I can do—"

"I'll let you know."

"You do that."

Davie's dad had drawn back a little, removing his hand from the hand of Mr. Ralston and getting too far away for Mr. Ralston to keep a grip on his shoulder. "If there's anything, business-wise—"

"Oh, no, Tom. God's sake, I wouldn't come here to bother you with money matters at a time like this. Everything's kind of waiting now, anyway, depending on what Whitney's going to do, whether he's going through with that deal with Jemmerson and Marks—my own opinion, we ought to toss our plans for that property into the ash can and forget it." Mr. Ralston had taken another cigar out of his breast pocket; he didn't light it but kind of rolled it around between his fingers, loosening it up, and this playing with the cigar covered a sharp, foxy look that he gave Davie's dad.

Thomas said rather quietly, "I don't know how that deal's getting along, Vince. As I said before, Bowman considers Whitney his own private province, and I couldn't influence things if I wanted to."

"I know, I know. I'm not trying to bug you in any way."

"You could just ask Whitney directly, couldn't you?"

Mr. Ralston smiled. "Well, that might look eager. And looking eager never gets you any bargains."

"I think Whitney has a pretty good idea of what his land is worth," Thomas answered. "After all, he's right in the path of all those new projected subdivisions. He'd be a fool to sell cheap. I don't think you'll get it cheap—you, or Jemmerson and Marks, or anyone else."

Mr. Ralston looked philosophically at the limbered cigar. "Yeah, you've got something there."

"I'll tell you what I'll do, though. If Bowman lets drop anything about the deal being final, I'll call you. And if he says anything about Jemmerson and Marks backing out—and if he doesn't make it plain the information is private—I'll call you then, too. I can give you that much of an inside track."

Ralston nodded. "If I just knew what's held it up for so long—"

"That I don't know. Maybe there's some complication over the title. Or it could be any of a dozen things."

"Like money."

"Yes, like money."

"Well, let me apologize again for coming in like this."

"It's quite all right, Vince; don't think anymore about it."

Davie, in the shadows of the hall, half out of sight, thought that his dad was making an extra effort to be friendly to Mr. Ralston, and that behind the effort was a kind of feeling sorry for Mr. Ralston, which was a silly idea because Mr. Ralston didn't seem to be in need of any sympathy at all. He was a plump, foxy go-getter kind of man. He got what he wanted. If anyone had said, "I'm sorry for you, Vince," he would have thought they were crazy.

"They'll find the freak who did this," Mr. Ralston was promising Davie's dad.

"I'm sure they will."

"I only saw your mother a few times, just to speak to in passing, but she seemed like a lovely lady." Mr. Ralston went over to the front door and took hold of the knob. "Give my sympathy to the wife and children, will you?"

"Yes. Thank you."

When Mr. Ralston had gone outside and closed the door behind him, Thomas Stoddard remained standing in the entry. Then he seemed to rouse out of some thought and, turning, saw Davie. "Davie, would you do a little job, please? Mr. Ralston dropped a cigar butt into the planter. Go get a piece of toilet paper to keep the smell off your hands, and pick it out of the planter and throw it into a toilet."

"Okay, Dad."

"Is Mr. Caldwell with your mother?"

"Yes."

"Let me know when they leave the den, will you? I've got papers in there that have to be moved."

Davie nodded. His dad turned away.

"I'll be in the bedroom, Davie. I've got this damned headache that just doesn't quit. Oh, and by the way, you heard what I said to Suzie about going outdoors, answering the phone or the door—"

"Yes, Dad."

"It applies to you, too. I've given Suzie permission to ask Vicky to run her into town to the library, to get some books to pass the time, and if you want, you can go with them. But that single errand is *all*. No stopping for hamburgers, no side trips to see anyone."

"Is Vicky back?"

"A minute ago. Hurry if you want to go with them."

Davie shook his head. "No, I guess I don't. I'm going to sort out some stuff I fooled around with this summer, models I didn't get finished and things like that."

"I've got to think about plans for the funeral. Got to notify the few relatives back East—not that I expect any of them will come."

His dad looked worried; Davie sensed that he was speaking to himself.

Caldwell accepted the chair that Margaret Stoddard offered him. She sat down a dozen feet away, on the couch. Caldwell was interested in the change in her. At midnight she had seemed quietly in control of herself. Since then she had changed her clothes, and her appearance had altered in other ways also. She now wore a suit and high-heeled pumps, as if she had prepared to leave the house and had forgotten or dropped the idea before getting around to her hair and face. Her hair showed signs of hasty renovation, and shaking hands had applied lipstick. She had separated the two of them with as much distance as the furnishings of the den allowed, reasonably, and she showed nervousness at his scrutiny of her. She asked if he wanted coffee, and Caldwell said that he'd had breakfast in town and was fine.

"Well, I—I suppose you're here to quiz me about whatever my husband has been telling you," she said, putting her chin up.

"Oh, just getting things straight." Caldwell decided that there had been a fight between the husband and wife, that perhaps Stoddard had said some things he wouldn't have said except in the first shock after his mother's murder. And Caldwell wondered why married people almost inevitably, in the face of tragedy, blamed each other. Sometimes only during the first stunned reaction, and sometimes forever. "How much had Davie told you about his phone calls and the other contact?"

"I don't know anything about another contact."

Caldwell told her of the note left in Davie's camp and of the forgetfulness on Davie's part which had caused the note to be seen by his grandmother. "That's where it all started," Caldwell explained. "That's where she got the idea of protecting all of you. That *was* her motive, Mrs. Stoddard. You might even say she died for love of you, her family."

She didn't soften. "How much better sense she'd have shown, to talk to my husband."

"Oh, of course, we can see that now," he agreed. "But then her reasons might have gone even deeper than that. She might have wanted to prove herself, to draw closer into the family circle

—to earn the gratitude of the rest. Or even just to be *noticed*."

Margaret Stoddard looked down at her hands folded in her skirt.

"Sometimes older people feel neglected and ignored," he went on, "even when others around them don't intentionally neglect and ignore them."

"No one will ever know what I put up with," Mrs. Stoddard said. Her hands were clenched now, and there was sudden color high on her cheekbones. "We added that nice suite of rooms, an apartment really. And it could have been attractive. People could have enjoyed being in it, visited her; only she had to stuff it full of all that ancient clutter. I don't think she left a stick behind. A whole houseful of outmoded junk—"

"To her it wasn't junk, of course."

"I never spoke to her about it; I didn't argue when it was all jammed in there at the top of the stairs. I did try to be patient with her. I don't care what my husband has told you."

Caldwell waited, letting the silence draw out. Margaret Stoddard drew several deep sighs; her anger seemed to subside, and her color returned to its gray pallor.

Finally, she said, "You have heard by now that since the baby's death I've neglected my husband and children—my remaining children—and have spent my time in a ridiculous shopping orgy."

"I hadn't heard this, Mrs. Stoddard."

"When my baby died under the care of my husband's mother . . . I was at first just—" She pulled a long breath into her lungs, waiting, searching for the right word. "I was crushed. I was disassociated from reality. Or that's the way the doctor put it. Then I gradually came back to—to life, you could say, and I became obsessed with the thought that I had to make this house so beautiful, so perfect, so wonderful to be in, that my family would find it a paradise. I did go to extremes. I must admit that. I did spend too much time and money and effort on the house. I overdid it all."

Caldwell smiled at her across the wide space between them. *Liars like to keep a distance between them and the people they lie to—it must make lying easier,* Caldwell thought. And Mrs. Stoddard was a liar. She was far too intelligent a woman ever to

confuse constant change and refurbishing of a house with a desire
to please or comfort her family. The shabbiest shack could have
peace in it and be a haven. She had been punishing someone. Her
husband? The children still left alive? Or all of them? And
through all of them, the old woman most of all? The old woman
who mustn't be allowed to forget that she'd been in charge when
the little boy had died?

"Your mother-in-law said something, briefly, just before she
died," he said, not commenting on what she had told him or his
conclusions about it.

Her brows lifted. "Oh? At the hospital, you mean? And what
was that?"

"She spoke about a reflection. 'It was the reflection.'" He
waited a moment, watching for any change in her, but could see
nothing. "Does this remark suggest anything to you?"

"No."

"It may not have anything to do with her murder. Or again,
it might. We have to try to settle what it means. And why she
should speak of it in her last moments."

"I can't help you," Margaret said, "but now we have arrived
at the meat of our talk, haven't we? What happened to her, out
there in the dark. And where I was, at that particular time."

19

Caldwell wondered if Margaret Stoddard were try-
ing baldly to move him off the subject of her mother-in-law's last
strange remarks. It seemed a forcible switch, but then perhaps
all this time she had been nerved for, and dreading, the direct
question. So inwardly he shrugged and let her lead him. "Did
you have any hint at all of what she meant to do last night?"

"No hint whatever. I didn't see her after dinner. Nor did I see my husband. He's told you that by now. And that's why you're here."

Caldwell rubbed the side of his chin with his knuckles. "I'm afraid you have a wrong idea there. I don't trot right away when somebody points. I'm not a bird dog. Of course, I need to talk to all of you, again and again—Davie most of all, but the rest of you, too—so that the bits and scraps all can be fitted together, can add up to the murderer. If they ever do."

She looked defiant. "You did come here direct from a talk with my husband. Don't deny that."

"Why should it make you angry?" he wondered. "No attempt is being made to throw guilt on you. Since you and your husband were not together at the time his mother was murdered, it's important to get everything straight and to find out where you were and what you could have seen and heard."

"I saw and heard nothing."

"You were here, in the den?"

"Part of the time."

"And where else?"

"Outdoors."

Caldwell almost didn't conceal the start of surprise. "Oh?"

"This was still twilight. There was a little glow from the sky. Not much. The clouds were heavy and dark. But I went out—there'd been a disagreement at the dinner table"—she stopped here and seemed to have a hard time getting past it, so Caldwell judged that the scene at the dinner table had been pretty rough. The family, he thought, had been falling to pieces for a long time—"and I walked around the deck that encloses the pool. I looked at the water. For a while I wondered if I had the courage to jump in. To force myself under, to breathe water. But in the end—" She hunched her shoulders.

"It would be almost impossible to kill yourself that way. Unless a person is drunk or drugged, reflexes take over. The lungs cough up the water, and the body fights to the surface, by instinct."

"I suppose so," she said dully.

"I want to get straight exactly what you did. You went outdoors as soon as you left the dinner table?"

"Well, no, not quite. I came in here and—and kind of got control of myself, of my emotions. I felt as if I'd been beaten, the things that had been said to me. I was . . . shaken up."

"Who had attacked you?"

"All of them," she replied flatly. "They were all in it together."

"What part did your mother-in-law play?"

"Oh, I don't know. I can't remember. I'd taken so much off her in the past, her slyness, manipulating Thomas—" She checked this line abruptly. "I don't think she said much. Actually she might have tried to smooth things over. I'd have to think about it."

"You left the others at the table?"

"You know that. My husband has already told you."

"Then came here," Caldwell said as if meditating, "and then went out to the pool. It was getting dark."

"The wind was blowing, too, and there were stray spatters of rain." She shivered, and her eyes seemed to look past Caldwell to that windy dark beside the pool.

"Did you see anyone else out there?"

"I wasn't looking for anyone else. Someone could have stood within ten feet of me and I wouldn't have seen him. I was just wishing I were dead."

Was it the truth, Caldwell puzzled, or was she wanting sympathy from him, a sympathy that might becloud any suspicions her husband had roused? "How long do you think you stayed out there?"

"Not long, I suppose. I remember thinking, I'll go to the den and shut myself in, and I'll have to get to it before someone else goes in there. Thomas worked in the den when there was something extra to take care of, and the children kept games and books in there."

"And that's what you did?"

"Yes."

"And you slept in here?"

"The hassock over there is hollow, it's for storage, and we keep a pillow and blanket in it in case anyone wants a nap."

"Did anyone come to the den during the evening?"

"No."

"Did you hear anything from outside?"

"I heard the disturbance—this was Thomas and the children, after he had found his mother."

"Did you see your mother-in-law before she was taken to the hospital?"

"No." Again the color rose in her gray face. "It sounds heartless. But Thomas warned me not to go to her. There was nothing anyone could do—outside of a doctor, that is."

Caldwell told himself that her attitude was one of complete rejection. She had turned her back on the rest of them. No disaster, no pity or compassion could change her.

Could he make a change? Was it even worth trying?

"Well, no doubt you were busy comforting your children."

"No. Thomas made them stay put. Except for Vicky. She went with him to the hospital." There was a sudden look of thoughtfulness, as if she realized that Vicky had played her role.

"No one cried or needed soothing?"

She shook her head firmly.

"Davie must have been pretty upset. He'd set it all in motion —not willingly, of course, just trying to obey the terrifying man who wanted his father's keys."

"I—I guess Davie was . . . terribly hurt."

"Blaming himself."

She didn't want to think about her son's feelings. She didn't want to put herself in his place. "Perhaps."

"Your husband and I have decided on a few things regarding Davie and Suzie, Mrs. Stoddard. For their own safety, we want them out of the reach of this man, and so they aren't to leave the house without telling you or their father. They aren't even to step out of the door. And they aren't to answer the phone or the doorbell."

She licked her lips. "That seems pretty drastic."

"Killing your mother-in-law was pretty drastic."

She nodded unwillingly. Caldwell sensed her resistance. She didn't want to share any changes here. She wanted to remain inside the cocoon, isolated in anger.

He went on: "As Mr. Stoddard pointed out, if the investigation goes on for very long, he'll have to leave the family in your charge and get back to his office. You'll have to assume the responsibility in his absence. You'll have to see to the safety of your children. That means you must understand the rules, you must make sure that they do, too, and you must show the authority to make them obey."

"But—but you'll be around," she protested, her glance flicking around the room, her face distracted. "And Vicky—"

"Mrs. Stoddard." He waited until she grew quieter, until her eyes were fixed on his. "No parent can resign the obligation implicit in being a parent. It's binding. It never quits. And you can't quit. It's not just a job. You can't draw severance pay and take up somewhere else. This is forever."

She had a lot to say on that point, most of it mutinous, he realized, but the words wouldn't come. She struggled, sitting there opposite him, her eyes full of fear and fury.

"These are your children, and they may be in terrible danger," he went on, keeping his voice neutral. "Their very lives may depend on what you do to control them and protect them." He waited, giving her a chance to get it out, the things he saw in her face, the rage and the rejection. But still she didn't speak. "Wouldn't you die for your children, Mrs. Stoddard?"

"Yes. Yes. Oh, gladly." She began to cry, hunched there on the couch. "Yes. A million times."

Now Caldwell had something to say and couldn't say it. He wanted to tell Mrs. Stoddard about all the people he'd known in his life who were perfectly willing to die for those they loved—but who wouldn't live for them. He sat silent while she gradually muffled the sobs and composed herself.

"I'm all right now," she said finally. "And I'll be very conscientious, Mr. Caldwell; I'll see that Davie and Suzie obey the rules."

"The one moment of carelessness may be the one he's waiting for."

"Do you think he's actually hanging around out there, spying and sneaking—"

"I don't know who he is. So I don't know where he is."

"Well, don't worry about my not taking charge of the children."

He stood up. "Thanks for talking to me, Mrs. Stoddard."

"Thank *you*," she corrected, "for thinking of my children's safety."

When Caldwell had gone, Margaret Stoddard sat on the couch for some minutes. She was still shaken by that moment when rage had almost engulfed, destroyed her, when Caldwell had dared to hint that she had resigned her duties as a parent. It had been by the greatest effort that she had kept from lashing back at him. And still, now that she had calmed herself, she could see how he might have got the impression that she was neglectful. He hadn't believed what she'd told him, that she had constantly fussed with the house in an effort to make her family happy in it. Well, actually she hardly believed it herself, though; who could say? There might be some truth in it. She'd have to think it over again later. Right now she had to act to destroy any lingering notion that she had been delinquent. She had to move.

She considered ways in which she could show concern and authority. She could order Davie to clear out his closets, for instance. He had a lot of junk, old summer projects, that should be discarded. She couldn't think of anything to tell Suzie. Suzie had been working on her school clothes and supplies for several weeks. She might order the two of them to clear the garage, but then that would mean leaving the house, technically, and she would suppose that Caldwell would expect her to stay in the garage with them while they worked, and somehow she couldn't see herself doing it.

She sat dejected, and it seemed that she had come to the end of her ideas.

It was all the old woman's fault, of course.

If the situation had been barbarous before, it was now unendurable.

"I won't cry anymore over it, though," she whispered. "This is *my* home and these are *my* children. I am the mother, and I have charge of this house."

Of course, changes had to be made. She remembered then that when Cootie had died, suddenly everything that the baby had possessed had disappeared. Thomas had stripped the nursery

without a word to her. Out of kindness. Anything that could remind her of Cootie was gone.

"I'll do the same for him," she said softly.

She got the business directory out of the desk and looked up
moving and storage firms. She chose one with which, in the past,
they had done some business or other. She sat down at the desk
and pulled the phone toward her, lifted the receiver. She began to
dial the number. She felt a sudden lifting of her spirits, and a feeling of gratitude toward Caldwell. *This is exactly what he would
want me to do,* she thought. *In fact, this is what he was hinting
about.*

A woman's voice answered, and Margaret asked about the possibility of having a moving van soon, explaining that she was an
old customer. The woman thanked her for calling, and then there
was a rustle of paper, and Margaret thought: *She's looking at a
schedule.* Then the woman said that it was possible they might
come tomorrow, if that was all right. There had been a cancella-
tion.

Margaret thought fast, her heart beating at an increased tempo,
an odd misgiving suddenly invading the feeling of cheerfulness.
Then she remembered Caldwell saying that Thomas felt he must
soon attend to business affairs again, and an inspiration came—
he'll go to the office tomorrow, not for the day but just for a few
hours, to check up on things that won't wait. In the morning.

"Could the van be here about eleven o'clock?"

"Yes, that's fine," the woman said, and Margaret explained
carefully where the house was located and exactly what was to
be removed.

"We'll be there at eleven!" the woman promised, as if she
herself might be driving the van, which was of course ridiculous.
She was just the office girl. Margaret replaced the phone in its
cradle.

"I'm doing him a wonderful favor," she said half-aloud, remembering with a painful twist how she had searched for Cootie's
things all through the house before realizing that Thomas had
sent them away.

When Thomas got home tomorrow, everything his mother had
owned would be gone.

A smile of blissful relief filled her eyes.

She rose from the desk chair and moved around the room, filled with new energy and restlessness. She had accomplished one thing, one very important thing, but there should be other things she could do. There must be other opportunities to show authority and good management, to prove that she hadn't resigned her post as a parent.

She blew some dust off the books in the bookcases and aligned the volumes in the shelves, and straightened the top of the desk, and emptied an ashtray into the wastebasket. The basket itself needed emptying, so she took it off to the kitchen, to the bin under the sink. Once in the kitchen, she was struck by dozens of things that needed to be done. Groceries and meats were low, for one thing—she could make out a list and telephone the order to town. Not many stores delivered anymore, and those that did were higher. But she had to stay at home and had no choice. She sat down at her little desk at the far end of the kitchen and got out pencil and paper.

I'd better collect a few things and run a load of laundry, too, she thought all at once, and jumped from the desk to rush out to the laundry room. There was no need to gather up anything; the big baskets there bulged with sheets, towels, and personal belongings of the children. She began to sort clothes and throw a load of white stuff into the machine, and then she stopped. What had Vicky said last night about getting help? Or had it been earlier, that bitter remark about not even having a cleaning woman anymore because she was showing them . . . showing them how little—

I won't cry.

But she did cry, a little, as she loaded the machine and put in soap and bleach and set the dials.

Then she went back to the grocery list.

"I could get a woman from an agency," she said, and chewed the pencil while she thought it over. Wouldn't it seem as if she had felt unable, though, to handle everything herself? Would it appear to her family and to Mr. Caldwell that true to form, she had sloughed off the responsibility, evaded it by passing it on?

She tried to make up her mind and then, still undecided, called a couple of employment agencies in town. Their replies were non-committal. Domestic help was in short supply, almost nonexistent, and where the Stoddards lived, transportation was a problem. Finally, she got a half promise of somebody in three or four days, at two dollars an hour, gas money extra, and extra pay for the time involved in getting out there.

The fine mood of lifted spirits was wearing thin. She felt tired. She looked at the grocery list and realized that she might as well discard it. You had to plan meals first, then order according to what you intended to eat. She crumpled the paper in her fist.

From away off in the laundry room, though, there was still the quiet and efficient gurgle and swish of the washing machine. Comforted, she began planning three days of meals and constructing an order list as she went.

She was still at the desk when Vicky and Suzie came in, both bearing an armful of books.

She looked up, all aglow with the triumph of accomplishment, of doing the necessary things that proved she loved them, and waited for them to notice, to respond, to speak. Surely they must know what she was doing, planning their meals, getting ready to order food for a week, and of course, they could hear the machine in the laundry room.

It was a shock, then, to see them passing her without a word, their quiet faces averted, their steps the only sound in all that stillness.

20

In Suzie's room they dumped the books on the bed. "She looked at us," Suzie said. "She looked when we went by."

"I know she did. I wanted to say something. But I'm tired right now. I'm too tired to fight."

"Maybe she didn't want to fight."

"She looked all ready for *something*."

"Do you think she's sorry about Grandma?"

Vicky was touching the books, lining them up on the bed, glancing at the titles on their backs. "Who knows? Why do you have all this stuff about Indians? *The Indians of California. Religious Practices in American Indian Life. Kiva and Kachina. Trails of the Bitterroot.* You've got eleven books here."

"I've got to have something to think about. I can't go outside; I can't talk on the phone or look out of a window. What am I, a zombie?"

"Well, you know all that's just temporary."

"How do we know?"

Vicky thought: *She could be right. They might never find him. We might live here the rest of our lives like people in a bomb shelter.*

Only I won't do it. I shouldn't have turned from Jeff today. What's virginity, after all? Isn't it really kind of sick in a woman my age? Isn't it sick to reject the man you love, shove him away as if he's offering you something dirty? I'm a fool. But right now I'm glad I'm a fool because I don't want that first time to be because I'm scared and lonely. I want it to be a glad thing from beginning to end. I want to start out with it glad and free, and no tears.

Only Jeff doesn't know how I feel. He thinks I turned away because I don't love him enough.

"Are you going to cry?" Suzie asked anxiously.

"Why on earth should I cry?"

"You just looked like you were getting ready to. Look, here's a picture of an Indian medicine man. He made magic spells and talked to spirits and cured people."

"He looks like something the cat dragged in."

"Well, I guess he looked good to another Indian," Suzie defended, drawing the precious illustration against her breast.

Vicky stood frowning, as if listening to some inner warning. "Suzie, you're not cooking up anything, are you?"

"Cooking up? What could I be cooking up?"

"Oh . . . one of your weirdies. Like the time you read

Dracula and wore that garlic around your neck on a string and made hocus-pocus affairs on your windowsills to keep things out. This isn't like that, is it?"

"I don't know what you're talking about," Suzie said loftily. "That was when I was ten, and some of that book was hard to read, I want you to know. The vocabulary was about one hundred years behind the times. I asked Miss Murphy about it."

"You didn't get *that* out of the children's library."

"Miss Murphy was surprised I could even read it. But she said there wasn't much in there to hurt me. Actually it's a very moral book, she said."

"You showed her the garlic you were wearing as a protection?"

"Oh, *Vicky*."

On a sudden impulse Vicky grabbed her, hugged her close, the book between them with its hard edges and papery smell. They stayed like that for a minute or more, suddenly close, and Vicky thought: *Why is it we can only love each other for such little whiles? And why not always?* But she released Suzie when Suzie's arm dropped, and she saw that whatever was behind all this information about Indians, Suzie didn't intend to share it.

"Have fun with your medicine man, and if you come up with a good cure for the daily drags, let me know."

"You can't have the daily drags. You're engaged to be married."

Vicky ruffled her hair. "That's right. Why didn't I remember that? But other people might have them." She would have left then, but Suzie put a hand on her arm.

"That night . . . that night I got the mud thrown on me—"

Vicky saw the sudden worry, fear, and suspicion. "It could have been. There's no way to know for sure now. Don't think about it."

"I didn't see anybody. It could have been a ghost."

"Well, that it wasn't. But don't start thinking back about every small thing that's happened lately. Get back to your medicine man."

Suzie shot her an odd, sharp glance, as if Vicky had said something inadvertently important, as if there were some connection here that she was hiding. But then she got busy with the books, putting them away in the closet shelves where she kept other treasures, and Vicky went to her own room.

I promised Jeff I'd call him about four, she remembered.

But what was there to say?

She was stretched on the bed and must have slept for a while, when she was wakened by a rapping on the door. She rose hastily, brushed back her hair, went to the door, and opened it. She must have looked sleepy because Caldwell, in the hall, said, "I'm sorry. Did I disturb you?"

"No, no. It's quite all right."

"Just wanted to ask a couple of questions, about the shopping trip with your grandmother, the hardware store."

"Yes?"

"When your grandmother came back to the car, was she carrying a package? Say, so big?" He indicated something the approximate size of a shoe box. "Had she definitely bought something there?"

Vicky hesitated, trying to remember. She had parked by Baker's; her grandmother had got out of the car; she had waited and had tuned in various stations on the radio. She thought: *I really didn't pay any attention to Grandma, I wasn't interested in what she wanted at a hardware store.* "I think she brought something back, something wrapped up, but I didn't ask her what it was."

"Did she carry it as if it were heavy?"

"I guess I just don't remember."

"Did she seem secretive?"

"No." *She just knew I wasn't interested and wouldn't ask,* Vicky thought. *She didn't have to be secretive. Who cared?* "She wasn't gone long, though." *She came back quickly,* her thoughts added, *because you'd get bored very soon, waiting for her.* "I guess I didn't realize until today how very little real attention we paid to her."

"Maybe that's why she died," he offered. "She died trying to get the rest of you to notice."

Vicky felt a surge of anger. Her father might have said the same thing, and she would have agreed. But Caldwell was an outsider. Then she thought, *Perhaps it's part of his job to make remarks like that,* and she answered civilly, "Perhaps she did."

"They're looking through the sales slips at Baker's Hardware. It would have been easy, I guess, but it happens they've put on two new clerks. And the new clerks don't know the regular customers by sight."

"I see. I wish I could help you. Thinking back, I can't think of a thing Grandma might have logically wanted at a hardware store. Dad has a toolbox in the garage, ordinary things like wrenches and screwdrivers and clamps and stuff. So perhaps she did want a new flashlight to take out into the yard to catch that man with."

Or, Caldwell told himself, she might have bought a tire iron or a good solid length of bicycle chain. Maybe she wasn't the peaceful little old nonentity everyone took her for. Maybe she was one of the spunky ones—had to be, considering the preparations she made. She was going to blow the whistle on him. Literally. Had it with her.

Caldwell went back to the suite of rooms at the top of the stairs and looked again for a journal, a diary, a letter to the family in case of accident. She hadn't foreseen any accident, he told himself. She had been sure of success. And still, for anyone of good sense, there should have been moments of warning—

The rooms felt stuffy and unaired. Neat, not dusty, just full of the smell of furniture that was full of years.

Caldwell sat down in one of the heavily upholstered old chairs and shut his eyes. He planned his evening. He would leave just before dinner, eat in town, check with the detectives who had covered other angles of the case, then go home to bed. Sleep until three. Then come back out here and park and wait as inconspicuously as possible, just in case something might be doing.

Tiredness dragged at him; the need for sleep stung his eyes. Someone bigger than he was or broader in the beam had sat in this chair long enough to shape its cushions. It was almost like lying half-erect in a cradle. Nice. The stuffy smell wasn't too bad, actually it smelled of safety and warmth. How could she have left this safe, warm place and gone out into the night to confront a blackmailer?

She'd loved her son, sure, but not enough to get along with his wife. And anyway, Thomas Stoddard was the kind of man who kept his thoughts on the job, provided well for his family, and wouldn't relish jolts and disasters—so it could be she had just wanted to be able to save the status quo and to get credit for it.

Don't be mean to her, his inner voice warned. *She died for something that posed no threat to herself. She left this nice safe place and stole out into the dark to battle for the rest of them.*

They could care less, he told himself. *Look at the way I have to interview them. One by one. All alone. Any other family, I could have gathered them there in that family room, and we could have talked it over together, sharing the pieces and fitting them together. This is a bunch of strangers.*

What had they been like before the smallest boy had died? I'll bet, he told himself, *just the way they are now only without the open animosity. A family doesn't shatter like this without warning. The parents build it all, brick by brick, with little unloving hands*

To hell with it

He must have slept, because he awoke with a feeling that the light in the room was subtly changed, and he himself felt as un-aired as the furnishings. *Add a shower to that program after dinner,* he thought. He looked around. The place had a waiting look. All these things that had belonged to Mrs. Stoddard sat here arranged for her return, the way she had wanted them.

If I were a religious man, he thought, *I'd say a prayer for the repose of her soul. I hope she's not hanging around here to see what happens to her stuff. I hope she's peacefully in heaven, if there is one.*

He glanced at his watch. It was time to leave for town.

Thomas Stoddard got up in the shadowy room and went into the bathroom. The headache was gone, but he felt fuzzy and ex-hausted, used up. He didn't want to think about his mother, but he did anyway, all the time he shaved, showered and dressed in fresh clothes. He thought of how she had died, and why, and wondered why he couldn't settle down to what Caldwell wanted and write out a list of names of people who might want to look at the files in Bowman's offices. The thing was, once he started, there would hardly be an end. Who *wouldn't* want to see what, confidentially, the lawyer had said and thought about his affairs?

Buttoning his shirt in front of the dresser, watching his image in the mirror, he decided that before putting down any names, he'd better talk it over with Bowman. If this had to be done, Bowman would have to know which names went on the list.

I won't phone him, Thomas thought. *I'll go in tomorrow morning, and we can sit down and hash it out together.*

Right now he had better check up on the kids, make sure that they were indoors and hadn't done any of the forbidden things. Before leaving the bedroom, however, he went into the bathroom, removed the huge red paper flowers from the vase, tore them into pieces, and flushed them down the toilet. Margaret should have taken them out, as he had asked, but she hadn't. And now they were gone for good.

It occurred to him to wonder how much of his money had just gone down the drain.

There were also his papers in the den.

He went to the den, rapped on the closed door. There was no reply. He opened the door. The place looked straightened, dusted, and he wondered if Vicky had been in here. He took all the folders out of the desk drawers and the portable typewriter in its case and went back to the bedroom and stacked them all on the dresser.

Vicky was in her room, her back to the door, sitting on the edge of the bed and reading something. He closed the door without sound and went on, passed the door of the vacated nursery, and opened Suzie's door. No one was in here. Davie's room was also empty.

He was wary about going on into the other part of the house. He sensed light, activity, and movement ahead of him, and suddenly it seemed that this was wrong and strange. Today was a day for darkness and quiet. He thought of going out the front entry to the garage, taking the car to town for something to eat there, alone in a café. But then, perhaps Davie and Suzie were trying in their unskilled way to get a meal together.

He went on, stood at the end of the hall in shadow, and watched what was going on in the kitchen and dining room.

The place glowed with light and smelled in a way that it hadn't smelled for a long time. Something had been baked. A cake, he thought, and then he noticed it on the sinkboard, tall, frosted all over with a caramel-colored frosting, dusted with shredded coconut. It glimmered there like a mirage. He could smell newer odors, too, meat roasting, potatoes being baked, vegetables simmering, a clump of smells like a bouquet, warm and mouth-watering, the very odor of a home. He could see Suzie; she was in the dining room. A fresh white linen cloth had been spread on the table. White china and polished glassware gleamed under the light. Suzie had a handful of silver.

Now all at once Margaret came into sight. And she too was incredibly changed. The gray look, the tiredness were gone. Her cheeks were pink, and she moved easily, quickly, happily. She had on an apron over the suit skirt, her blouse sleeves were rolled to the elbows, and there was flour on her arms. For a moment he didn't recognize her; he thought that some neighbor woman must have come in to help them out.

But the neighbors, remembering the hell and ferocious intrusion of the previous disaster, were decently keeping their distance. This was Margaret, after all. His heart lurched for an instant and then began to pound, rising in his throat, a beat that surged all the way up to hammer behind his eyes.

At last he forced himself to move, to go on into the lighted and warm-smelling kitchen. Margaret stopped when she saw him; he noticed now that she had dough rolled out on a board, was getting ready to cut biscuits. In the dining room, Suzie caught sight of him and gave him a big smile. The smile didn't register, didn't make sense.

He tried to think of something to say and got out harshly, "What in the hell are you celebrating?"

Margaret too had begun to smile, just before he spoke. Now she blinked and looked at the floured board as if she had just noticed it.

"As if I didn't know," he said.

He picked up the board and tilted the rolled dough into the sink, ran water from the faucet, and started the garbage pulverizer. He took a fork from a drawer to guide the biscuit dough into the opening of the disposer. When the biscuit dough was gone, he reached for the big cake. He made chunks out of it by slashing with the fork and washed the chunks into the disposer. Suzie was saying something from the dining room, but the vibration of the appliance muffled her words. Margaret just stood there.

The biscuits and cake all gone, he went to the range and opened the oven. A gush of heat spilled out, and inside in a wide shallow pan was a big beef roast, deliciously browned, nestled in a ring of baked potatoes, sizzling gently. It would be quite a job getting the big piece of meat down the pulverizer, and probably he would burn himself cutting it. There must be a quicker, less troublesome way. He looked around for the potholders, thick shabby pads that were usually to be seen scuffing around the sink somewhere. The old ones were gone, but he saw a couple of new ones, brightly colored, and he wondered briefly what on earth had got into Margaret that she should buy anything for the kitchen.

He used the new fluffy pads to protect his hands, and pulled the big pan out of the oven. "Suzie, go ahead of me and open the back door, will you?"

She said something in a choked voice, and he thought: *It's too bad. But it isn't a half of what I really feel like doing.* He remembered the moment when Margaret's skull had seemed to shatter in his hands.

As he turned with the big pan, to follow Suzie, he looked through into the next room, and there was Davie sitting on the floor in front of the television set. He sat quite straight, as if startled, and his eyes were on Thomas.

"Davie, go tell Vicky to get ready to go to town. I'm taking the three of you to a restaurant for dinner. Come on, get moving."

He carried the big pan with the beautifully browned roast and the potatoes out into the darkening twilight. He propped the pan on the fence while he opened the back gate. He went up the barranca a way, and where the brush was thick he suddenly threw the pan and its contents in a wide arc. The whole thing vanished into a thicket. For a moment he caught a drifting odor, the deliciousness of the meat. He turned then and went quickly back to the house.

In the kitchen he wound up the whole business by emptying the pot of simmering carrots and peas into the pulverizer.

The kitchen was empty, and it seemed to Thomas that it was beginning to smell like its old self again, insipid and sterile, a place where cans got opened and where the contents got a brief warming, a room to walk through.

A grave.

21

Margaret lay curled on the couch in the den. She hadn't put on a light. The room was dark, with only the faintest glow through the draperies, the beautiful new draperies with their splashes of sea color. There was no sound from the rest of the house. By now Thomas and the children were in the restaurant, in town, eating dinner.

In a stunned way she thought back through the events of the afternoon. When Vicky and Suzie had entered the house, had passed her without a word, she had at first wanted to do what she was doing now—retreat, curl up, hide. But then she had thought of Caldwell and of what he had told her, that she must maintain her position as parent in this home, and she had gone on to finish the list of needed supplies. Then she had telephoned the order to the store, promising a bonus to the deliveryman if he would bring the groceries out right away. As a final thought she had also ordered new kitchen towels and holding pads, matching sets that would dress up the kitchen cheerfully.

While she had awaited the arrival of supplies, she had finished the second load of laundry and sorted the first for ironing. She had even set up the ironing board and iron. The big hampers were noticeably emptier. She hurried from job to job. The shelves that held laundry supplies, soap and fabric conditioner and starch, were a mess, since the laundry jobs had been taken over by the children and done haphazardly of late. She dug out clean shelf paper, threw away empty containers, arranged the still usable supplies in neat clusters.

Some things which had been mixed in with the laundry—old shower curtains discarded months ago, Davie's pants worn beyond repair, ragged towels and sheets—she had bagged to be sent away with the trash.

The whole room looked busy, clean, shipshape, and inside herself there seemed to be a sort of singing, of coming alive, renewal, like awaking from a disabling illness. Vicky and Suzie hadn't spoken to her, had passed without a look, but she would show them. She would prove that she *was* their mother and that she did intend to look after them.

The man had come with the boxes of groceries and other supplies, and she had glanced over the account and had written him a check, giving him his bonus in cash, for which he had thanked her with a gratitude almost never encountered anymore. Then, as she sorted the food, putting away all the new things, the makings of all those wonderful meals she had planned, it had seemed that the inward singing reached a crest of joy. She felt that if she put her arms out, she could fly.

I'm so glad . . .

I've been dead, and now I am alive again, she thought. *I've been in a dark place, and I have come out again into the light.*

She'd wanted to dance, but instead, thinking of the surprise she would prepare for all of them, she got out the bowl and beater and began to make the cake.

Davie had come first. He had come into the kitchen, really on his way through it, and had stopped to watch the cake being taken from the oven, this such an unfamiliar thing, his expression implied, that it was like seeing an excavation taking place in the middle of the floor.

She had hummed softly, had hidden her smile.

She had let Davie scrub the potatoes for her, dry them, grease the skins with butter, and when the cake had cooled and she'd frosted it, he had taken the frosting bowl to lick out with a spoon. There had been a puzzled but delighted air to Davie, as if something he had dreamed of had unexpectedly come true.

Then Suzie had come, yawning with boredom, ready to complain about being shut in and deprived of freedom, and she'd given Suzie the job of fixing up the table. Suzie had even pressed one of the newly washed linen cloths, had taken out china that hadn't seen the light of day in more than a year.

And then, in the midst of the warmth and happiness, *he* had come, and it had all ended.

The words he had said—*"What in the hell are you celebrating?"*—hadn't made sense. She wasn't celebrating anything. She was doing what Mr. Caldwell had said that she must—she was maintaining her place as the mother of the family.

In the dark, she whispered, "I won't cry."

What she could do next wasn't exactly clear. She would have to do things that Thomas couldn't find fault with, perhaps wouldn't even notice. She would have to win him over slowly, carefully, with a long series of little things. She might try to do some of them through the children, suggest jobs to them, outline how they should be done, supervise without being obvious about it. Until the day would come and Thomas would suddenly see—

She checked the train of thought. There had been a sound from somewhere in the house.

Or had there?

She lifted her head off the pillow. Had Thomas and the children returned so soon?

But no . . . with the den right at the end of the house next to the garages, she would have heard the car.

She lay with her head propped up on one hand, trying to hear something more.

There was nothing. The house was utterly quiet. It had been her imagination.

But the supposed sound had taken her out of her thoughts and made her aware of her surroundings. She thought: *I ought to get up and put on a light. Lying here in the dark wouldn't*

*seem right to anyone like Mr. Caldwell. He would say that I was
retreating, I was abandoning the job my life had given me. I
mustn't just lie here hiding and defeated.*

*I could go to the kitchen and tidy up any disorder left from
that dinner I tried to fix.*

*I could make some snacks, sandwiches or something, and leave
them in the refrigerator covered with plastic wrap. I could make
some lemonade, and Davie and Suzie would have something to
eat and drink later, before they went to bed.*

She sat up in the dark, put her feet on the rug. And then again
she heard something. It was a noise, she thought, like something
big and scaly brushing against a wall.

Terror jolted through her, there was a convulsion of heat and
pressure inside her head, and she wanted to scream. She opened
her mouth, but her throat was locked, and not a sound came out.
She sat there voiceless, straining, fingers digging at her face.

Across the room, an oblong of shadow against the pale wall,
she could see the door. If the door should open, if the thing or
whatever it was—

Big. Hideous.

Put on the light . . .

*No. I won't look at it, if it comes. I won't turn on a light because
then I'd have to—*

The noise came again, closer and bolder, a thrashing kind of
noise, a huge, tail-swinging noise. A weak cry was squeezed from
her lips. She felt herself turning cold, felt her senses dissolve, and
knew that she was going to faint. She was going to pass out here
and lie helpless—

Then she knew all at once what the noise was.

It wasn't inside the house at all—it was outside; it was shrubbery being dragged back and forth against some outer wall. The
wind had come up. And she had been a fool.

Calmed now, but exhausted, she lay back and listened to the
rubbing and scratching of twigs.

A fool. What on earth had got into her?

I'm going to put on the light, she told herself. *In a minute or
two, as soon as I get my breath back. And then I'm going to the
kitchen and do the things I thought of doing: Davie and Suzie*

can find the sandwiches and lemonade, and they'll have sense enough not to say anything to their father, not after that awfulness tonight over the dinner. And they can share a snack in front of the television set, before they go to bed.

I wonder what made me so afraid?

Why should I imagine that branches being scrubbed against the wall were something else? Something . . . monstrous?

She shivered; she tried to put a name to that horror she had half imagined and could not. The helpless terror had come out of the past, out of one of the nights when she'd been eight or ten or so, when her father had gone off pier fishing and her mother was attending evening services to sing in the choir. The small isolated beach town had no crime, and they'd always reassured Margaret that she was perfectly safe to stay alone, and yet when nine o'clock came and it was time to close the book and go upstairs, she'd always been afraid. The sea winds had made the old house creak and stir, and sand scouring the front porch had hissed like snakes. There had always been something wrong with the upstairs lights. Her father had shrugged off the trouble—who needed lights in a bedroom, which was for sleep?—and so she had had to climb the narrow stairs and find her room and get into bed in the dark for years.

She lay, lost in memory, with her eyes shut.

That's why I got so upset and silly a minute ago, she told herself. *I remembered those nights when the stairs creaked, when I watched the door as long as I dared and finally covered my head because I couldn't stand any more.*

And of course, the reason I thought the noise from the shrubbery was indoors was on account of that other sound, the first sound, because it had *been—*

She frowned, and tensed. What had that first sound been like? It hadn't been dragging, scraping. But what? She tried to remember that first noise, the one that had aroused her, but nothing remained that she could pin down. And now that the wind had died for a moment and the branches had quit scraping, the house was as completely quiet as before.

She got off the couch, moving a little uncertainly, and went to the lamp beside the desk and switched it on. The room sprang into familiar focus, and she thought, *I ought to replace the desk; it's shabby,* and then out of the past she remembered her dad's desk, the old rolltop antique with the pigeonholes, and her mother's indignant tirades over it—her dad had inherited it from his father, who had also been a lawyer, the same kind of lawyer that his son became, one that liked to fish and dream and own a patched-up boat, and the thing that had driven her mother into pinched-mouth frenzies was the fact that the old desk was marred all along its front rim by the burned tracks of forgotten cigars and cigarettes. Her mother's church, the one where she sang in the choir and sewed for the missions, had been totally dead set against smoking. Dancing and drinking, too, Margaret remembered, but if her father drank, he did it while he pier-fished or went out in the boat, and in the small beach town, overblown with weeds and sand, there just hadn't been any place to dance.

She looked at the desk again and remembered that Thomas had made as firm and reasonable a stand in its protection as had her father for his. It was not to be changed for anything new and better.

The lamp needed a new shade, though. But then she thought of all the criticism, backbiting, she had endured of late, as though the buying and rearranging of furnishings had been a way to punish the rest of them, no gratitude or understanding whatever, and she made up her mind to leave the lampshade as it was. So let them have stained, frayed, shabby stuff, and let them see how long the house looked pretty—

What was *that?*

The branches were twisting against the wall again, but only a little, and the new sound, a noise like a thump, was quite different. She backed against the desk, put her hands over her mouth, the pulse of heat coming back into her skull and flesh growing cold.

Something was *in* this house. In here with *her.* Thomas and the children had been gone long enough, they should be returning, they should—*please, God*—be driving up, turning toward the garage, this very minute!

The thud came again, from far away, from the other end of the house. It was like a summons. It called her; it demanded that she come and see.

Do something, she commanded herself. She opened the door to the hall.

The light from the den spread a little way and then was lost.

She ran to the entry where there was a big shallow frosted bowl up against the ceiling and switched it on. The ferns and philodendrons sprang out, greener than life. The inner side of the front door gleamed white, the brass knob set into a plaque of ornate metal and the brass sill protector giving a gleam of gold. She was tempted then to run out into the grounds, to hide somewhere outdoors until the others came home.

There was thick shrubbery out beside the pool, and from there she would have a view not only of the house, but of the driveway, and be able to see the car as soon as Thomas drove in. She had her hand on the big knob, her arm trembling with the urge to get the door open and be gone, and then that inner voice came, that voice that seemed to be more and more like her mother's when her mother had been talking about smoking and drinking and dancing, and the voice reminded her that she was the responsible one here, the parent. The tone was her mother's, but the words belonged to Mr. Caldwell.

You can't go out and hide like a scared child, a terrified baby, because you are the parent, the one in charge, the defender and protector.

This is the home that you were given to look after. This is your place. Whatever it is over there at the other end of the house, banging and knocking, it's your job to go see about it and stop it.

She took her hand off the knob and rubbed her fingers because both her hands were so icy. And both her arms shook. But then she turned her back to the entry and went again to the dark hall and walked down the hall to the point where she could see into the kitchen. A light burned here, after all, the light in the hood over the range. But half the length of the kitchen and all of the dining area and the family room were dim and shadowy.

The knocking was farther away and to the right, and something about it struck her as random, wind-driven like the scraping twigs, aimless. She couldn't have said why the impression was so strong, but she felt sure—it wasn't a deliberate pounding. There was no pattern or intent.

She switched on the big overhead light in the kitchen and walked on through the big laundry and storage areas, the air around her growing colder and more night-smelling as she went.

The back door hung fully open, and when the wind hit it, it thumped the wall with varying degrees of impact. She switched on the light, illuminating not only the entry area, but also the paved space outside, and part of the yard, and away off in the night the dim shape of the fence.

She thought, *He's come inside,* and turned swiftly to glance behind her. But if he were inside, hiding, would he betray it by leaving the door open? She decided not. He was *outside.* She was afraid to look out there, afraid of what she might see, but she told herself sternly, *I won't show terror. To anyone out there I have to seem just curious and a little surprised. He didn't know that anyone was home. He thought we'd come and that one of us would find the open door and be afraid. Davie, maybe. Davie always rushed in first.* After a minute, willing herself to be composed, she moved casually to shut the door and lock it and turn off the light.

If he was out there, he had a key and could come right in again. I couldn't stop him.

Thomas must have thought of having the locks changed, and then in the press of all those other things, he forgot. I'll remind him tomorrow.

I won't worry him about it tonight. He must have locked up before leaving with the children; it would disturb him to know what happened here. I won't tell him. And when they're asleep, I'll bring the blanket and pillow and sleep lying across the doorway. No one could open the door without my knowing it.

It occurred to her then that this was the spot where her mother-in-law had lain dying. Someone had mopped up the traces of blood. There must have been some. Had Vicky done it? Thomas?

Vicky, she decided. Thomas wouldn't have thought of it.

22

Caldwell awoke. Something was buzzing softly around the room.

But then he thought: *It's the damned alarm. But it can't be two thirty yet. I made a mistake; I didn't set it right.* He rolled over and lifted his head to see the illuminated clock face in the dark, and sure enough, the hour hand was between two and three and the minute hand was precisely on six. "Got to get up," he groaned, and reached to silence the alarm, and shut his eyes just for a minute, and when he finally struggled awake again, it was almost a quarter to three.

He went into the bathroom and did brutal things to his face and neck with cold water, and dried, feeling the grainy need for sleep still there behind his eyes. He looked into the mirror and said to the bleared form there, "You bastard, you knew it was never going to be a picnic. And you've been lucky. You've never taken a slug in the gut or been sapped or razored. So cheer up, little buddy. Life is just a bowl of cherries."

He dressed. The clothes felt tired, as if they'd been asleep, too, and didn't want to wake up any more than he did. He had a back bedroom, private entrance, breakfast included—that was a laugh —in the home of a very kind and respectable police widow, Mrs. Wampers. The reason breakfast was a joke was that since he'd made detective, he didn't often get a chance to eat it. He finished dressing, tying his tie in front of the dresser mirror, made a last smoothing motion over his thinning hair, checked his pockets for keys and wallet, and let himself out by way of his private entrance without making any noise.

The Wampers house wasn't too far from the downtown area, where all-night neon made a glow in the sky. Caldwell headed for a diner he liked, a twenty-four-hour place, and had some coffee and scrambled eggs, not feeling hungry but needing help in getting really awake.

He drove out of town, along silent streets where an occasional intersection blinked red with a warning to make a stop. He ignored the red warnings; he was the only one out anywhere. He headed for the long rise that led up to the valley, Warren's land, and he remembered for a moment that even up until ten years ago the place had been Warren's alone. The whole valley and the ridges that surrounded it, a private kingdom, and at the top of the rise at the valley's entrance there used to be a big sign, NOT A THROUGH STREET. People went up there and picnicked anyway, and give Warren credit, he never had run them out. He must have married around that time. Caldwell frowned, trying to recall just when he'd heard of Warren marrying that Eastern society girl, the one whose family owned a shipping line. Must be about ten years. She'd never really lived at the enormous place Warren had built for her here. She'd commuted from it to New York and Europe and had had two kids—not here, either—and had left Warren flat and gone to live . . . Paris, wasn't it?

For a few moments Caldwell, driving in the dark, amused himself by wondering what it would be like to be married to a rich bitch like that, somebody who'd had every damned thing she had ever wanted, who didn't really understand what *wanting* a thing was, because at the first stirring of a whim, the thing that the whim was half directed toward immediately appeared. What had Warren's life with her been like? Warren hadn't grown up with his wishes being instantly translated into fact; he'd had a pompous old fool of a father who had wanted a barony here in the brush-covered semidesert of southern California, who had kept them in poverty by diddling around trying to grow lilacs and English oaks, and who had built an enormous swan pond surrounded by acres of miserably misclimated bluegrass, peonies, rhododendrons and iris . . . such stuff as had struck the occasional stray wanderer up from town bug-eyed at the effort and waste and had made the name of Warren for a long time a spur to winks, finger windings against the head, and even guffaws.

The kid must have had good sense and tact, Caldwell decided, to have won the old man over from his diehard compulsion to be a duke, to have scraped up financing, planned the layout of groves, the plowing and planting, and all the rest of it to make a little citrus empire up here, a million times more practical and profitable than his old man's cock-eyed countryseat. And now Warren even had oil to play with, or would have, when he made whatever decision—concerning or not concerning his wife—which now seemed to keep him from going after it.

Caldwell's car topped the rise and started down. It was all a dark cup under the night sky. The big white houses on the rim were pretty well concealed by their shrubs and trees. He thought he could smell through the open window the orange trees and eucalyptus.

"A really pretty place to live," he commented half-aloud, "provided you've got the right people living with you."

He swung right into the curving road that led past Warren's big home, past some vacant land and two or three other places, to the Stoddard house.

He cut the lights and the motor before he got close, let the car drift to a slow stop, and shut the door silently. The night felt cooler and more damp than it had from inside the car, and a sudden sweep of wind sent the tree branches dragging across the roof of the car, a noise that reminded him of surf. He stood quietly, letting his eyes adjust to the dark.

He moved off, keeping to the side of the pavement. The cement drive led him toward the garage doors, and there he cut across the front of the house toward the pool. He tested the big double glass doors; they were locked tight. He rounded the back corner, picked his way through shrubbery, stopped at the rear door to listen. There was a light inside, not right at the entry; the door had a frosted glass panel, and he could see that inside was not completely dark. He thought that the light might be in the kitchen, and not a bright one at that.

He turned the knob soundlessly. He thought that in answer there was movement of some kind, a rustling, stirring, low and near the inner sill. His first instinct was to leap backward. He didn't believe in ghosts, but that was where Mrs. Stoddard had lain dying. He felt the prickling of his scalp as his hair rose.

He waited, listening, and had the uncanny sensation that someone inside was listening to *him*. But there was no further sound at all, and finally, he went on, promising himself to keep an eye on that rear door for a while.

Thomas Stoddard should have made some arrangement about changing the locks or should have reinforced them temporarily with bolts, but Caldwell made a bet with himself that Stoddard had done neither; the day's troubles had overwhelmed him.

The windows along the rear wall were lightless, and shut. No gleam showed, and no curtains stirred. The Stoddard family was in there like people in a fort, closed up against danger, and he felt a wry moment of sympathy for them. He retraced his way to the path that led from the back door out to the gate. The white fence showed up distinctly, even in the dark, and beyond the cleared area was the opening to the barranca, a wedge of blackness, and the rising tumble of brush beyond. He leaned on the gate for perhaps fifteen minutes and heard nothing above the occasional burst of wind except a single coyote yelp from far back in the hills. When the wind came, it seemed to gather itself first far down in the valley, to circle there with a noise like a rising sea, and then to flow up the crest like a tide and sweep the trees and make whistling sounds along the rim of the roof.

He went out by way of the side path to the pool and walked all around there, expecting nothing, just trying to keep awake. Something little scuffled off through the shrubbery, a rabbit or even a possum. Even in this light he could see how much debris there was already on the water's surface.

He went to the front entry and tried the door there, remembering that he had neglected to do so on first arrival, and it too was locked as fast as the others. He was turning away when a voice spoke from inside, muffled, the words indistinct. Then the door opened a crack, and the voice said, "Who's out there?"

It was one of the girls. Suzie, he decided. He said calmly, "It's Detective Caldwell. Just checking around a little."

"What time is it?"

"Must be getting on to four o'clock in the morning."

She yawned. "Have you found anything?"

"Not a thing. It's all as quiet as a church."

"Have you been here long? Were you around in the back a little while ago?"

"Yes."

"Did you hear that coyote?"

"Yes."

"He was way up near the Indian burying grounds. Did you know that? If an Indian were here, he'd think it was one of his dead ancestors calling."

"Is that so?" Caldwell said politely.

"May I come out and talk to you for a little while? I've been awake for ages, and everyone's asleep in here, and I'm tired of reading, and anyway Dad said the lights had to be out—we need our rest."

Caldwell thought swiftly. Would Stoddard approve of his youngest daughter being out in the night with a middle-aged police detective? There was a certain ambiguity here, depending on the kind of mind you had. But Suzie was the one he hadn't had a chance to talk to yet, and she was the one toward whom the threats had been directed. "You'll have to put on a coat," he said. "There's a lot of wind now and then."

"I have on a robe."

"A coat," he repeated firmly.

"Just a minute. Don't go away!" The door didn't shut, but he sensed that she had gone. When she stepped out a few minutes later, she had on something dark blue or black, and above the neckline her face was an oval paleness. "I'm sorry if I'm acting like a kind of pest. I wanted to come out ages ago and breathe the wind and look at the sky, but I couldn't because of the rules. I'm glad you're here, and I won't bother you too long."

"Do you come out at night often?" Caldwell asked. "I mean, slip out without anyone knowing?"

"Well . . . not often. But sometimes."

"You understand that you mustn't do it now?"

"Yes."

"Do you want to sit on a bench by the pool? Or walk? I have to take another look at the back door. Something there puzzled me."

"Mother's lying on the floor there, inside," Suzie said promptly. "I heard her go by, and it sounded as if she were tiptoeing and dragging something. I'd been reading. That was before Dad came and said to go to sleep. I waited until she was gone awhile, and then I went to find her, and that's where she is, wrapped in a blanket and her head on a pillow. Right against the door."

Caldwell didn't comment on what Suzie had told him, but he checked his progress toward the side of the house and turned instead to a bench on the decking near the pool. "How's this?"

"Fine." She sat down, and then, with a suppleness he found himself envying, she tucked her legs under her. She was dark, Buddha-like on the end of the bench, the paleness of the young face turned toward him. "Are you here because you thought that man might use the keys and get inside the house?"

"Not exactly. I just thought I'd better check around."

"You don't want us to get scared," she decided.

"Being scared is all right," he pointed out, "as long as you don't panic and do something foolish. Being scared has saved a lot of lives. A smart way to be scared is to look ahead and to plan— for instance, to plan how you'd have to get out of the house in case of fire. Or what to do if you think there's a burglar. Make up your mind what to do and then stick to the plan no matter what, and half the battle is won."

"What should I do if I think that man is inside and might be coming after me?"

Caldwell considered in silence. She was intelligent and should be able to follow a sensible course of action once it was laid out. "If there's a place to hide, a place you can get to quickly and without making any noise, a place where he wouldn't find you right away—"

"My closet?"

"That's too obvious. He'd go there first."

"Under the bed? I don't think I could squeeze under there anyway; it sits so low. Behind a chair?" She put her head back, turned her face to the sky; he could make out her profile dimly. She sat quiet for a time and then said, "I guess there isn't any good place at all. I'd have to try to run, wouldn't I?"

"If you get the chance, yes. And scream."

"I'll have to think of something. Do you know that the Indians made charms, magic things that protected them from danger? Mostly they wore them in a pouch around their necks. The stuff they used was pretty simple, really. It was the combination of things, and what you said and thought over it while you were getting it all together, and when you did it, like during some phase of the moon. The full moon. Or the opposite of the full moon, whatever that is."

"The dark of the moon? I'm not sure just when that comes around," Caldwell admitted.

"And where," she went on. "You were supposed to call on the spirits. That was the main idea. So you went where the spirits might be expected to stay."

"A burying ground?" he guessed. He was going to remind her that any trek to the burying grounds in the hills was far off limits right now and then decided that she already knew it and that she didn't have any plans of hiking up there anyway. What it was, she'd been reading Indian lore and just needed to talk about it to somebody.

23

"Some of the things they put in those little pouches were pretty *ugh*," Suzie said. "I couldn't cut up a lizard or a snake. But then, there were other medicine charms that just used little stones and feathers and pinches of special kinds of earth."

"Earth must have meant a lot to them," Caldwell agreed. "I read somewhere not too long ago the Indian people always felt a great affection for the land. Their love of the earth is the basis of their religion, their sense of belonging here and that the Great Spirit has given them a place of their own."

"That's almost exactly what my books said! Don't you think

that a great many Indians might have lived right around here
where our house sits?"

"I don't know much about local Indian lore," Caldwell answered, wondering how to lead her off the subject. "I suppose the
library might have some material along that line."

"Yes, they have some. Do you think this man might be hanging around right now, watching us?"

Caldwell sat very still. "Do you feel as if he might be?"

She turned slowly as if to listen or as if to tune in on something
beyond sound or sight. "When I'm out at night like this, the world
seems a million times bigger and quieter than it does in the daytime. Mysterious. With strange people and things out in it. As if
all the familiar things have been tucked away. He has to be somebody we know, doesn't he? A man who comes here. Someone
who knows a lot about Davie and me, so he could scare Davie
with what he knows. Davie won't tell me all of it. I think the man
told him something awful. I think what he said was so bad it made
Davie sick. When I ask Davie to tell me just exactly what it was,
he turns a funny color and he won't look at me."

Caldwell thought: *There are jerks in the world who wouldn't
mind a bit telling their sister what might happen to her. Give
Davie credit—and give his mother credit, lying there on the cold
floor in a blanket. Here are two, surprisingly, who are in their
own way protecting the others.*

And then he remembered: *That's what Mrs. Stoddard was doing, too, out there in the dark last night.*

He asked quietly, "Do you have any ideas about this man? Who
he might be?"

While she hesitated, he heard the wind again, gathering itself in a whirlpool down in the valley, making the trees sing. "No,
I guess not," she said at last. "Not really. I don't want him to be
anyone we like. I've figured out he didn't really come to kill
Grandma. That was almost like an accident. He wanted the keys,
and maybe if she hadn't been out there, we would never have
known the difference. He was going to use the keys, according
to Davie, and bring them back. That was all."

"You've done a lot of riding on Mr. Warren's horse. Did you
ever feel as if you were being watched and followed?"

"Yes. Sometimes."

"By someone else on a horse?"

"No. Just someone who was up there to look around maybe."

"You saw someone?"

"I kind of—of heard things."

"Things they wanted you to hear? Or not?"

Again she waited before answering and then said, "Sometimes I just knew the noises weren't rabbits or other animals."

"And no ideas at all about who made these sounds?"

"I thought . . . I shouldn't say it, but"—she coughed on a nervous note—"I thought of Jeff."

"Jeff?"

"Jeff Norbert. Vicky and Jeff are going to get married. Didn't you know that? My dad wanted Vicky to go to the University of Arizona. It's in Tucson. He wanted her to get away from home, what it really was, so she wouldn't get married at all. Or for years yet, anyway. But now she isn't going to the university; she's going to marry Jeff and move right out, soon."

"Where does Jeff live? Oh, wait a minute . . . Norbert. He lives across the valley on that other ridge."

"Yes."

"He won a scholarship, some big school—"

"He's a brain, just *brain*," she agreed.

"And so why did you think it might have been Jeff up there looking around?"

"Well, for a long time it seemed as if Jeff was in love with Vicky, but she was only kind of halfway in love with him. Do you know what I mean? She still looked at the books about the university classes and she shopped for things to wear in that hot weather over there, and you could see she still hadn't made up her mind. And I think sometimes he kind of hung around, and when she came out, he'd coax her to walk up there with him. Kissing, that kind of stuff. You know."

The adult, condescending tone made Caldwell smile, there in the dark. "But you didn't actually see him?"

"No. And I don't mean that it was Jeff who might have followed *me*. If he was around here, he was looking for Vicky. If anybody was looking at me, it was someone else. And I don't know who. And maybe I just imagined the—the noises and the feeling of being watched, because it's kind of spooky when you're up there all alone, even in the daytime."

"Do you ever go up in the hills on foot?"

"No, hardly ever," she said. "You have to go up through the barranca, and there's some real prickly brush in there. It even scratches your legs when you're on a horse. I walked to Mr. Warren's place dozens of times, of course, but that's not up in the hills; that's just cutting behind the neighbors' fences and through the land where nobody's built any houses yet. Of course, I got mud thrown at me—"

"When was this?"

"Two days ago now. It might have been the man who did it —he'd know Davie would find out. If it was the man, he was doing it to show Davie he meant business. Vicky helped me clean up. I asked her today—yesterday, I mean—if it could have been the man, and she said not to worry about it. Maybe it could have been him, but how could we know? And so I shouldn't spend time being scared about it now."

"Very sensible. You didn't see who threw the mud?"

"I thought it might have been some kid playing a dirty trick, a joke. You know, some kid about nine or ten, a brat showing off."

"Davie knew of this when it happened?"

"Yes, and now that I think back, he acted pretty quiet. He acted as if maybe he knew more than we did. Isn't it against the law to make telephone calls like that? And doesn't the phone company do anything?"

"They do all that they can." *Mainly,* he concluded to himself, *they advise you to get an unlisted number. Should Thomas Stoddard get an unlisted number? Probably not. The creep might be frightened enough now never to make another call. And he could also easily be one of those to whom the new unlisted number would be given as a matter of course.*

He's close here. I know it, Caldwell told himself.

"I guess you want to think," Suzie said. "I'd better go in anyway."

"If your mother is still there on the floor, tell her I'm out here, will you? Maybe she'll go to bed."

"I don't think I'm supposed to know what she's doing," Suzie said after a moment. "Did you ever notice? Sometimes we can spoil something that somebody else is doing for us by telling them we know all about it."

"You're right." He was surprised by Suzie's insight. "Don't tell her then."

He accompanied Suzie to the front door and listened as she shot the lock inside.

He did want to think, but he might as well walk while he was doing it. It was past four now, and there was the faintest hint of grayness in the air, a breath almost like fog; the water in the pool had subtly changed color, and the trees showed stark against the horizon. Would anyone come now, this close to morning? He wanted to smoke his pipe; his fingers touched it, the smelly relic, there in his coat pocket. But better not to. Wait.

He went around the house to the back, all the way out to the gate. Some of the dead brush high on the flank of the hills was the color of cotton, frosted with a light that seemed to come from nowhere. The horizon toward the east was paler, but not much. Morning came in a funny way, he told himself.

Davie had a camp up in the barranca, he remembered. The final message had been left there, a note stuck on a bush. It wasn't going to take the creep long to find out that none of the kids was answering the phone anymore—provided he got up his courage, or was determined enough to try to reach Davie that way. So maybe the campsite was worth a look.

The smell of pipe smoke might run off anyone prowling around the house. But up in the barranca, where the rising ground caught the full sweep of the tide from the valley, smoking ought to be safe enough. He'd stop there for one pipeful.

He pushed his way through the brush, climbing in the ruts left by rains, gravel crunching underfoot. After a couple of minutes, dodging thorny twigs and trying to keep his ankles from turning on scattered rocks, he paused to draw breath and to look back. The

Stoddard place seemed to lie directly below and in the paling light to be even closer than when he had entered the barranca. Well, if Suzie were right and if Jeff Norbert had hung around up here to watch for her sister, he had had a good view. You could even see past the house at the far end, to the point where the driveway joined the street. The houses down there looked drowned in all the greenery of citrus trees.

He suddenly felt the strain of the climb and thought: *There won't be anything in Davie's camp. I can stand right here for my smoke and then go back to the house, and as soon as it's fully daylight, I'll head for home and have forty winks and a late breakfast. I'll surprise Mrs. Wampers for a change. Bacon and eggs. I wonder if she'll mind my asking for breakfast after eleven o'clock. She shouldn't; she's saved enough on my breakfasts in the past.*

He took out the pipe and the tobacco pouch and opened the pouch and smelled the spicy odor of the tobacco, a smell that had nothing to do with the richness and relaxation of the smoke but was a pleasure all in itself, a promise, an introduction.

Then with a thoughtful air he closed the pouch and dropped it and the pipe back into his pocket. *I should have had a look at this camp of Davie's a long time ago. I must be slipping to have put it off like this.* He looked at the crowding thickets ahead of him with a grim expression. "Well, do your damnedest. Nothing I've got on would even make the racks at a rummage sale."

He climbed, and got scratched, and felt his clothes being snagged. He broke a branch that would have hit him in the face, got thorns in his fingers, swore some. But finally he was there— there couldn't be any mistake; the earth was beaten down in a semicircle close to the overhanging clay bank and the little stone fireplace was black with old smoke. He saw scattered hoofprints, a sheet of paper speared on a twig, some scratchy writing on the paper, and more important—much, much more important—a big silver-colored flashlight all frosted with damp, its case bent and the lens busted, lying in the sand under the bush.

Caldwell didn't enter the packed-down area. He stayed on its fringe, moving, looking at everything over there against the bank. The writing had been made with a scorched stick or a piece of charcoal, he decided, and the paper had been here all night, long enough to become blotched and wrinkled by the fog. As near as he could make out, the writing said

Too Bad
for
Your
Sister

and the broken flashlight lying below it completed the promise of what was to come.

Thank God Davie didn't see it, Caldwell thought, and then grew suddenly still, his eyes narrowed. A camp such as Davie had described should have some kinds of supplies in it. The little fireplace had been built to heat food on, to roast wieners, to play at having a home in the wilderness. Davie had been here, then, and cleared it out. And so—maybe he'd seen the note and the flashlight after all. It was time to find out.

He took a final careful look around, in case anyone might be coming along to change things. Then he pushed and stumbled his way back down the barranca. He knocked loudly on the rear door, and it took a minute for Mrs. Stoddard to come in answer, so he judged that she'd got up from her vigil on the floor and had gone to the kitchen, and sure enough, when he got inside, he could smell the coffee.

"I need to use the phone, Mrs. Stoddard, and then to see Davie."

"Oh." She moved back, leading the way toward the kitchen, and any surprise she felt at his unexpected appearance was masked by the effects of the night without rest—she had a withered, exhausted look, eyes puffed and dull, and she moved unsteadily. "The phone is here—"

"Thank you, I know. Will you bring Davie, please?"

He called police headquarters and requested the squad, on the double, that took casts of footprints and other marks and collected physical evidence. There wouldn't be any fingerprints on that flashlight, but they could try.

He went on into the Family Area, which was dark, the curtains drawn against the big glass doors at the far end, and he walked around impatiently, wanting the pipe worse than ever, until after a moment Davie came in, wrapping a robe over his pajamas.

"Good morning, Mr. Caldwell."

"Good morning. Davie, I've just been up to your camp in the barranca." He waited, but Davie was still half-asleep. He hunched his shoulders, suppressing a yawn, and then coughed a couple of times. "Let's sit down," Caldwell suggested. He took a chair, and Davie settled in a corner of a couch. "There's a paper up there, fastened to a twig on a bush. Do you know anything about it?"

The look of strain and embarrassment that he remembered from their first talk appeared suddenly on Davie's face. "Yes."

"You went up there? You saw that paper?"

"I brought all my camp stuff down yesterday. It's all in the garage, in an old basket I kept it in. I saw the paper there, and I read it, but I didn't touch it."

"And you didn't tell me about it. Did you tell your dad?"

"No." Davie huddled deeper into the cushions. "I knew that I ought to. I knew it was what I should do, and I kept thinking I'd find a way; I'd say to myself, 'Do it now.' And then I didn't, I just put it off because I was so . . . scared." There was the gleam of tears under his lashes, a sudden brimming that he rubbed angrily away.

"It's hard to know what to do sometimes," Caldwell said sympathetically. "And the note was a threat without really saying what was going to be done or what you could do to avoid it. He was mad, all right, because things had gone wrong. But he's not telling you what to do next. What about that flashlight? Didn't you realize how important that was?"

Davie looked at him blankly, his face, eyes, his whole body growing still, and then a flush of color rose in his skin, and Caldwell knew what he was going to say, and he remembered the silver metal frosted with dew and he cursed inwardly because he hadn't risked damaging other signs to walk over and get the flashlight. He should have brought it with him. Damn it, suppose when the crew got up there—

"I didn't see any flashlight," Davie said slowly.

"Lying right below the note."

"It wasn't there yesterday."

"I'm going back up there right now. I want you to get some clothes on and follow me. I won't be far ahead, and I'll keep an eye out below. Now hurry, will you?"

24

A couple of gray doves had come down out of the brush and were investigating a red-berry vine at the corner of the fence. It was almost full daylight now, a clear, colorless light that made the white fence, the brown earth, and the hills extraordinarily sharp and distinct. Caldwell rushed up the barranca, heedless of thorny growth, and a few minutes later Davie arrived at a run, and Caldwell stopped him at the rim of the camp by grabbing his arm. It all looked exactly as Caldwell had left it a few minutes ago except that there was more light and he could see it better. "We'll wait here until the men come from the crime lab." He thought: *And let's hope that they find more than what I can see. It doesn't look like much.*

There were scuffs, drag marks—left probably by Davie when he'd cleared out his stuff—and a few old hoofprints. Where the soil wasn't pounded hard, too hard to take a print, it was too soft and sandy to hold one.

"Is that . . . is that flashlight the one that—"

"My guess is, yes, it is. I imagine it's been wiped clean of any traces of the man who handled it, or it wouldn't be here."

"Why would he leave it?"

"Well, you didn't take the note away or burn it the way he instructed you to do with the other one. You just left it. In a way, you ignored it. And maybe he thinks you didn't pay enough attention to it. He wanted you to show more reaction, and he wants to make sure you understand."

"Understand *what?*"

"Since there are no further instructions, my guess is that what you're supposed to remember is something he told you previously. Something he made pretty clear, such as, you aren't to spend time thinking about his voice and where you'd heard it before. Wouldn't you figure that's what he's warning you about?"

Davie nodded thoughtfully. "The only time he got kind of upset and nervous was when I said, 'I know you!' That's when he got so excited he almost forgot how to talk. He almost forgot to keep talking in that phony way of his."

"And have you thought about his voice?"

"Yes."

Caldwell waited, but after a moment Davie shook his head in a frustrated way. "Sometimes it seems as if I'm going to place him any minute."

Caldwell suppressed his own feelings into an attitude of patience. If you tried to force the kid, he never would remember. "Well, Davie, I hope that this business here"—he gestured toward the note, the flashlight—"will impress on you how important it is to obey the rules that your dad and I figured out for you. For you and Suzie and Vicky. This man is afraid that you'll remember who he is, and he might be watching closely, and it won't be long before he understands that you aren't answering the door or the telephone or going outdoors alone. And then he may try to reach you in some other way. And you are to tell your father or me—phone me if I'm not around—the very instant he tries anything. Do you get this?"

"Yes, sir. I won't keep still about anything again."

"Good."

They waited until the first of the lab men appeared, and Caldwell pointed out what was new and told him what he hoped they could get, and then Davie and he went back to the house.

Margaret Stoddard had followed Davie to the back entry and had watched him run into the tangled brush of the barranca. She supposed that something new and important must have been found, that Mr. Caldwell had been exploring up there—he must have come out from town very early—and that now perhaps they would find who had killed Tom's mother and the man would be arrested and everything would be ended, even before the mobs had time to build up the way they had before, drawn by the scent of mystery. If the old woman hadn't pretended that she had seen a strange enigmatic figure out in the yard, drawing Cootie to his death, the whole thing would have been passed over as an accident, a child's rash mistake, and maybe after all, the old woman's lying attempt to pass the blame had been what she, Margaret, hadn't been able to forgive. It had been even more unforgivable than letting Cootie die in the first place.

When you were to blame for something, you should just accept it and take your punishment.

She'd have to think about it some more, some other time, because right now she was so tired, so sleepy and even tottering, that she had to go lie down on the couch in the den.

She went back, picking up the pillow and blanket in passing, and in the kitchen she checked to make sure that the percolator was keeping hot. She turned from the range in the direction of the big dark empty family room, and for a moment it seemed that some half-visible shape moved over there against the glass doors, against the shadow of the trees outside. She stopped with a jerk and waited; it seemed to her that she could hear her pulse, hear the thud of her own heart.

But the motion, the half-seen beckoning shape, now seemed to have dissolved. She shuddered, and gooseflesh ran up her arms and into her scalp. It was all so silent, so full of menace and strangeness. She wanted to scream. Instead, ready to bolt, she forced herself to take one slow step after another until she was out of the kitchen.

Someone had drawn the draperies without permission, that was all. It would be better to keep them closed in case people came to stare.

Had *she* drawn them?

She paused in the hall and tried to remember. She had got up off the floor dizzy with exhaustion, after a night of fitful dreams and of rolling this way and that in an effort to find comfort. Had she automatically drawn the draperies to let in the light? It was a gloomy room, really, unless the draperies were open and you saw the vista of trees out beside the pool and the shine of the water. Or unless, as at night, the lamps were lit. The room was poorly

planned, she thought, taking up her progress toward the den at
the other end of the house. The architect hadn't foreseen what the
room would be like by daylight without the draperies fully pulled
back. It was a mistake. His mistake. Like adding the suite of rooms
for the old woman so that she could pack them with all that junk
of hers. How much better to have added a single tiny one-room cot-
tage out back, complete with a small bath and one of those com-
pact units that had range, refrigerator, and sink all together, a
miniature kitchen that could fit into a closet.

And then instead of leaving empty space to be filled, to have
bought some good but simple furnishings, modern things that were
sleek and quiet and invited orderliness—

For an instant something tugged at her memory; it concerned
the stuff in the old woman's rooms, but even as she tried to pin it
down, she saw that she was passing Suzie's room. She stopped,
wondering if she should look in, and she remembered the
friendly warmth of last night, Suzie's pleasure in arranging the table, the whole lovely atmosphere of the dinner being prepared,
the cake so fantastically beautiful, the children involved and
cooperating— She touched the knob, ready to peep in, and then
she thought of the aftermath, the shocking things that Thomas had
done. The cake chopped and destroyed, the roast and potatoes
thrown out God knew where, pan and all, like garbage, like worse
than garbage . . . The nice vegetables down the disposer. And
then the coldness that came after, the strangeness that made her
want to hide and cry, Davie and Suzie not looking at her but hurrying after their father.

I'd better lie down right now.

I'm sick.

*There is something about all that furniture up there in her
rooms, I almost remembered whatever it was, but it's gone now.
I forgot it when I touched Suzie's door.*

I'll rest a while, and then I'll remember.

She went on to the den and shut the door behind her.

*I'm so alone. I wish I had someone to talk to, someone who
would try to understand.*

She placed the pillow on the couch, lay down, and spread the
blanket over herself. As soon as she shut her eyes, she seemed to

be floating away on a cloud, her senses whirling and all the aches and bruises left by the hard floor softened by drowsiness. *I'll rest until about eleven o'clock,* she told herself, and wondered why the time had come into her thoughts with such impact.

Sleep, she commanded herself.

I tried to explain to Mr. Caldwell, I wanted him to understand my side of things, but he didn't believe me. I could see by his eyes that he didn't believe that I had wanted the home to be so beautiful and perfect that living here would take away all the grief over Cootie's death.

Ever since that time, when Cootie died—it seemed to Margaret that she looked back through a dim narrowing tunnel—*I've tried so hard to please everyone.*

And now, with the old woman out of the way, it could be better—

For just a moment a blurred image came, the old woman creeping out into the dark to face up to the danger, to confront the man who threatened all of them, and in that moment Margaret trembled on the brink of something like shame. It was a feeling she couldn't endure. It was too menacing, too filled with destruction; it made her hurt and shiver inside, deep inside where the little girl waited in the lightless house, still waited after all these years, and finally covered her head with the bedding.

Davie and Mr. Caldwell came back to the house, and Mr. Caldwell said he would enjoy a cup of coffee, and Davie found that the percolator was hot and filled with fresh coffee, and he poured a cup for Mr. Caldwell. He also offered to fry eggs and pancakes if Mr. Caldwell wanted them. Suzie came into the kitchen about that time, and she offered to make Mr. Caldwell sausages and waffles.

"We learned to cook," she told Mr. Caldwell. "We're like orphans, sort of. We had to learn to cook and to do laundry, and I learned to iron. We had to take care of ourselves. It happened when my little brother got killed riding his tricycle through those glass doors. Did you know about our little brother?"

Mr. Caldwell nodded over the cup of coffee. "Yes, Suzie, I knew."

"Were you one of the cops up here then?"

"No, but I heard about it."

"Our mother had a nervous breakdown. Isn't that a polite way of saying she went kind of crazy?"

Davie burned with embarrassment at the stuff Suzie was saying to Mr. Caldwell. He thought that Mr. Caldwell was embarrassed by it, too. Mr. Caldwell was smiling a little bit, the way you do when you wish somebody would switch off. He didn't answer and say yes, a nervous breakdown was the same as going crazy. He asked Suzie about the rules that her dad had told her about, and then he talked about the flashlight they'd just found up in the barranca. He explained that finding the flashlight like that meant that the man was still hanging around and might still do something pretty bad, and the rules about not answering the phone and the door and not going casually outside were more important than ever.

Suzie looked patient as if she were being bored. Davie knew all her looks and what they meant. She thought that Mr. Caldwell was talking to her as if she were a baby. She was pretty grown up, this look said, and after all, she had heard all this stuff before from their old man.

Apparently Mr. Caldwell could read that look about as well as Davie could, because all at once he broke off. Then he added, "Of course, you're old enough to realize the danger and what has to be done about it. I don't have to go over all these rules again."

"No, you don't, really," Suzie said, using the voice that meant that she was much older than she looked—about twenty years older than their mother, even. And so old that Davie was a mere baby. "I thought, of course, that you were reviewing all that stuff for my brother's benefit."

"He was talking to you," Davie said hotly.

"Oh, was he? Mr. Caldwell, did you know that our grandmother fell down those steps to her rooms and broke her leg in some awful way? And was crippled after that?"

"Hmmm," Mr. Caldwell said, meaning yes, he knew about it.

"Was she pushed, do you think? Or a string tied across the top of the stairs, a strong black thread that she couldn't see in time? Something to make her fall and get hurt and to punish her for letting Cootie cut himself all up in those glass doors?"

"Did you see Cootie after he died?" Mr. Caldwell asked interestedly.

He thinks she's got a gruesome imagination, Davie told himself.

"I didn't see the body," Suzie said in her grown-up way, "until the mortician fixed it all up. Cootie looked quite nice. He was pale, but of course, that was on account of all the blood he had lost. Do you think somebody deliberately made our grandmother fall, Mr. Caldwell?"

"Do you?"

She tapped her fingers on the tiled sink and tried to look as if she were thinking deeply, and Davie wanted to yell, "Hey, knock it off, you look like a kook." "Well, there is another idea, Mr. Caldwell—that Grandmother could have had a guilt complex. Surely you've heard of them. She might have wanted to fall down those stairs, to be hurt, maybe even to die."

The smile left Mr. Caldwell's lips and seemed to creep up behind his eyes, half-hidden there, a funny private expression that Davie thought might mean that Mr. Caldwell didn't want to be laughing out loud. "I see that you've been reading psychology books, too, Suzie."

"Oh, sure," she said airily. "I do all the time. My views are quite broad. My interests, I mean. I'm interested in all kinds of things. And this family of ours is full of things to be interested in, don't you agree?"

He went over and put the empty coffee cup under the faucet, rinsed it out, and left it in the sink, clean. "These ideas you have about your grandmother being hurt, that fall—do you know what I wish you'd do about those ideas, Suzie?"

She smirked and got very bright-eyed, and Davie thought in disgust: *She thinks he's going to ask her to keep her ideas a secret—they're important and dangerous. Oh, brother!* He grabbed the cup out of the sink and wiped it hard and fast with a towel and slammed it back into the cupboard. Mr. Caldwell must know that Suzie was a kook. He had to know it by now.

"I want you to talk these ideas over with your mother as soon as you can. Find her where you can be quiet together, you two, and have a good talk."

There was complete silence in the kitchen. All the brightness and smartness washed out of Suzie's face, and she looked young and pale. She licked her mouth a couple of times and swallowed. She put her hands behind her, caught together, like a kid.

"Talk to *her*? But . . . but I *couldn't*—"

He touched one of Suzie's hands gently in passing. "Don't get the wrong idea; don't think I want you to go to your mother like a small child, like someone too young to understand grown-up things. That's not *you*, Suzie. You're practically a young lady. It's time that you took your place as one, and I'm not saying that you haven't been." He smiled, a real smile that made Suzie smile in return. "I guess I'm having a hard time saying what I mean without putting my foot in my mouth. But I do want you to have a quiet, sensible talk with your mother and ask her opinion on these thoughts of yours about your grandmother."

She looked confused, almost afraid. She glanced at Davie to see how he was taking it, and Davie congratulated himself on keeping a poker face. He didn't twitch a muscle, didn't bat an eye. *Let her do her own talking now; she's been so high and mighty and tried to make me feel like a silly baby—*

"If you want me to, I will."

"Thank you, Suzie."

"Shall I come to you afterward and tell you what she said?"

"Your mother? No, that won't be necessary. This is going to be a conversation just between the two of you. You don't have to talk about it to anyone else."

She was absolutely baffled, Davie thought with inner satisfaction. There went the dream that she was going to be some kind of kid detective and make reports to Mr. Caldwell and all that junk.

Davie wanted to hug himself.

25

The detective turned to go, but Davie spoke. "Mr. Caldwell, could I ask you a question?"

"Why, certainly."

"When you and my dad were outside yesterday on a bench by the pool, were you talking about the rules for us? About not answering the phone and all that?"

"Yes, Davie, that's what we were talking about."

Davie wanted to ask, "You weren't talking about my mother at all, were you?" but he couldn't get the words out. Mr. Caldwell waited a minute, standing there in the doorway.

Finally, Mr. Caldwell said, "There's an important point I want you to get straight. The man left that flashlight for you to see, and he knows that you would know what it meant, the threat implied in his leaving it. In other words, he is close enough to you, to the family, to have found out that we are investigating what happened to a certain flashlight and that the theory is that your grandmother was killed with such an instrument. Do you understand this point of reasoning?"

"I—I guess so, sir."

"And do you understand that this closeness and familiarity makes him a thousand times more dangerous than if he were a stranger?"

Davie nodded. Suzie looked scared.

"I hope that both of you keep it in mind," Mr. Caldwell said, sounding serious but perfectly friendly.

"We won't forget," Davie promised, and Mr. Caldwell said thanks for the coffee, and went out, probably back up the barranca, where the other men were working.

Suzie said, "Well, he wouldn't eat any breakfast. But I'm still going to make sausages and waffles. I just feel like doing it."

"Maybe Mom will get up and fix breakfast."

"No, she won't. She slept all night on the floor by the back door. She'll be worn-out, I bet."

"Why should she do that?"

"To protect all of us." Suzie opened the freezer compartment of the big refrigerator, poked around in its frost-covered contents, and came up with a package of link sausages. "How many for you?"

"Three. Why should she think somebody was coming in that way?"

"How should I know? Here, take these and put them in a skillet over a low fire, will you? And I'll be mixing the waffle batter. After you put the sausages on, you can get the waffle iron out and plug it in."

"Gee, thanks. I thought you were getting breakfast."

"I am. I'm doing the brainwork, silly. The thing is, just watching a door isn't enough. And Mr. Caldwell waiting around outside isn't enough. Oh, I forgot to tell you—he was out there while it was still dark. I heard him and went out, and we talked."

"And you told him how to do his job," Davie put in. He'd taken out a skillet, put it on the range, turned on the gas under it, plopped in the six links of sausage. "So he thanked you kindly for your advice."

"Oh, go jump," Suzie said with a disgusted look. "But it's true, they think because they're grown up that they know what is best, and what has to be done, and so they do sensible things—they think."

He put the waffle iron on the counter and plugged the attached cord into a wall socket. "And you know something that isn't sensible but would work?"

"I sure do," Suzie agreed, "and I'm going to do it. You'll see." Davie paused to look at her fixedly. "You heard what Mr. Caldwell told us."

"I heard him, but—" She broke off because Vicky came in.

Vicky had on a short black skirt and a white blouse, her hair was brushed back and tied with a pink scarf, and she wore makeup, as much as she ever used. "Hi, kids. Coffee hot? Whatever you're doing, make enough for me.

"Where are you going?" Suzie asked, dumping more pancake mix into the bowlful she was stirring now.

"I might go out a little later," Vicky said, frowning slightly as if she wished Suzie wouldn't ask. "Or I might not."

"Do you think there's going to be some more people up here today? Crowds, like when Cootie died?" Suzie wondered. "Does it matter if the waffle mix has lumps in it? They bake out, don't they? I guess I haven't made any waffles lately, and I've forgotten. Here comes Dad."

"As for the crowds," Vicky said, "I suppose there might be a few more people today—they've had a chance to hear all about Grandma on TV and the radio and to read about her in the papers — Hello, Dad."

He too was dressed for the day. He went directly to the coffee percolator and poured himself a cup. "Good morning, everybody."

Vicky said, "Do you have to go to the office so soon?"

"There are a few things that won't wait, things I have to explain to Bowman so that he can handle them while I'm away." He sipped at the rim of the cup, smiling at Davie and Suzie and Vicky in turn. "Of course, I'll be back early, and I'll be with you for the rest of the day. Don't get any idea you'll be on your own to do as you please."

"Mom's here, too," Suzie said, bending a little lower to examine the contents of the bowl.

Their father didn't answer her. He finished the coffee, looked at the electric clock on the wall over the desk, checked the time with his watch, and pulled at his cuffs and tie, getting everything straight. Davie thought: *They're never going to make it up. It's finished with my dad and mom. He shouldn't have thrown out all that food. She wasn't really celebrating; she was trying to make up a little for all the times she hadn't cooked for us.*

A stinging came into his eyes, and he got busy setting the table in the dining room so that no one would notice him.

I've got to tell Dad about Mr. Caldwell and the flashlight. Mr. Caldwell will want to see Dad before he leaves.

I'll follow Dad outdoors and tell him when he goes.

Vicky was saying, "Why don't you stay and eat a bite, Dad?

We'd love to have a few minutes with you. We need to feel as if we're still a family—"

He touched her chin gently with a fingertip. "You're the one who's getting out."

"I'm not leaving today."

He grabbed her hand, made the big diamond glitter by turning it from side to side under the light. "Do you think I didn't notice? You're going to marry Jeff. And I'm not going to be a damned fool and tell you that you can't, you mustn't leave us, you're too young and you ought to finish college, and I still want you to be my little girl, which I do, of course, but I'm not going to whine about it, and I'm not going to put any stumbling blocks in your way, none at all. I'm going to wish you good luck and all the happiness in the world, and I'm not even going to explain my own ideas about marriage, which you don't need to hear anyway because your marriage might not turn out the way mine did. Now—is everything clear, darling?"

Her mouth trembled. "Oh, Dad, I love you so much!"

He pretended to be surprised. "After all these years, you've found that out? But there comes a time when all the little birds have to fly, you know."

They were facing each other, their father mocking and gentle and Vicky's eyes brimming with tears, when Suzie's voice cut across sharply. In the dining room, Davie started. Suzie said, "You won't care when I go."

There was a strange silence, while the words seemed to die slowly, and Suzie lifted the top of the waffle iron to see if the inside were hot enough.

Then she added, "I mean, I won't be the first one, that's all. I won't be the first one to go. The first is the worst."

"Yes, Suzie, the first is the worst," echoed Thomas. "It makes you see what you don't want to see, that all your children are growing up and that they'll soon be at a stage when they won't need you, maybe even won't want you. I look at Vicky and I see one who is ready to go, but when I look at you and at Davie, I see people who only have a little while left to be children, who are going to pop into adulthood practically overnight. And leave. And leave, Suzie."

Suzie put down the spoon and ran over to her dad and threw herself at him, hugging hard, her head boring into his shirtfront.

He stroked her hair. "Well, I'll stay for breakfast on one condition. That I can cook the last few waffles, get them just the way I want them—"

"Burned black," Vicky said, with a shaky kind of laugh.

"Well, let's say, finished with my own special touch," he corrected. "So I like well-done waffles. How about it? Okay?"

"Okay," Suzie said, muffled against his shirt. *She's embarrassed now,* Davie thought; *she feels silly because she wanted him to notice her.*

Davie realized with a shock, with a touch of grown-up changing insight, that he wished his dad would notice him, too. He stopped fooling with the silverware and stood looking through into the kitchen, where his dad and the girls were making a three-way project of the waffles now. His dad was insisting that the batter needed an added dash of sugar so that the waffles would brown nicely, and Vicky was suggesting a touch of vanilla to give them class.

"There isn't any syrup!" Suzie suddenly cried, clutching her mouth with both hands, in despair, wracked.

"I'll make some," her father told her. "Get out more sugar, and hand me that vanilla, Vicky. You're going to be surprised at how good homemade syrup can taste!"

Right then there was a rapping at the back door, and everyone froze. Davie knew who it was. It was Mr. Caldwell come back to tell his dad about finding the flashlight. And of course, everything would change. They all would remember now about Grandma's murder and the man who was afraid that Davie would remember his voice. The sausages would frizzle away into shrunken dismal rods. The waffles would never get made; the batter would go flat in its bowl. All this because Mr. Caldwell had to come back right at this minute.

Oh, bull, Davie said to himself, full of revolt.

He turned, and something white moved and disappeared in the shadows of the hall, and he realized that his mother had been there, watching and listening, and now was hurrying away.

He wanted to go after her but was restrained by a desolate sense of not really knowing what to say to her or of how even to let her know that he wanted her to be with them. Mr. Caldwell was coming into the kitchen, Vicky bringing him, and Davie noticed how Mr. Caldwell took in everything at a single glance and then looked straight at his dad.

"There's something I want to talk to you about before you leave, Mr. Stoddard. No hurry at all. Go ahead with your breakfast. I'm going to have a peaceful pipe out beside your pool."

"Won't you join us for breakfast?" Thomas asked.

"No, thank you. I ate in town earlier."

"You've been out here for a while?"

Mr. Caldwell and Suzie exchanged a glance, and Davie thought that a kind of secret smile passed between them. "Yes, for a while. I don't want to talk about it right now. I'll go right on through to the pool. Take your time. It looks as if you might have some expert cooks here, Mr. Stoddard."

"Oh, they'll do, I suppose," Thomas said. He sounded sort of proud, though, Davie thought.

Mr. Caldwell excused himself and went on through the Family Area. Someone had already drawn the draperies, and the trees made a shadowy background that showed Mr. Caldwell's advancing figure reflected in the glass doors. He paused about halfway across the room and stood quiet for a minute, as if thinking about something, and then slowly went on, pulled open one of the doors enough to pass through, closed it behind him. Before he got out to the pool, though, Davie saw another man approach him and say something, a man who must be one of the other detectives. Mr. Caldwell and the other man spoke together for a minute or so, and then the other went away, and Mr. Caldwell went on to the bench.

Vicky had been watching Mr. Caldwell. "I'm going to close those curtains before somebody comes to stare in at us," she said all at once. She crossed the room, walking fast, and then instead of closing the draperies, she opened the door as Mr. Caldwell had done and went right on out.

Thomas said, "Well, let's get started. Those sausages are done, Suzie. How's the table, Davie, all set?"

"Yes, sir."

"Okay, Suzie, pop in some batter, I'll boil some syrup, and everything's go."

Caldwell had seated himself and taken out his pipe. He had wanted to pull the draperies in passing, so that the Stoddards could eat together without seeing him out here, but neither the draperies nor the house were his, and perhaps pulling them would be taking a liberty, something that might jar, might be remembered and resented even slightly, something he couldn't afford. He heard the glass doors open, though, and glanced up and saw Vicky coming. He rose, dropping the pipe back into his pocket.

She stopped, and seemed to search for words, and finally began. "I guess every little bit could be important. This isn't anything, really. Not what you could call a clue. It isn't what I saw, even; it was told to me by Jeff Norbert. He's my fiancé."

"He's a fortunate young man," Caldwell said, trying not to sound formal or stuffy, an old bachelor talking about something beyond his experience.

She smiled at his small gallantry, briefly, worriedly, and went on: "I'm not sure that Jeff would appreciate my telling you about this. But all at once I felt that I must."

"Won't you sit here next to me?"

She sat on the edge of the bench. The light wind caught a strand of hair and threw it across her eyes so that she looked at him through a veil, beautiful eyes looking at him through a mist of lovely hair, and for just a moment Caldwell wondered what it would be like to be young again. "Jeff was awakened early yesterday by an officer in a patrol car. The officer was going from house to house over there on the other ridge, I guess, asking people if they had noticed anything odd or out of the way happening over here. It was just a long shot, Jeff explained that it was really too far away to make out anything very clearly, and the officer left, and then Jeff decided to come over here. He'd gotten out of the officer what had happened. Mr. Caldwell, don't you want to smoke your pipe?"

"It wouldn't bother you?"

"No, not a bit."

Caldwell thanked her, took out the pipe and pouch, and set to work. "Did he come to the house?"

"No. He parked some distance down the road and came over here through that vacant land. And before he got here, he saw Mr.

Warren. Mr. Warren was standing where he could watch the back of the house."

"Hmmm." Caldwell nodded and carefully kept any expression out of his face.

"And this is what I mean, Mr. Caldwell, when I say that this really isn't anything. All Mr. Warren did was to watch, standing quite still, and then go away briefly and come back leading his horse, and head up one of the smaller barrancas. When Jeff went over to where Mr. Warren had been standing, to see what he'd been looking at, he said that there was an excellent view of the back of the house and the yard and that two men were out there talking and that one of them had a big camera. He must have been a reporter."

"And the other one was me." Caldwell struck a match, lit the tobacco in the pipe, took several satisfying puffs. "Jeff didn't speak to Mr. Warren?"

"No."

"And Warren didn't appear to notice him?"

"No." She shrugged, embarrassed, apologetic. "It didn't amount to anything. Of course Mr. Warren has a right to cross his own land and to look at anything he pleases—"

"Of course. I'm glad you told me, though. Are you seeing your young man today?"

"I—I suppose so."

"Tell him I'd like to hear about this directly from him, will you?"

"I'll tell him." She stood up, a slim and lovely silhouette against the brightness all around them. "If I don't see him, I'll phone him and tell him that way."

He rose and thanked her, and she walked back to the house.

Caldwell sat down again, and smoked, and didn't enjoy it as much as he wanted to. He was going to have to tangle with Warren, and the prospect was dismal. Besides all that money, Warren had friends in high places and influence where it counted. Caldwell began to plan how he should move.

26

Margaret opened her eyes and looked at the clock in the den. It showed about twelve minutes before eleven o'clock. She sat up, throwing the blanket aside and putting her feet on the floor. Her body protested the movement; she was stiff, bone-tired. Her mouth tasted dry and papery, and her eyes stung. She went into the small bathroom, aware of its closed-in water smell, and freshened her face, brushed her hair, tried to find a lipstick and gave that up, and returned to the den, where she folded the blanket and put it, along with the pillow, into the cavity of the hassock. She found herself staring at the clock again. Six minutes had passed. There was something breathlessly urgent, something just beneath the surface of her thoughts that she couldn't quite remember, and it had something to do with this particular hour, eleven o'clock.

She stood in the middle of the room, frowning, pressing her hands to either side of her hot, aching head, and it seemed that she could feel time ticking by with an enormous series of sudden jolts. Something was coming closer. And she didn't know what.

I'll go to the kitchen and have a cup of coffee, and then I'll remember. I'm fuzzy because I lay on the floor all night and couldn't sleep, and now this morning the sleep was too deep, and I'm in this hateful dazed condition, as if part of my brain were missing.

Thomas would be in town, at the office, by now. There would be things to take care of, matters he couldn't expect Mr. Bowman to cope with because Bowman was older than God and, in spite of an increasing childish befuddledness, remained the tyrant he had always been. Give him credit, he paid Thomas a remarkable salary to be afraid of him.

She left the den with a sense of deserting a shelter, a haven, and went down the hall, pausing at Suzie's half-open door. Suzie was in there with a pile of books and a pad of paper on which she

seemed to be making notes. She didn't look up, and Margaret
didn't speak. There seemed something embattled and formidable
about Suzie, as if she had made up her mind about a course of
action and were engaged in the initial design.

The kitchen had been cleared and straightened since that early
breakfast Thomas had shared with the children. Margaret plugged
in the coffee percolator, then stole a look into the dishwasher—their
plates, the silver and the cooking utensils were there, all shining
and still a little warm. The pancake mix, the waffle iron, the eggs,
syrup, butter, all were out of sight.

Perhaps they don't even want me to know, she thought. *I won't
ever tell them I watched from the hall. It was a happy sharing time
for them, and they didn't need me. Perhaps they didn't even want
me.* Her thoughts twisted, and she remembered starkly that moment when she had looked into the swimming pool and had longed
to drown in it. Mr. Caldwell said that you couldn't do it, the reflexes took over. But really wanting to die might make a difference.
Had she really wanted to?

No, she told herself; *I couldn't do that to them. Not after
what happened to Cootie and to his mother, I couldn't. They are
trying to—to heal themselves, to cure the agony—the breakfast
this morning, sharing the preparation of the food and then the
meal, was part of it. I have to leave them alone* . . .

She poured herself a cup of coffee and stood by the sinkboard
to drink it, rubbing one foot up the other calf in the nervous way
that had become a habit.

Davie must be in his room. Thomas had left strict orders about
any wandering around outside.

She finished the coffee, rinsed the cup, and then heard the doorbell chime in the hall. She retraced her way to the front entry.
As she pulled the door inward, a flashbulb went off, a dazzling
burst that left her blinded for a moment. When her sight cleared,
she found herself facing a tall man in white coveralls who carried
a clipboard with a sheaf of papers and a pen. He was just turning
from looking over his shoulder at a fat man. The fat man was
retreating, winding a camera with an air of sly satisfaction. He
wore brown shorts, soiled across the belly, and a torn green shirt.
A skinny knob-kneed woman also in shorts waited for him out

beside the road; she had straw-colored hair and squint eyes, and she too was grinning at the fat man's accomplishment in getting a picture.

"Good for you, Bob," she called. She had a voice like a rooster's.

The man in white coveralls looked disgustedly one more time at the fat man behind him. Then he said, "Mrs. Stoddard?"

"Yes."

"We're here for the furniture."

"Oh?" In her confusion she had thought that the fat man, the straw-haired woman, and this man in white coveralls were together, part of some weird tableau, but now she understood that the fat man had simply been one of the watchers, the picture takers, a ghoul drawn by the old woman's death, and that this man who remained had some business here.

"For the furniture—what you wanted put in storage." He referred to the clipboard, obviously checking the address, then glanced at the house number on the white wall beside the door. Then he again turned and waved an arm at someone out in the street. A moment later a motor roared, and the back end of a big van inched around some shrubs and began to angle toward the driveway. The movement of the truck scattered a small horde of sightseers, ill-dressed men and women and barefooted kids, who rushed ahead of the rear wheels and fanned out across the lawn. The fat man with the camera who had taken Margaret's picture ran with a vast jiggling of his belly.

Margaret was terrified. "What is the truck doing?"

"Backing in, ma'am. I judge you're not storing the whole houseful." He looked appraisingly the length of the house. "They'd have sent a bigger truck."

She remembered then. It all came to her, the phone call she had made, the thought behind it of saving Thomas the grief and trouble of disposing of his mother's belongings. It seemed ages ago that she had made the call; it seemed that she had been someone else, a silly fool, an optimist full of plans, a dreamer without wits. But now she must go on with what she had begun. She must pick up the pieces, finish it. "It's the—the things my mother-in-law owned. Her furniture and belongings."

"You'll have to show me where they are, ma'am."

"Yes." She started to go out, to lead him by way of the front of the house to the big double glass doors, through them to the stairs that led up to the old woman's quarters. But she was suddenly aware of the staring eyes of the people on the lawn. The straw-haired woman had her head pulled up, stretching her neck, alert, and the fat man clutched his camera, ready for a second shot.

Margaret drew back, feeling sick, and the moving man understood. "I'll come through this way," he offered. "You've got an ugly little crowd out here."

"There was a—a crime. My mother-in-law was killed," she said hoarsely.

"I believe I read about it in the papers."

She let him in and took him through the hall. Suzie heard them and came out of her room to stare after them. When they got upstairs, there was another surprise—Davie was there, sprawled on the couch, reading one of his grandmother's books. He looked up, studied the man in the white coveralls and said uncertainly, "Hi."

"I'm going to store these things, Davie."

She thought that a pallor and a look of shock spread over Davie's face. "You're going to *what?*"

"Store her things. Put them away."

He stared around him, still with the air of disbelief, of being aghast. "You mean, it's all going to be empty? There'll be nothing up here at all? Nothing left?"

"I'm so tired, Davie. Don't pretend not to understand. It has to be done; the things have to go; it's not fair to leave them here for your father to have to deal with them."

"But he said we *wouldn't,*" Davie cried in an anguished voice.

She looked at the moving man, thinking he might help her. "This is your load," she told him. "Everything up here. Some of her belongings will have to be packed, put into boxes. Can you do that?"

He frowned. "It wasn't in the original order, but I'll see what we have in the way of boxes. We might have enough." He went over to the closet, where the door was ajar, and looked in. The clothes hanging inside were neat, but drab-colored and somehow forlorn. The moving man reached in to touch a coat, lifting the sleeve and then letting it drop, and Davie sprang away from the couch and ran for him.

"Don't you touch her things!"

"Davie! Behave yourself! He's doing his job. He's doing what I asked him to do."

The man fended Davie off with his free hand, keeping the clipboard out of the way so that Davie couldn't run into it. "Hey, fella. I guess you loved your grandmother, huh? And it hurts to see her things sent off. But the time comes—"

"It's too soon!" Davie wailed, and Margaret shrank toward the door, unable to cope with the situation. She heard someone come up the stairs outside, and then there was Vicky. When Davie saw his sister, he left the moving man and darted toward her. "Stop them! Stop them!"

Vicky put an arm around Davie and stood there in the doorway with an expression of anger and outrage. "Mother, is this something you planned? Why do I even bother to ask? Of course it is. She isn't even buried yet. Had you thought of that?"

"But I'm doing it for your father."

She couldn't meet Vicky's eyes. The accusation there was too terrible, the judgment too complete. The room teetered on some strange axis, threatening to stand on its side, threatening to dump them all out the door and down the stairs with the furniture rolling to crush them at the bottom. *I'm so tired,* she whispered to herself, *and everything I do turns into a nightmare, and this seems to be the worst of all, I'm caught here, and I can't deny what I meant to do; there's no way to say that I intended something good and kind, something for the benefit of the family.*

Vicky spoke to the moving man. "I doubt very much if the police will let you take my grandmother's things before their investigation is complete. And I know that my father will just absolutely blow up—he might even sue you. He's a lawyer, and he would know what he could do."

The moving man looked from Vicky to Margaret. "Well, to me, miss, it's just a job. The order came in, and the office girl took it down, and my partner and I came out with a truck. That's all it is. We aren't planning to get into any trouble. We don't want to be involved in any family fights. I can assure you of that."

"We could just say that there has been a misunderstanding," Vicky suggested, speaking without looking at Margaret.

As if, Margaret thought, *I'm not really here.*

I wish I were dead . . .

The man shrugged. "Calling it a misunderstanding is okay with me. I don't care what you call it. The problem is, there's the matter of the time we've already put in. On a storage job we count charges from the minute we start rolling with the truck. There is already some money involved. I'm sorry about this, but I can't help it, and I can't just turn around and go back to the office and tell them it was a misunderstanding. I hope you can see that."

Vicky stood there, dismayed and perplexed. Finally, she said, "Do you know how much it will be?"

He glanced at his wristwatch. "Well, offhand I'd say between twenty and twenty-five dollars. Oh, maybe less. They figure these things at the office. We will have to drive back into town, empty, and turn in a work sheet on this job, in your father's name and directed to this address, and then they'll figure the costs and mail your father a bill. Of course, it will be a whole lot less than if we'd stayed here, and given each item a numbered tag, and written down the numbers and the item to match as we have to do, and packed some of the loose stuff, and carted everything down to the truck, and stowed it so it won't get damaged in transit. It won't be anywhere near that much."

"I should imagine not," Vicky said, with an edge to her voice. She wouldn't look at her mother. She looked at the moving man, letting him see her anger and resentment, both of them knowing that all the time it was Margaret at whom she was angry.

Margaret thought she couldn't speak, couldn't get out a word, but she heard herself stammer, "I'll pay the bill, whatever it is. Just please ask them to send it here to me."

"Perhaps I can take care of it," Vicky said, ignoring Margaret.

"Why do you pretend I'm not here?" Margaret asked, surprised again that she could get the words out. "Why do you act as if I'm some loathsome thing, a stranger, an interloper—" Her voice died; her throat seemed tight, knotted with misery, and here in the room with Davie and Vicky and the strange, embarrassed man, with Suzie now peering in through the door, she felt completely alone. No one listened. No one heard. She spoke and the words vanished. She was a woman who was not.

For some reason, or for no reason, she remembered at that instant that there had been many times when old Mrs. Stoddard had said things and when she had pretended not to hear. Even before Cootie died, she had tried to ignore the old woman into silence. After Cootie died, she had deliberately, day after day, made occasions not to hear. And now, suddenly and scaldingly, she knew exactly how the old woman had felt. To speak and not to be heard made one as a ghost, a nonbeing, took away the human right to communicate.

And I did that . . .

The pain of knowing was too awful to be borne. *I can't endure it,* she told herself. *I won't look,* she thought, and knew then that it was at herself that she could not look. It was the Margaret of these last few years that she couldn't endure to see.

She stumbled through the door, bumping into Suzie, who tried to jump aside. She ran down the stairs, half falling, grabbing the banister to keep from going head over heels. The kitchen went by as a blur, and she was in the family room, her only need that of surcease from the inner horror.

I won't look . . .

She wanted to close her eyes, as if thus to shut out the sight of what she found within, but she had to guide herself through the room. Halfway across, she saw her reflection moving with her against the glass, running to meet her, a shadow woman who trembled there in the shadowy gloom, a phantom. And Margaret was astonished to feel the great instant upsurge of hatred for that image, for herself.

She stopped, gasping, but the agony seized her, squeezed tears from her eyes, cramped her within so that she felt she must bend double. *I can't endure it . . .*

She fell against the glass doors, tugged them open somehow, got outdoors. The open air felt cold, and the gray sky seemed full of a vast light that made her naked and exposed. She wanted to wrap herself in her arms, cover up, put down her head. The people who were scattered across the lawn, the idle small crowd, stared at her, and she was aware of every eye as she limped in the direction of the pool.

She stood above the water; it was gray, cold-looking, and her skin contracted at the thought of the plunge. Behind her she heard a babble of voices, beginning low and growing louder, the tone astonished and pleased. She sucked in a deep breath, shut her eyes, fell forward with her body stiff. Something struck her, and it took a moment for her to sense that she had hit the water. Her eyes opened involuntarily.

Breathe . . .

She tried to inhale the water.

All at once without knowing how it happened, she had ejected herself and was head and shoulders above the level of the pool, her thrashing body whipping a froth around her. People were running toward her, their faces greedy, enlarged beyond life, with popping eyes and open mouths. *Go away, you fools* . . .

She got control of herself, stiffened, gritted her teeth, and slowly sank. Bubbles went past her eyes.

Breathe . . .

A vast lethargy seeped into her, and strength and energy flowed away. A heaviness started in hands and feet, and she was dragged down, her face toward the bottom of the pool, as the heaviness worked its way toward her heart. *This is dying,* she thought. But not quite. Again her body began to twist and thrust with a life of its own, rejecting what she had willed for it. Lungs bursting, she again found herself with her face abovewater and gulped air.

But the heaviness remained, as if a part of her had accepted death and were waiting for it.

All I have to do is to sink again. And perhaps again.

A vast splash filled the pool, and a tubby body fastened it-self to hers. Shocked, she found the fat man here in the water with her. The broad face with puffed-out cheeks and gleaming eyes was no more than in inch or two from her own. She choked with the insufferable indignity. How dare he interfere with what she was doing?

He was strong. He gripped her, trod water, kept her from sinking. When it seemed she was quiet, he freed one arm and headed for the edge of the pool, and several people there, Vicky among them, pulled her from the water.

She shut her eyes. She felt herself lifted and let down, felt the deck hard beneath her, her clothes streaming water, her hair heavy against her head, the breeze cooling her wet face. More than ever, she wanted to die. To be laid here like a *thing* . . .

"Ma'am—"

She opened her eyes a little. The fat man was bent over her now, staring at her. *Gross, horrible,* she thought. *What have I done to suffer this?* And then through her half-shut lids she saw something more. In the fat man's eyes was an expression of concern. He was worried. He didn't want her to die.

"Please look at me, ma'am."

His voice was gentle, the kind of voice you used to someone who was sick or hurt. And she saw, too, that his wife, the rooster-voice woman, was also bending, along with Vicky and Suzie and Davie, with an anxious air of wanting to be of help. Behind them were other faces, a few of them grinning and avid, but many showing that they didn't want her to drown and that they would assist in saving her if they could.

I have so much help. And Thomas' mother didn't have any.

She turned to Vicky. "I'll be all right. I'd like to go indoors. And I want you to call Mr. Caldwell. I have something to tell him." Her voice came out choked and indistinct, but she saw that Vicky understood.

"I think you should lie still for a while, Mother."

"No. Please. I'll be fine. It was just a—a moment's upset. I won't try it again." When Vicky didn't do anything except pick up her wrist and chafe it between her hands, Margaret insisted. "It's no fun lying here with these people watching. Please."

"All right, then. But you have to go to bed, and I'm going to call a doctor."

"Please don't get a doctor out here," Margaret begged. "I'll lie down for the rest of the day; I'll do anything you want me to do."

In the end, the fat man carried her to the bedroom. Vicky turned down the bed, and he laid her between the sheets, wet clothes and all. Vicky drew the bedding up to her chin. The fat man patted her shoulder in a gentle, kindly way. She wondered what he had done with his camera, and then noted that his wife had it, along with Margaret's shoes, which must have come off in the pool.

After some comforting remarks, the fat man and his wife and a few other stragglers withdrew. Vicky went out after them, and Margaret heard her telling Davie and Suzie to go to their rooms and stay in them. For her part, she was going to make sure that the house was securely locked up and call Mr. Caldwell.

Margaret lay and cried, weak tears that mingled with the wetness left by the water of the pool. She had made an utter fool of herself, of course. More than that, she had committed a criminal act. It was against the law to try to die. Perhaps Mr. Caldwell would arrest her when he got here.

I'm too tired to care . . .

In the hall, Suzie was giving Vicky an argument. "I don't see why Davie can't come into my room and stay with me. We have some things to talk over."

"Such as?" Vicky asked.

"Just things . . ."

"You aren't planning anything foolish, are you, Suzie?"

"Of course not."

"Davie, is she up to something?"

"How should I know?" Davie muttered, so low that Margaret could scarcely hear.

"We've had quite enough disturbance for today," Vicky told them. "And by the way, did either of you see what became of that man who came here to move out Grandma's things?"

Davie replied, "He got in the truck with the driver, and they left. He looked scared. He thought somebody would blame him for what Mother did."

"He'll send a bill anyway," Vicky concluded. "All right, Davie, you and Suzie can spend some time together, for an hour or so. And now scat. I have to check the house to be sure we don't have any unwelcome callers. And I'm going to phone Mr. Caldwell."

In the bed, damp now from her clothes, smelling faintly of the chlorine from the pool, Margaret turned her head on the pillow and, with a long sigh, fell asleep

27

Suzie stalked into her room and went to the windows to look out, then half drew the draperies. She glanced slyly over her shoulder at Davie, as if she had some teasing planned or meant to test him in some way. "Come on in and close the door. Make sure it's shut."

On the bed were heaps of books and scattered note papers, plus the remains of a cheese sandwich on a paper plate and a couple of candy wrappers. Suzie went over to the bed and sat down at its foot, waiting while Davie shut the door to the hall and then came with an unwilling, suspicious air to stop several feet away.

"Well, don't stand looking like a lost cat. Sit down," she said, pointing to a spot beside the pillows.

Davie moved slowly. "Somebody ought to phone Dad. He ought to be told what happened, what Mom did. Maybe somebody like a cop or a reporter will go and tell him. If you were Dad, how would you like that?"

"Oh, don't worry. Vicky will call Dad and tell him all about it. And anyway, there are so many evil influences floating around this house now that what happened today is just practically nothing. We could even have something terrible. An earthquake. Another murder. Don't you feel the mind of that man searching for you?"

Davie clenched his mouth stubbornly.

"I'll bet you do," Suzie said. "I'll bet you feel him all the time. When you remember who he is, he'll know it even before you can tell Mr. Caldwell. He'll be here in a flash, and he'll take you away. And we'll never see you again."

"I don't believe it."

"It's going to come true unless we do something to stop him."

Davie squirmed uncomfortably on the edge of the bed. He thought the room was stuffy, and he could smell the cheese left in the crusts of the sandwich. There were other smells, too, odors like dried weeds and dust, that seemed to come from beneath the bed. "What can we do? We don't even know who he is."

"We don't have to know who he is," Suzie said, lowering her voice so that she sounded mysterious and aloof. "We can protect ourselves, even against the unknown. There are charms. There are spells. Not magic spells like a witch cooking a toad and bat's wings and the left hind leg of a newt along with some sulfur and brimstone. That's all hogwash. It was all right for its time and place. Castles. Knights and dukes that couldn't even read and write."

"Is this what you had me come in here for? A crazy lecture?"

"No. I'm going to share with you some of the things I've learned from all this research." Suzie waved a hand toward the scattered books and papers. "It's been work. Hard work."

"What's so good about Indian magic? How's it any different? And by the way, I don't remember hearing about all those Indians who could read and write any more than your knights and dukes."

"My research," Suzie said softly, "has led me into the presence of a great truth. All the so-called Indian magic was based on nature, on things found in the Indian's own world, and its purpose was simply to put everything in tune the way it ought to be. The charms they made and wore simply put them in tune with their surroundings—"

"Have you made us some charms?" Davie interrupted.

"Not yet. I've been gathering the materials. It takes time. You have to be careful. You have to gather things that belong together. That was the whole point of Indian magic and worship."

"I think you're just kind of nuts."

"So make fun. Mother didn't drown, did she? Even what I've done so far, simple as it is—"

"You've been outdoors!" Davie accused, suddenly enlightened. "You've been out since Dad told us we couldn't go. You disobeyed him even after he told us how important it was not to do it."

Suzie gave him a conspiratorial look, and at the same time Davie felt a strange kind of dread, a touch of coldness, the beginnings of belief. It had always been this way, and even after previous bubbles had burst, a kind of trust in Suzie's hocus-pocus remained. She said, "Are you going to tell Dad on me?"

"Of course I won't. But you've got to stop."

"If I stop, all the bad things will happen."

"No, they won't. Mr. Caldwell won't let them."

"He's like everyone else. He can't see past the end of his nose. The world of mysterious influences is all around him, and he doesn't even sense it."

"But you do!" Davie hooted, wanting desperately to sound offhand and cynical. "You're the original witch! Why don't you make yourself a black hat and a cape? Why not fly around on a broom? Mr. Caldwell would sure believe that if he saw it!"

"You're just a little kid, of course," Suzie sighed, plucking at a spot on the bedspread.

"All right," Davie agreed impatiently, "so I'm a kid. I'm not a *little* kid, though. And I'm old enough to ask: Why should all this Indian stuff be affecting us? We aren't Indians. We don't live in tepees and wear war paint and hunt buffalo. So—"

"When we moved out here," Suzie said portentously, "we intruded into the Indian's world. It was all here just as he had left it. Probably there was a village right along the ridge. Why not? He could see enemies coming and game that strayed into the valley—it would be a good place to settle."

"What about water?"

"There might have been springs that dried up later. Water was there all right. In the ground. Mr. Warren's father drilled for it and found it. And not very deep, either. Why do you want to ask all these questions? Why not just help me and see what happens?"

"What are you going to do?" Davie asked, afraid of what she might answer.

"We have to go to the burying grounds."

"Now wait a minute! That's a long way off! That's not the same as sneaking out to the barranca and picking a twig or two off some of the bushes or gathering stones—"

"Well, where else could we find a human bone?"

"A *what?*"

"A human bone."

Davie sat there, chilled, unbelieving. "You mean something out of a *person?*"

"Oh, don't be such a knuckle-skull. Of course, I mean out of a person. What would a human bone be out of? A cow?"

"That's gruesome."

"I never told you this before," she said solemnly, "but I've been to the burying ground. All the way. And somebody had been digging there, and bones were lying around. It's very important that we have a real bone."

"No!"

"It isn't the way you think, Davie scared-cat. There's no bad smell. And no meat hanging on the bones. The bones are just clean and white. They even look kind of sterilized."

"I don't care!" he cried, horrified. "I won't touch them!"

"I'll do the picking. I just need you to come along to—to watch in case Mr. Caldwell or somebody is following us."

"You're scared, too," he accused.

"No, I'm not, but I want you to come. We'll have to borrow Mr. Warren's horse because it's too far for us to make it there and back before they'd miss us. We'll slip over and get the horse."

"In the daytime? Mr. Warren will see us—"

"Not in the daytime," she corrected irritably. "At night. We'll take matches along, and when we get to the burying grounds, we'll make a fire to see by. And it won't take any time at all. We'll be back, and nobody will even know we've been out of the house."

"I don't think we ought to do it."

"If you won't help, I'll have to go alone." She sounded defiant, but kind of lonely, too, as if Davie were failing in some trust she had put in him, as if he weren't quite the brother she had thought he was. And Davie, who knew all her tricks, all her little acts, realized that he was going to fall for this one.

He thought of one last objection. "This'll be robbing an Indian grave. How are you going to make any good magic by doing a thing like that?"

She shrugged. "I don't know why it should work, either. But it will. The Indian spirits will hear us."

"And nothing bad will happen?"

"Nothing bad *can* happen," Suzie informed him, looking heavenward.

Well, why not? Davie asked himself. He surveyed the piles of books. She had certainly been reading a lot. More than he could wade through in a year. And the books must have told her things.

"Will we bring back a whole skeleton?" he asked, with a sudden disturbing vision of the two of them riding homeward on Mr. Warren's horse with a third—bony—companion up behind.

"Of course not," she scoffed. "A bone, I said. A little tiny bone, like maybe part of a finger." She held up her hand and measured off a joint.

"Don't tell me what it's part of!"

She smiled, a little wise smile that barely curled her lips. "But you are coming along tonight?"

"Yes." To himself he added: *The more fool me; they'll find out. And then will we catch it.*

"You can bring the matches," Suzie said, "for the fire."

When Margaret awoke, she was confused for a moment. She was in bed, the big bed that she had shared with Thomas all these years and that she had not shared last night, and the bed was damp and smelled of chlorine. The light was dim, but she could see Thomas and Mr. Caldwell sitting near, both of them looking at her.

"Margaret—"

She had to say something, but what? She could tell him that he was embarrassing her, sitting here with Mr. Caldwell, whom she hardly knew, in the privacy of the bedroom. God knows what she looked like, dragged from the pool and stuck here, and the attitude of the two men, solemn and watchful, made her think of a pair of judges staring at a felon.

She wanted to hide. She wanted to hide down under the bedding the way she had done when she was very young, when the old house had creaked with its empty lostness, when she had known herself quite alone and without any lights at all upstairs.

She heard herself speak in a hoarse, ragged voice. "My father would never do anything around the house. He just let things go. There weren't any lights upstairs for years and years. He shouldn't have treated us like that." When she had finished speaking, she waited for some reaction from the men. Mr. Caldwell had a pipe in his hands, but he wasn't smoking; he was just fooling with the pipe to have something to do. Thomas looked tired; he slumped; his eyes had a blurred, worried expression. "When you won't do anything for your house," she found herself explaining, "it simply means that you don't care anything for the people in it."

Thomas said slowly, "I'm not going to argue with you anymore, Margaret, about what you want to do with the house. If you have to buy and fix constantly, it must be something you feel compelled to do. And we won't fight about it again."

"I want to think it over," she told him.

"Mrs. Stoddard—" Mr. Caldwell sounded kind, concerned, and Margaret flinched. She had broken the law by trying to kill herself, and Mr. Caldwell had a right to be severe and disapproving. But he wasn't. He was leaning forward in the chair, putting away the pipe in his coat pocket. "Do you have something to tell me?"

"Yes."

"Something about the murder of your mother-in-law?"

"Two things," she said. "First, last night that man came here and unlocked the back door and left it swinging open. Thomas and the children had gone to town to have dinner. I was lying down in the den. The house was dark. He thought that we all were gone. He wanted us to come home and to find the door open, and to realize how helpless we were—"

"How do you know he didn't come inside?" Caldwell asked. "Came in, and figured out somehow that someone was here, and ran? Ran so fast that he forgot to close the door?"

"There wasn't any way he could have known I was here. I—I didn't put on a light right away. The shrubbery was blowing, and I thought it might be something else. I was confused. I just lay and sh-shook."

"I see." Caldwell went on looking puzzled and doubtful, however. Margaret waited for further objections, but he didn't say anything more.

He thinks that because I tried to drown myself, I'm not reliable, she thought. "I really am telling you the truth. I'm not imagining things, or at least not now, and jumping into the pool this morning was just—just because I couldn't endure to think about things I knew I had to face. Like the way I treated Thomas' mother. No, please don't interrupt and tell me not to feel guilty. And that regret never cured anything. I want to feel regret and grief—as much as I can. And getting back to my mother-in-law, I know now what she meant by that last remark. The one about the reflection."

A flicker showed in Caldwell's eyes. His hands on the pipe grew still. And at the same time, she thought: *He knows what I'm going to say.*

"The day Cootie crashed through that glass door, she was running toward him, to stop him. At the last moment she thought she saw a dim figure outdoors, just beyond the glass. She saw the figure, all right. But it wasn't outside. It was the reflection of herself. I saw my own reflection this morning when I was on the way to the pool. Upset and feeling the way I did, I thought for an instant that someone was rushing toward me, to stop me."

"I've noticed that effect in the glass," Caldwell said quietly.

"The reflection was what she saw, but she didn't realize it until almost at the moment of her death. And that's the whole point, Mr. Caldwell. There at the very end she wasn't even thinking about herself. She was still worried about Cootie and why he'd had to die—" Margaret's voice grew too choked to speak. She turned her head so that they wouldn't see her tears.

"She had had a bad time over the baby's death," Thomas

said. "We *gave* her a bad time. I thought at the moment that I was doing all that I could to reassure her, but I guess what I did didn't amount to much. She was isolated there at the top of the stairs—"

Margaret lifted her head from the pillow. "I didn't forgive her and I didn't hide how I felt. I know now . . . when it's too late—"

For the first time Caldwell looked uncomfortable. He coughed slightly, moved on the chair, and glanced at Thomas as if asking if it were all right to go. Plainly family accusations and breast barings were not to his taste. Thomas said, "My wife and I have a few things to talk about. Before you go, I would like to know what you think of that business last night, his unlocking the door and leaving it for one of us to find."

Caldwell was standing, still holding the pipe, and he gave Thomas a quick glance as if to discover whether he believed the story exactly as Margaret had told it. "Well, I can't help thinking that there's something . . . uh . . . immature"—he paused and frowned—"almost childish, in the action. I'm not referring to the motive. The intent was to frighten, of course. To intimidate. But too, it's almost as if he's saying, look at me, see what I can do. I think of . . . for some reason, I think of a kid showing off to other kids by walking a fence." Thomas started to say something, and Caldwell held up the pipe in a motion to silence him. "Don't get the idea I think he's harmless. He can be even more dangerous—is almost certainly more dangerous—for being immature and a braggart."

Thomas said, "I'm going to attend to the locks today, install them myself if I have to. There won't be any more incidents like this."

Caldwell nodded his agreement and went out and shut the door after him. He stood in the hall; the house was quiet. He heard a murmur of voices from some room nearby, and by listening closely, he identified them as those of Davie and Suzie. He let himself out by the front entry, making sure that the door was locked behind him. The onlookers hadn't increased in number. He decided that a few had gone and a few more had come. A uniformed officer stood beside a police cruiser at the curb and occasionally asked the strollers politely to move on.

Caldwell went over to the pool. Mrs. Stoddard had warned him of what was in her mind; he should have spoken about it to the eldest daughter and the husband. She was a woman who had to confront a few things about herself and couldn't somehow endure to do it. She had hated her mother-in-law down through the years, she'd made the old woman's life as miserable as possible, and now it was time not only to admit to herself what she had been and had done, but to recognize that the same things could happen to her in her turn. *Nobody,* Caldwell thought, *stays forever on a plateau, invulnerable, in control, needed and wanted, and the most certain thing about the human condition is that it changes.*

The death of the older woman had caused a cleavage, a break, in a family already half-destroyed by the tragedy of the child and the withdrawal of the mother. And the mother, who had wrapped herself into a frantic consolation with the house, had to understand that her children were now withdrawing from *her.* And the husband, though he was gentle and compassionate because she'd just tried to kill herself, wasn't going to continue being blind.

"They'll have to work it out somehow," Caldwell said softly, staring into the water of the pool. "If they can . . ." He knew that it was time to go see Warren. All the other leads had petered out. The flashlight hadn't yielded any clues. The old lady's final whisper had simply meant that she was still dwelling on the baby's death. Any footprints had been pocked into distortion by the rain. Davie couldn't remember where he had heard the man's voice before.

What do you do then?

You start pushing.

If there's someone too important to push, someone with influence, friends upstairs, you shove him quickly before he can get in touch with the ones who matter. And you watch yourself carefully, so that when he repeats what you've said or describes what you've done, it won't sound like anything but the routine of a conscientious detective. Warren might not even be the type who complained. Caldwell suspected that Warren's image of himself was that of the good cowboy, the benevolent cavalier who dispensed justice, exacted atonement, rewarded the grateful . . .

A man like that, Caldwell mused, a man on a horse, a man

who rode above other men, might even get to thinking of himself
as a kind of king. And might even consider himself above the law.
Or—might not.

It was time to try to look behind the façade. It was time to see
if the good cowboy was a grown man who indulged himself in a
pose without taking it too seriously or if he was a tall kid with
a popgun. Caldwell began to fill the pipe. He would have a smoke
before he walked over to Warren's place.

28

Vicky ate a late lunch in the kitchen, a bread-and-
butter sandwich and a hastily brewed cup of tea. She had just
come back from town. As soon as her father had arrived, she had
left on a rush trip to the storage firm, where she had made sure
that the charges for the men and the truck would be sent here
in her name instead of her father's.

Her mother might tell her father what she had meant to do
about their grandmother's things, but perhaps not, or not just yet.
Vicky herself, in phoning the office, hadn't explained just what
had triggered the suicide attempt. And the bill from the storage
firm, arriving a week or so later, might rouse questions no one
wanted to answer. She would take care of it.

Caldwell had been gone quite awhile, and her father was still
in the bedroom with her mother. "Please, God, let them begin
to be happy together," she whispered. It had been such a long
time since there had been any closeness, any love, between them.

She didn't want to remember that morning, her mother's
ghastly attempt to drown herself, the thrashing agony in the pool,
the slow sinking that betrayed the deliberate will to die. It seemed
that a scream had ached in her throat ever since, that her eyes
burned with unshed tears. But in spite of herself, she found her
mind fixed on a vivid memory of the fat man, the one who had

dived into the pool and had swum with her mother to the edge of the deck. He had really been kind and had really wanted to help.

She was filled with a sudden overwhelming desire to see Jeff. *I'll go over now,* she thought; *I won't phone first, I'll just go. I'll tell him what happened here this morning.* The desire to be comforted, to be held and loved, brought the tears brimming into her eyes. *When Jeff and I are married, we must never,* never *come to the point where we can't tell each other everything. That's when you lose people,* she thought, *when you can't tell them your thoughts, your real thoughts. The first hesitation about what to say, the first shading of what you really mean—you'd have to recognize that point and to know where you were headed.*

That's what happened to my parents.

Finishing the last of the sandwich, she found herself wondering if the point of hesitation, of subtle change in what you started to say, might slip by without awareness, might be gone by days or weeks before you looked back and thought: That was the beginning.

I won't let it happen to Jeff and me.

She rinsed out the cup and saucer, dried them, and put them away. She carried her purse to her room, where she freshened her makeup and smoothed her hair. The tears had made her eyes puffed; it couldn't be helped. She went outside to her car, still in the driveway. She glanced toward the road. A police cruiser which had stayed there most of the day was gone, and so were the casual onlookers. It must be after three o'clock. Perhaps if the reporters played up her mother's attempt to drown herself, a fresh crowd would be here tomorrow. Trying to kill yourself could seem an admission of guilt if it were written up in the right way.

But we're really old stuff now, Vicky thought, getting into the car. *People who gobble up such things know all about us from the time Cootie died. Grandma's story of the mysterious figure in the yard gave them something to wait for, watch for. And nothing happened.*

They'll get tired of us, whether the police find Grandmother's murderer or not. There will be something more interesting or more cruel to do.

Backing the car toward the road, the house receding in front of

the car, its lines gracefully balanced under the sunlight, against
the hills, a house beautifully planned for its site, Vicky was seized
by a sense of unreality, a feeling that none of this could be happening to them. They were such an ordinary family, fitted into
ordinary lives. There was nothing about any of them deserving
of attention. Even her mother's behavior this last year—there
must be many other women who reacted to grief in unconven-
tional ways. Her dad, the lawyer all business, hadn't a single out-
of-the-way attribute to make him conspicuous.

We're people involved in an accident, Vicky told herself,
*caught up in something without reason or preamble, a freak thing.
We've had a double dose, but when this is over, we'll sink back
into obscurity forever and ever.*

She turned the wheel as she backed into the street and headed
for the main road into the valley. She crossed it some minutes
later and began to climb the opposite ridge. These homes were
older, a little more thickly surrounded by trees and tall shrubbery.
She passed two houses before it occurred to her that she didn't
know for sure whether Jeff's father and mother were still away.
She wanted to see Jeff, she wanted to be in his room again, warm
with love, but she didn't want to see his people. There was an
old road, scarcely more than a track, which led up between two
walls, passed behind some of the houses and ended at a small
gravel diggings, long abandoned.

Thick weeds scraped the underside of her small car as she
turned into the old disused road, and something small and slim—
a lizard, probably—skittered along the cement-block wall for a
moment, keeping pace. To her left the ridge lifted in a final crest
of worn rocks, almost barren of green growth. Ahead, above a
surf of brush, lay the weathered heaps left from the worked-out
gravel deposit.

She pulled to a stop under a stunted pepper tree and got out of
the car. She was struck by the unusual quiet, the feeling that the
country lay here wild and lonely the way it had been at the beginning, without man. A faint breeze stirred. There was an uncertain cricket sound that began, then stopped. A fringe of trees cut
out any view of houses below or of the valley filled with orange
trees and scattered blocks of homes. There was nothing here but

rocky bareness, the silence, the smell of dried growth and faraway dusty canyons. She stood for a couple of minutes, savoring the feeling of strangeness, unwilling to start walking, to break the quiet with the noise of her steps.

Jeff's home should be right below. She shrugged off the unwillingness to get started and walked down through scattered eucalyptus and live oaks and suddenly saw the roof of the big house.

I'll scout around quietly first, in case his people are home.

There was a final barrier of lantana and plumbago, head-high, allowed to grow wild and to form a fence that enclosed the rear lawn and the shrubs Jeff's mother had chosen to place here. Vicky pushed through it, then stopped to brush herself; it was thoroughly dusty. She saw happily that Jeff's windows were open wide.

He's home then.

She hurried down the slope toward the open windows. She leaned on the sill, drawing the odor of the rooms—Jeff's odor—into her lungs. "Jeff . . . Jeff. It's me, Vicky. Are you in here?"

There was no answer. She called again, "Jeff!"

It seemed to Vicky that the room had something about it which seemed recently vacated, as if Jeff had been here a moment ago and had left something of himself to linger on the air. The posters and sketches glowed down at her from the walls; the room had its casual air of being liked, lived in, well used; the bed pillows were not covered by the top of the spread and looked as if Jeff might have been stretched out, resting, just before he got up.

She thought: *His father or his mother have come home, have just arrived, and he's gone to meet them at the front of the house.*

She got a good grip on the window ledge and pulled herself over and into the room. It took on a more familiar perspective. The pillows looked more as if someone had punched them into shape than lain on them. The desk was still a mess. Something had been laid across the scattered papers and other clutter.

A gun.

She had seen it before, she remembered. Jeff's rifle. He had come by the house one day and had told her he'd been out target shooting in the hills. Shooting at cans and paper-plate targets.

She walked to the desk and stroked the gun, drawing her finger-tips along the burnished wood of the stock. It looked newly pol-ished, clean and glowing, handsome.

Standing beside the desk, she was aware of the empty quiet of the house. If Jeff were in it somewhere, greeting one or both of his parents, there should be some trace of sound. She lifted the gun, being careful not to mar the blued steel barrel with finger-prints, and hefted it gently, not quite sure what she should do.

Should she go? Come back later?

She walked to the window, still holding the gun, and looked out at the long lawn, the tangle of border, the bank of trees be-yond. She wanted Jeff to walk into the room behind her, to be surprised and pleased, to take her in his arms and to warm her with the sense of shelter, protection.

It seemed to her that there was a sound of talking somewhere. Not from inside the house. From outside.

She put the gun down on the foot of the bed and crossed the bedroom and entered the hall. There was no sound except the faint echo of her footsteps, and nothing moved. The rooms held their shadowy vistas, long polished floors and dark furniture, with a gleam admitted here and there from a space left between the velvet draperies. There was the monastery smell, she thought. Neither Jeff's father nor mother was here, nor was Jeff. The house waited, empty and somehow faintly melancholy, filled only with silence.

She entered one of the rooms that faced the road. The draperies were drawn here. She moved through deep shadow to the win-dow, pulled an edge of heavy ribbed silk aside. The afternoon sunlight seemed brilliant as gold. Outside was Jeff, with his back toward the house. With him was Mr. Caldwell. Two cars were drawn up in the driveway. One she recognized as Jeff's, and the other must belong to the police detective.

Jeff was here after all. No doubt Mr. Caldwell was asking him about his seeing Warren and Warren's behavior on the morning after the murder. And Jeff would be repeating the story he had told her. It shouldn't take long.

Her breath fogged the glass, spun the sunlight into misty splen-dor. "I love you," she whispered. "I love you so terribly much."

Jeff was taller and leaner than Mr. Caldwell. Caldwell, turned toward the house, was holding his pipe and looking up into Jeff's face. Jeff made a gesture with both hands, throwing them outward with fingers spread, the way he did when he couldn't quite put something into words or expected the other person to understand without his saying it. Jeff's blond hair looked damp; he'd just run a comb through it. He had on a brown knit short-sleeved shirt, much faded, and white pants cut off raggedly at the knees. He was barefooted. Beside him, Mr. Caldwell in his plain business suit and white shirt and discreet blue tie looked like a figure from another world.

Vicky thought: *Mr. Caldwell mustn't get the wrong idea about Jeff. He mustn't just see the clothes and the beard and think that is all there is.* But then she thought: *Of course, Mr. Caldwell knows about Jeff, how brilliant he is, his scholarships, his school records.* Mr. Caldwell knew everything about everybody.

She had forgotten to tell Jeff that Mr. Caldwell wanted to talk to him about seeing Mr. Warren watching their house the morning after the murder. But it didn't matter now. Mr. Caldwell would find out all that Jeff knew, and thinking about it, she thought it didn't amount to much. Mr. Warren had come to see what he could see. Hadn't almost everybody?

"Please be quick," she whispered for Mr. Caldwell's benefit. When Mr. Caldwell left, Jeff would come inside and find her. She remembered with a blush of warmth how their last meeting here had ended. Well, it wouldn't happen that way today. She needed all the loving and the security and shelter Jeff could give. "Come inside, Jeff, and put your arms around me. I won't turn away. I'll never turn from you again . . ." She blew him a kiss through the tiny opening in the draperies.

But the talk outside between the two men went on, and Jeff no longer made the funny half-exasperated gesture with his hands, and Mr. Caldwell finished his pipe and knocked out the ash against the heel of his shoe and kept on talking while he slid the pipe into his coat pocket. He seemed to speak shortly and to wait for Jeff's replies, and Jeff's back looked straighter, his shoulders back, so that the faded shirt hung in a big fold from his neck to his belt.

Vicky walked away from the window, promising herself that if she went around the room, slowly, that when she got back to the window, Mr. Caldwell would be saying good-bye and getting into his car. She walked carefully next to the shadowy wall, passing a couple of pictures—there was a big solid dark refectory table and eight chairs out in the middle of the room—and counted her steps and pictured to herself how Mr. Caldwell was nodding his farewell. And it worked.

When she peeped out, sure enough, Mr. Caldwell was getting into his unmarked police sedan. Jeff raised a hand in a mock salute, and she heard the hum of Mr. Caldwell's motor.

Jeff would be coming indoors now.

She should be just inside the door when he came.

So . . . let him die of shock!

Only he wouldn't, of course. She had never known him to be caught off guard. No matter what happened, what surprises developed, it was as if Jeff already kept hidden such a vast hoax that nothing could top it, nothing could shake him. His response to the inadvertent was mockery. And Vicky thought: *That's one reason I love him so much. He's so different from me. I'm too literal, too down to earth.*

Outdoors, Jeff waited while Mr. Caldwell backed his car and drove out of sight. It was time to leave her peeping place and go to the front entry. But she lingered, hating to give up even a moment's sight of the tall figure that stood unmoving, his gaze apparently fixed on the houses across the valley.

He's thinking of me, she thought. *He's looking at my house, and he's wondering if I'm there and what I'm doing.*

Her hand was slipping off the edge of the stiff silk when he turned. His glance went toward the house, and she had a moment's shock, the feeling that he had seen her. But quickly, without hesitation, he went to his low black sports car and lifted the lid of the trunk. He took something out and turned at once to the street. A low concrete-block wall crossed the front of the yard, and he headed for this and, to Vicky's puzzlement, jumped up on it. She still could not see what it was he had taken from the car.

He braced himself on the low wall. He stood still, and Vicky thought that he seemed to be listening. She wondered if he expected Mr. Caldwell to come back.

Jeff took a long look to the left and then to the right. Then he lifted something to his face. It was a moment before Vicky realized what it was. He had a pair of binoculars. He swung them in a wide arc, his fingers busy on the focusing mechanism between the lenses. They were big binoculars, powerful. Finally, as if the focus had been adjusted to his satisfaction, he aimed them across the valley.

He's looking at my house, Vicky thought—an echo of what she had told herself only moments ago. Only now, somehow, the warmth and sense of loving protection were melting away. She found her mind full of scattered thoughts, lame and half-formed justifications for Jeff, and at the same time she was remembering what he had said he'd told the officer who had first come, the one from whom he had found out about the murder.

He's bought the binoculars since. What the officer suggested gave him the idea.

Who's he keeping track of?

I won't think of it that way; it can't be something ugly, she scolded herself. *If he watches all the time, why didn't he see me heading here? Why wasn't he waiting for me?*

The road dips, her thoughts reminded, *and there are a lot of trees where you join the road that goes to town. If he saw you leaving in your car, he thought you were headed out of the valley. And he's still watching. He's still watching for somebody.*

I should go out there and speak to him.

On the low wall, Jeff had suddenly taken the binoculars from his eyes and had assumed the listening look. After a moment he stepped down from the wall and went over to the car and stooped and seemed to examine one of the tires. A big sedan went past in the street, and a middle-aged man and woman in the front seat both looked over at Jeff and waved.

Jeff glanced up and waved back with his left hand. His right, holding the binoculars, was out of sight behind the tire.

When the car was gone, Jeff waited, still half kneeling there. He must have waited until all sound of the car had died, until the silence reassured him. Then he went back to the wall.

Vicky left the shadowy room and went out into the entry. She put a hand on the big brass knob. The metal felt smooth and cold against her palm. She turned the knob, and the door began to swing open, and she could smell the odors of the sunlit yard, and then she could see Jeff. He was on the wall again, watching her house.

She left the door ajar and went back through the house the way she had come.

In Jeff's bedroom she stopped and stood motionless, feeling the empty quiet of the house as she had before. The gun lay across the foot of the bed, its blued steel barrel and glossy stock reflecting the light in prisms and streaks. A bee had flown in and was resting on one of Jeff's pillows. The array of posters and sketches and maps flowed around the walls like a river.

The room speaks of Jeff, she thought. *I know him and love him. I'll wait for him here.*

Everything will be all right.

She went over to the window to sit there to wait, and then as she sat down, she abruptly swung her legs over the sill and dropped to the ground. Off-balance, she clung to the wall. *It was so easy,* she thought, *to leave like this. You just swung clear and dropped. You dropped because you didn't have enough love and trust to see you through. You left because all those ugly wounding years while you watched your father and mother had taken away the ability to put your trust in someone else. It's easy to disengage,* she thought. *You just let go.*

Blinded by tears, she ran for the car.

Lantana snagged at her clothes, scratched her skin, showered her with pollenlike dust and dry twigs. *I can still go back. I can even drive up to the front door. Jeff will hear me coming. He'll get rid of the binoculars somehow, and they wouldn't matter. It's something he just started doing today. He would be the way he always is, loving and sheltering. We would go to his room and settle that business we started the other day, and it would be wonderful and complete because we love each other.*

She got into the car. She put her crossed arms on the steering wheel and laid her forehead against them and shut her eyes. The tears crept out between her lashes.

She felt the heat of the westering sun on her hair, her shoulders. *I must quit crying and get started. I have to tell Jeff about mother.*

You don't have to tell him about your mother.

He saw it all through his binoculars.

She shivered, and then all at once the tentative cricket noises quit, chopped off by silence, and a few seconds later there seemed to be a crackling in the lantana thicket that bounded the Norbert yard. Someone must be coming. For an instant she remained with her head down, frozen to the wheel, feeling helpless and exposed, and then reflexes took over. She jabbed the key to the on position, and the motor hummed. She choked the motor, which was still warm and didn't need it and promptly died. She spun the starter again. And again. Her head pounded. The motor caught for a second time. Wild with a terror that had no sense behind it, she jammed the car into gear, backed, ran over stones which rocked the chassis, braked with a squeal, changed gears. The car lunged forward. She was looking back over her shoulder and barely missed a big rock that would have burst a tire.

"Don't let him . . ." she was whispering to herself. *"Don't. Don't."*

She drove down the rutted track heedless of rough spots, turned between the two old adobe walls, came to the street. There was a frightful moment while she inched out onto the pavement. She couldn't remember whether this turn was visible from the front of Jeff's house or not.

It wasn't. The street curved, and there was a clump of pepper trees there that almost overhung the road. She swung right and began the descent from the ridge. At the bottom of the slope was the intersection, where the roads from the ridges met the street that led down out of the valley. Again she looked, and what she had thought was true. The dip and the tall trees hid this place from anyone on the height behind her.

Should she go to town? Stop in the library, for instance, and hide herself in some study spot behind the stacks and stay there until she could think straight? Or go to a coffee shop and compose herself over a cup of coffee . . .

I just want to lie down. I don't want to think. I want to sleep.

She crossed the intersection and headed for the rise. The street climbed past empty land, past clumps of eucalyptus and pepper trees and old wild oaks that had been here since before the Spaniards came, and then past Warren's big impressive house, set far back, and other houses and more vacant land, and across empty space she saw the wild clump of brush where someone had hidden to throw mud on Suzie, to dirty her, to frighten Davie, and something rose in Vicky's throat, a knot of fear that almost choked her.

She pulled to a stop in her own driveway and got out. Her legs shook. She had to slam the car door twice to make it shut. She wanted to run into the house and get as far as her room, close herself in, and throw herself on the bed. And forget.

What a nothing kind of thing I am, she thought. *I'm a piece of jelly.*

She kept a grip on the car until her legs steadied. Then she stepped well away from it and turned, turned so that she faced across the valley. She lifted her head. She wanted him to see her face. She tried to keep fear out of it.

She felt the touch of his stare like the probe of a burning beam.

She curled fingers and thumbs and made binoculars out of her hands and lifted them to her eyes. She swung to one side and then another as he had done, and then settled the aim on his house across the valley. It was no more than a stamp-sized white blot in the far distance; her curled fingers brought it no nearer. She couldn't make out the stone wall or his figure, though she knew they were there. She could see a blur of greenery and the tiny white rectangle, shadowed now, and behind it the rocky crest of the ridge. She stood for a full minute with her pretend binoculars on his house, and then she dropped her arms, took her purse from the car, and walked away.

You've condemned him without a hearing, the inner voice protested. *How do you know it isn't something he started doing today? Since the crime? And how do you know, for sure, that his motive isn't loving and protective?*

She stood for a few minutes, looking at the glassy surface of the pool. In the kitchen she poured a cup of cold coffee and sipped it a little at a time.

I'll have to tell Dad, or Mr. Caldwell, about Jeff's binoculars. They have to know. But first I have to think, to decide. I have to figure out how I feel about Jeff now.

In the kitchen, the phone rang, but Vicky did not answer it. She sat down at the desk and took a sheet off a note pad and lettered a message, which she taped to the wall.

I don't want to talk to anybody.
                                                    VICKY

Then, walking slowly and quietly, she went to her room.

Suzie paused in the hall to size up what was happening. Her mother was busy fixing something for dinner. It looked like canned soup and grilled sandwiches. Her dad was in the dining room setting the table. She didn't see Davie. He was the one she wanted.

It was past seven, almost dark outside.

She went into the dining room. "Is there something I can do, Dad?"

He paused with a stack of plates and looked at her. She thought that he seemed awfully tired, and his eyes had an expression as if something inside him were hurting—had been hurting a long time. "I guess not, but thanks for asking. Maybe your mother could use some help."

He put down the plates and went to the cabinet for the silver. Suzie was sorry for him because he looked so awful, but she couldn't help wishing that instead of the wretched soup and sandwiches, they could have had the dinner her dad had tossed out into the bushes. That roast had really smelled divine. And what had he proved, anyway, chopping the cake and throwing the rest of it down the disposer?

He proved he was just about fed up, she answered herself.

He proved he would rather show how mad he was than eat.

So we didn't eat, either. We went to the restaurant and fiddled around with turkey on toast, and mashed potatoes with lumps in them, and stringy carrots, and half-melted ice cream, and at the end we had to tell him how good it was because of the way Vicky was looking at us. Thinking of Vicky, she said, "Is Vicky going to eat?"

He blinked and looked puzzled. "Go and see, will you? But wait a minute. Wasn't there someone here late this afternoon?"

"Jeff was here."

"Asking for Vicky?"

"Yes. I didn't open the door to him because it's against the rules," Suzie pointed out virtuously. "I talked to him *through* the door. He asked if Vicky was at home and I said I'd see, and I did, and she told me to tell him she had a headache and didn't want to talk to anybody. There's a note about it beside the phone, too. I guess she put it up earlier. So I told Jeff, and then I watched, and he sat in his car for ages. He looked all tightened up, if you know what I mean."

"They've had a lovers' quarrel," her father said, as if he were remembering something as long ago as his first day at school.

"Well, she didn't talk to him."

"All right," her father said, "just run along and see if she wants to eat with us. Tell her it's just a snack, grilled cheese and tuna, and soup, and a salad."

Suzie went away and was gone about two minutes. She didn't reenter the dining room. In passing, she said to her father, "She'll be in in a minute if she feels up to it. But we're not supposed to wait."

Her mother was spreading filling on the bread, getting the sandwiches ready to grill. She didn't look hungry, Suzie thought. She looked as if God or somebody had told her to get busy and feed her family the way she ought to. *They spent all that time together today,* Suzie thought, *and you'd think it would be the way it is on television or in the movies—they emerge at last hand in hand, and they've both sort of found their place again . . . they were in the bedroom after Mr. Caldwell left, for hours. And so what?*

So they didn't come out laughing and looking in each other's eyes and wanting the world to know that they were in love again. They'll never be in love again. It's a lost cause.

She looked for something to do and didn't see any obvious openings and walked on through the kitchen to the Family Area. The big room had been darkened by pulling the draperies across the glass doors. The TV set was on, and Davie was in front of it, squatted on the rug. He glanced at her as she flopped down beside him.

"Don't forget," she told him.

He pretended his leg was cramped from sitting on it and moved away, but Suzie wasn't fooled.

"Feeling chicken?"

"Bull."

"That's a vulgar nasty word."

"I don't know why," he defended. "It's just the name of an animal."

"It's tonight, remember. You've got to start yawning right after dinner. We can't wait till too late. We'll go out your window."

"We can't go too early, either, or Mr. Warren will come out to see who's rustling his horse."

"Keep your voice down. That horse won't make a sound. I took a fresh apple from the refrigerator and a dozen or so sugar cubes. He'll drift out of that corral and follow me as if he has wings. I'll snitch the bridle. We'll ride bareback. Don't forget matches to make the fire. That was your job."

"It was?"

"There'll be leftover sandwiches from dinner, and we'll take them. And a jug of water. Do you have any candy in your room?"

"What's this supposed to be? A picnic?"

"Let's just be prepared," Suzie said in the voice that implied she was much more experienced than he.

He was waiting at the window in the dark when she came in. "Did you get the matches?"

"Yes. In my pocket. And I've unhooked the screen."

"So? Give me a boost." She got up on the window ledge, belly down, and he saw the shadow of the screen lift out, dimly. She was carrying an old cloth shopping bag full of stuff. She dropped it outside. He was holding her leg, firm inside the tight pants, gingerly trying to guide her upward and outward. "Don't push, doggonit," she whispered. "Hang on. I don't want to plop headfirst into the bushes. If we make a noise, Dad will be here in a minute. He and Mom are in the bedroom, talking."

"They talked all afternoon."

"For all the good it did." She writhed across the sill, swung erect by grabbing the frame, took her leg out of Davie's grip. Suddenly she was gone, and to his relief there hadn't been any noise at all. He in his turn wriggled up and gripped the open frame of the window and got across the sill. She held the screen out for him.

It felt suddenly cool. From the big town on the far side of the range of hills, light reflected into the sky, enough light so that he could see Suzie's face, the pale oval of it, and the dim shape of her, a little taller than himself.

"Are you really going to steal Mr. Warren's horse?"

"Borrow, silly. Stealing is keeping. Come on. Don't run into things and bang yourself and squawk."

He stuck out his tongue at her back, then followed quickly as she led the way to the gate. Suzie was caution itself, opening the gate an inch at a time, making shushing noises at Davie. They got through, and she closed the gate in the same gingerly manner. Then she hissed some instructions at him—keep low; listen, if the horse nickers, we'll have to wait; if you see a light, *drop.*

"Oh, for Pete's sake."

"No talking during this part of the operation."

"What part are you playing now? A doctor or somebody?"

"Operation can mean something besides—" To Davie's satisfaction, she turned her ankle on some rock or clod and yelped with pain. Then she danced on one foot, mumbling the cries she didn't dare utter.

"We can go back," Davie suggested, "and you can soak your foot."

"You can soak your head. I'm all right." She forced the foot to the ground and went limping off, almost lost at once in the dark. He ran to keep up. He couldn't let her out of his sight, he told himself; he had to stay with her and watch over her, his crazy sister with her itch for magic and humbuggery. She needed an Indian bone like she needed two skulls.

If she had two, Davie thought, they'd *both* be empty.

It took quite a while to get to Mr. Warren's house because they had to make detours up into the fringes of the hills to avoid any glow of light from the houses they passed. But finally, they were behind Warren's, and Davie could smell the odor of the paddock and stalls. Mr. Warren had built a double stall and a tack and feed room and a small corral for his horse. The horse was waiting for them now with his head over the gate. Suzie gave him a sniff of the apple.

"Now, Davie, you feed him a couple of sugar cubes. Here, hold the apple, too, or he'll follow me to the tack room. I have to get the bridle. I'm dropping my bag here. Don't walk on it."

"What's in your dumb bag?"

"Stuff we'll need." She climbed the fence, dropped to the other side, walked off, and disappeared into the darkness of the miniature barn. When she came back, Davie heard the metal chink of the bridle. She coaxed the horse to turn and got the bridle on him.

"This gate squeaks like mad," she warned. "So just pray that Mr. Warren is watching television and it's noisy."

The gate was not locked; it was kept shut by a leather strap looped over the gatepost. The hinges did squeak, but Suzie worked slowly, and brought the horse out through the narrowest possible opening. She maneuvered the horse over to the fence. "I'll get up, and then you hop on behind me. Be careful, and don't dig your heels in there just in front of his leg. He's real ticklish there."

"Aren't you going to give him the apple?"

The horse was trying to nuzzle the apple out of Suzie's sack.

"I'm giving him the apple at the burying grounds. Half of it, I mean. He'll hang around for the rest of it until we're ready to go home. Otherwise he might just get bored and leave us."

She climbed the fence and slid a leg over the horse and spoke softly and patted his neck. Davie thought he could see her more clearly up there against the sky. She settled the cloth sack in front of her, balancing it against her stomach. Davie climbed the fence in his turn and got up behind her. He put his arms around Suzie's waist. Below, he could make out the dark shapes of shrubbery and trees, and beyond that, lower on the slope toward the road, were the lights of Mr. Warren's house. Mr. Warren had a Japanese couple, Davie remembered, who came out five days a week, by the day. They lived in town.

"Hold the sack steady," Suzie told him. She put the top of the cotton bag into his fingers. "It's our lunch and everything."

She clucked to the horse and moved a foot along his side, and the horse went willingly enough. Small rocks rolled under his hooves, and Davie grunted in alarm a couple of times when it seemed that the horse was losing his balance. Above the barranca the land leveled off into rolling, brushy rises that took them steadily higher. It seemed to Davie that as they went higher, the sky grew lighter. The glow from the towns on the far side of the range of hills seemed nearer, and he could even make out the general contour of the land.

"Where's the dumb burying ground?"

"Away off west. You're holding too tight. Let up, you aren't going to fall."

"He almost stumbled back there."

"Well, he was a heck of a long way from falling down. He can see better at night than we can. Just try to balance yourself according to what he does. It's like riding a bicycle."

"Not much. What's he puffing like that for?"

"If you'd carried two people the size of us up through that steep barranca, wouldn't you puff a little? It's nothing. And besides, he smells something. I can tell by his ears. He smells something, and he's trying to hear it or see it."

"Smells what?"

"How should I know? A coyote probably."

"Or a bear?" Davie suggested, drawing his legs up so that his feet were farther from the ground.

"Bear!" Suzie said, disgusted. "What in holy smokes would a bear be doing here down out of the mountains? There isn't a bear any nearer than the Sierras. And you know where they are."

Suzie clucked to the horse, and Davie heard her patting him. The horse just finally came to a stop and stood there making the snuffling sounds.

"What's he doing now?"

"You can see what he's doing."

"Well, what's he thinking then?"

"He's very curious. Not scared, curious. There's something up ahead. My guess is it's not moving; it's just waiting, maybe watching us. And he doesn't want to get any nearer until he's sure."

"Sure *what?*"

"I don't know." Suzie's voice remained calm and matter-of-fact. She whispered to the horse and stroked his mane and neck.

Davie strained his eyes against the dark. And it *was* dark, he realized. That false glow in the sky showed how the land lifted, showed a glimmer of lightness along the tops of ridges, but left everything below in utter black. He tried to make out some kind of shape on the rise ahead, and thought he saw something, and had an instant of heart-thumping fright, before he decided that the unmoving vague form was just a clump of sage or other growth.

"I wish he'd go." To his shame, his voice quivered.

"Oh, he'll go in a minute. He does this all the time when I'm riding him. Sometimes it's only a jackrabbit. Mr. Warren says he has the biggest curiosity bump in the horse kingdom, and he's right. This horse has to know everything is okay before he goes anywhere."

"We could go back."

Suzie didn't answer the cowardly proposal by even so much as a shrug. "Come on," she coaxed to the horse. "Whoever it is, you're a lot bigger than he is. You're a *horse.*" She slapped his neck softly. "Look, Davie, look at the way he's moving his ears. Like antennas."

There was enough glow from the sky for Davie to see the silky ears, twitched this way and that. The horse took a slow step and then another. Gravel crunched under the iron shoe.

"Where, where is it? The thing, or whatever he saw?"

Suzie answered, "I told you, it was probably a coyote, and

they're awfully curious too, and when the coyote figured out that what he was looking at was a horse, he went away."

They descended into the upper reaches of one of the barrancas, rocky and shallow here, and the horse picked his way carefully over the rough ground. Davie was growing tired. His eyes stung, and he thought of his bed at home. His arms ached from his close grip on Suzie, and the inside of his knees had begun to feel raw.

"How much farther, for Pete's sake?"

"After this rough ground, only a couple of miles, mostly level."

"I'm tired."

"You're not used to riding. When we get down and move around, and build a fire and have a rest, you'll feel fine."

"This was a crazy thing to do."

Suzie was silent for a minute, as if considering. "Well, it might seem foolish to people like Mr. Caldwell. He's very literal-minded. He takes things just as he sees them. He doesn't try to see under the surface or examine the inner workings of things. Take us, for example. He and Dad decided on some rules for us, and Dad explained them, and Mr. Caldwell just takes for granted that of course we'll obey. He doesn't understand that when a silly rule is imposed, a person's instinct is to find out if they can break it. Break it and get away with it, I mean."

"Is that what we're doing?" Davie said, his anger rising. "I thought we were out here on serious business, like getting an Indian finger bone to finish up your crazy charm."

"Of course, that's the *real* errand," she assured him. "Don't get all bent out of shape over it."

Her back felt stiff and unfriendly. *She's mad, Davie thought, because I can see through her. All the time it was a game to see if we could do it without getting caught, and she picked the burying grounds because it was the farthest she'd ever come on the horse, and if we got up there and back without being found out, she could crow over it. She'd feel like she made a fool of Dad and Mr. Caldwell and proved how smart she was.*

And proved what a boob I was, to believe what she'd told me.

To his surprise, Suzie promptly reined up the horse. "Davie."

"Yeah."

"Would you get off here?"

"Wh-why?" he stammered.

"There's something off to the right that I don't understand. It's like a shadow. I can't really see it if I look straight at it. But I keep noticing it out of the corner of my eye. It's a shadow, but it moves along with us."

Davie looked out to the right, toward the high ridge that seemed light along its upper reaches and was pitch-dark everywhere else. "There's no shadow. Everything is just black as the inside of a cat."

"I told you you couldn't see it if you looked right at it," she said, a hint of nervousness coming into her voice. "It's when you *aren't* looking. You see the movement. You get off and go over there without making any noise and see what it is. I'll go along slowlike until you get back."

"Why don't you go and have a look and leave me with the horse?"

"Because I know how to ride," she snapped back.

"I know enough to just let the horse go at his own speed," Davie argued. "Mr. Warren let me take him up the barranca. He just plowed along and I hung on. What's to that?"

"You act like this horse has gears or something, and you just put him in low and sit back. Suppose I yelled for help? Could you turn him and get him to gallop? And come in just right for me to jump on but for whatever else was there not to?"

"So now you're a trick rider, like in a circus."

"No, but the one who stays with the horse has to control him, or he might even just decide to go back home."

"That would suit me fine," Davie declared. "I really don't care what it is sneaking along over there in the dark. I don't care if it's a coyote or an elephant or a mouse."

"I think it's a man," Suzie said practically. "Somehow."

"It's Mr. Caldwell. He's not as dumb as you make out. He's going to come up to the campfire and ask for a snack."

"Mr. Caldwell wouldn't act like this—this thing's acting. He would have stopped us at the corral. He wouldn't be ducking behind a bush right now."

"How can you tell?" Davie whispered angrily, trying to see something in the blackness beneath the ridge. To his eyes there was nothing but the dark. Hair was rising along his neck in a reaction to fear he couldn't control. "You're making it up. You're pretending, just to scare me."

"If you won't go and have a look we'll have to think of something else. If it *is* a man, maybe he doesn't know where we're headed. Maybe he won't think of the burying grounds. He'll just think we sneaked out to prove that we could do it."

Which is the truth, Davie thought, *as far as you're concerned.*

Suzie went on, "So if we pretended to turn back—"

"Why pretend? Why not really turn back?"

"I need an Indian bone. *They* used them. So it's no crime."

"I think I read somewhere they also ate their enemy's liver and stuff like that," Davie offered. "Are you going all the way?"

"Don't get me off the subject. We can't just stay here. It might come closer, whatever it is." She clucked to the horse, and after they had gone a few yards more in the westerly direction, she began to turn the animal little by little until they were headed southwest. "He's behind us now. *It's* behind us," she corrected, "so I can't see what it's doing. Look up toward the skyline, and let your eyes sort of rove back and forth. Don't strain. Just keep your eyes roving, and try to feel relaxed."

Davie turned his head. If something eleven feet tall, lit up with neon and covered with green hair, had been directly behind with arms outspread, ready to leap, he would not have been surprised. Instead there was nothing. The sound of night bugs, a chirping noise, came faintly on the wind. The horse made crunching and sliding sounds, and a stone occasionally rang on the iron shoes. Davie thought, *There's nothing but the empty night,* and he grinned, and then as his gaze shifted, it seemed that something moved; a shadow detached itself from another to stand suddenly clear, alone. His eyes instantly switched back to the spot, and there wasn't anything; it was as if a brush full of black paint had smeared a window through which he was trying to find a thing which wasn't there.

But the movement—if there had been a movement—had been nearer than he had expected from Suzie's talk.

His mouth was dry now, and his body trembled.

"You saw it?" Suzie whispered.

"I saw . . . something. Or maybe I didn't. When I looked at it, it wasn't even there."

"There's something called peripheral vision," Suzie explained in a low tone, trying to sound knowing and unafraid. "Our science teacher told us about it. You see things in the edge of your eyesight that you wouldn't notice ordinarily, I think she said motion was the main thing, and in the dark a speck of light. The lesson was about . . . uh . . . optics, I think it was."

"I don't care what your stupid lesson was about," Davie raged, shaking with fright. "I want to get home. As quick as we can. So get this horse running!"

"Well, if the thing is a man, and he's been following us, and he sees that we're headed back now, and if he wanted to, he could cut us off. There are a couple of dry washes ahead of us and the sides are too steep and deep for us to cut across, so we have to go around them. The way we'd have to go, he could be there ahead of us because he could jump or climb the sides of the washes. If he wants to, that is."

"There must be another way out of this."

"There is. We pretend to start back, and then when we get to some old live oaks I know, we switch back and go north to the burying grounds. Meanwhile, he's leaping and climbing in those washes. And breaking his neck—if he's got a neck."

"What do you mean by that?"

"Oh, for Pete's sake," Suzie exclaimed, exasperated, "hasn't it occurred to you that we've come to rob a grave?"

"I pointed it out to you a long time ago," Davie defended.

"Well, how do we know a spirit, left to guard the burying grounds, isn't following and watching?"

"Oh, for the love of—" Davie itched to dig his heels into the horse's flanks and send him headlong. "Anyway, ghosts are white. Snow white. Where are those *doggone* oaks?"

"Up ahead. We'll get off there and wait. We'll see if our shadow thing is with us or not."

"I've got another idea, better than that," Davie said. "Let's get off the horse and give him a slap on his rear and send him on—

the way they do on television—and let the spook follow the horse. And *we* get busy jumping the walls of those washes."

"Oh, I thought of that a long time ago. But we've got a kind of advantage, up here, and if things came to a showdown, the horse could always outrun a man."

"So let him *run*."

"He could step in a hole and fall, and I'm not taking Mr. Warren's horse back with a broken leg, thank you."

The old live oaks made a tent of darkness that closed them in, shut out everything but the trees' own dusty odor and the faint rustle of their prickly leaves. Suzie pulled the horse to a halt, and the two of them sat there straining their ears, tensed with the effort to hear. *It won't fool him,* Davie thought. He felt the horse's sides expand with a huge sighing breath, the clink of the bridle as he shook his head. Suzie patted the horse's neck and whispered to him and then said softly to Davie, "It's all right. We'll get off."

She looped the bridle strap over a low stubby branch. Davie's eyes were adjusting to the intense dark now, and he could make her out dimly. The horse had his head down, trying to find something to eat.

"I'll give him a chunk of the apple." Suzie took the cloth sack and felt around in it, and a moment later Davie heard her teeth crunch off a piece of apple. "You take the sack up the tree, or he'll be after the rest of it. He's hungry."

Davie thought, with surprise: *So am I.* This last half hour or so had left him empty and shaky.

"Which tree?"

"This one. It's easy to climb. I've been up it myself."

Davie climbed. The bark was rough, smelled thickly of dust, and occasional stiff leaves jabbed his hands. He climbed until he came to an open space that looked out, as near as he could tell, toward the way they had come; he could see the rim of the hills against the faint glow of the sky. He sat there, straddling the limb, for some minutes. He let his eyes rove and tried to catch any motion at the rim of vision, and then he thought: *The spook can come from any direction at all. If he passes the oaks in the dark, thinking he's still following us, and finds out we're really not up ahead of him, then he'll come back from the south. And I won't see him. We won't have a chance.*

Something touched him, and he almost fell off the limb.

"What's the matter with you?" Suzie whispered. "Are you scared or something?"

"Let's go. Let's just go back the way we came and figure he's jumping around in those washes looking for us."

A light came on below them, shockingly brilliant. The horse stood bathed in the light, all gold and bronze, and lifted his head and looked into the light and whinnied softly. "Steady, old boy. Steady, now."

Whoever held the light came in closer under the trees, and the light searched this way and that. "Suzie? Davie? Where did you two get to?"

A terrible fear pounded through Davie, a feeling that a hammer had struck him inside somewhere, stopping his heart and breath. He tried to speak, tried to whisper to Suzie. The reflected light showed him her face, not two feet from his own, and her eyes that shone with astonishment. "It's him," he got out, and saw that she didn't understand. "It's the one on the telephone," he added. Still no awareness showed in Suzie's face, and he realized that he'd stammered and whistled the words in such a way that she couldn't grasp what he meant. Frantic, he let go of the branch and made dialing motions and then the gesture of lifting the receiver to his ear, and a change took place in Suzie. Everything in her face seemed to sharpen, to grow narrower and more intent, and he saw that she knew the full danger at last.

"Hey! Kids—" The light moved on, passing the tree in which they crouched, and they could see the dark form that followed. They could see the shape of his head, and how tall he was, and the way he walked, and Suzie put her hand over her own mouth to choke back a scream.

He went on still farther, so far that they couldn't see him, and Davie thought: *He's looking for footprints, to see if we left the horse and ran.* The light made long beams out across the country, losing itself against clumps of sage and ocotillo.

Dimly, Davie saw that Suzie was leaning close to him. "Didn't you *know?* Didn't you realize who he was?"

"No. I—I just didn't, somehow."

"He's going to come back," she whispered, her voice quivering, "and he'll think about looking up into the trees, and he'll find us. We've got to get down right now and start running."

"He'll find us, with that light."

"Then, when he does that, we've got to split up," she said. "Do you understand, Davie? When he gets us in the light, we have to run in opposite directions. And yell, Davie. Yell with everything you've got."

They scrambled down, tearing their clothes and skin in their hurry, and Davie dropped the last part of the way with a jolt that stunned his teeth and made lights blink behind his eyes. He stumbled, and almost collapsed, and Suzie grabbed his shirt and pulled him with her. And then, finally, it was all for nothing. The light brought them up short, straight ahead of them, and above the light that blinded them the shape of the man's head and his long legs below.

"Going somewhere, kids? What's the trouble?"

"You leave us alone," Suzie yelled, and the man laughed.

30

In that moment, choked with fright, it occurred to Davie that he had left the sack up in the tree. *We forgot the sack,* he told himself, and tried to pull his eyes away from the light, tried to look behind him and up into the tree to make sure that the sack was still there. And at the same time, knew that wanting to look for the sack was just a way of trying to get his mind off what was going to happen next.

Suzie poked him. "Run," she hissed. "You run right and I'll run left. He can't chase us both."

Davie started to say, "He'll chase you. He'll catch you and do those things to you that he—" But the words came out garbled, because something was flying at him. The man hadn't bent to pick up anything, so what was flying at Davie had been in a pocket, or a sack, or somewhere on him. The first rock flew by Davie's head like a bullet. Davie ducked, not soon enough if the man's aim had been good.

"He's going to hit you," Suzie screeched, "if you don't get going! Run!" And then she did the craziest thing of all; she threw herself directly at the light and the half-seen figure that held it.

But two more stones had let fly, and the first one, the big one, caught Davie on the side of the head, and he felt the terrible blow, the jar that seemed to loosen his eyes in their sockets, a flash of fire that lit up the inside of his skull. An instant later something stung his left ankle. It seemed like a sting at first, but as he fell and lay groveling, the sting changed to a breaking burst of flame, a fiery agony that grew, and he chewed his tongue to keep from screaming and tasted the funny flat taste of dirt, and finally a stifled cry came out anyway; he couldn't help it. And he could hear the scuffling going on. The man had Suzie and was going to do those things to her if he didn't stop him. He was going to do everything he'd promised to do. Those times on the phone—the words crackled through Davie's mind like firecrackers going off, red flashes full of pain and fear, and Davie got up on his hands and knees and tried to crawl.

Suzie let out a cry, a little one, but furious and full of outrage. Davie fell flat, and his mouth filled again with dust.

The light was lying on the ground over there, he'd seen that much. The light was lying on the ground so that the man could see what he was doing. And Suzie was on her back. The dark shape was over her, holding her.

I've got to get up, Davie told himself fiercely.

He flailed his arms, seeking a handhold, a grip on anything to give him enough leverage to pull by, and he found a rock. It could have been the rock that had hit him in the head. It felt about the right size.

I'll throw it back at him. I'll get him *in the head.*

He gripped the rock, but then he had to crouch and make himself small, make himself less a target for pain, had to suck in several breaths, and let them out slow enough so that they wouldn't turn into screams. When the red fire had swept through and ebbed, he got himself up on his knees. He lifted his arm to toss the rock and tried to make it fly true, and the rock dribbled out of his fingers and lay about a foot and a half away, a lump of darkness between him and the light.

He forced his legs to work, forced his brain to ignore the angry tearing feeling that raced up his leg from his ankle.

He half crawled, half fell, and got a grip again on the rock, and lifted it, and was suddenly surprised by the weight, the solid feeling of it, and the knowledge that it was a weapon as good as any the man had, unless he had a gun, brought a sense of strength. He could save Suzie. Nothing could hold him back now.

He got all the way to his feet and stood for a moment, off-balance, almost falling again, and then again the heft of the stone gave him confidence. He tottered forward. The man's head was bent, and above his shoulder Davie could see Suzie's face, starkly lit in the glow from the flashlight nearby, her eyes wide with shock.

Davie brought his arm up. *The first blow,* he told himself, *the very first one has to do it because he's going to turn; he'll feel me behind him; he'll turn in another instant and brush me away.*

Davie brought the rock down hard.

A flame licked at his leg, and the exertion set off fiery explosions behind his eyes, but he thought: *I've got to do it again. And again.*

It's not hard, he thought, and it seemed that a long time went by while his arm lifted and fell like a machine, a machine wound up too tight to stop. Suzie was screaming. She was screaming something that sounded like, "Don't. Don't. Don't," so that Davie thought: *He's still bothering her.*

His hand grew wet, and what Suzie was screaming now was, "Stop! Don't do it anymore!"

Somebody's hands, big firm hands, took Davie by the shoulders and lifted him, and set him down gently, and when he looked up, he found Mr. Caldwell floating there in the beam of the flash, and Mr. Caldwell said, "Yes, Davie, you must stop now."

"He won't hurt Suzie anymore?"

"I don't think he'll hurt anybody anymore, Davie."

Davie tried to think of what it was he wanted to say, the most important thing of all, and then he got it out. "Promise you won't tell Vicky, please. Promise you'll never tell her it was Jeff."

Mr. Caldwell didn't promise, though. He didn't say anything for a minute; he just kept feeling Davie's pulse, and squinting into his eyes, and touching the ankle gently. But at last he said, "I think Vicky has already guessed." After another minute he added, "I'm sorry I got here late. You threw me off when you hid in those trees."

"Did you know *he* was following us?" said Suzie in a hoarse whisper.

"No. But I figured he could be. And I knew you'd go out sooner or later and that he'd probably be waiting."

"You *knew* we'd go out?" Davie asked.

"Well, to kids your age, especially kids Suzie's age, though she's actually more of a young lady"—Mr. Caldwell sounded tired, kind of patient, elderly—"to people your age, rules are made to be tested."

He remembers, Davie thought in surprise, in spite of the pain and the fuzziness in his head, with a kind of astonishment at the insight —*he remembers all the way from when he was a kid himself.*

31

It was past two o'clock in the morning when Thomas rapped softly at Vicky's door and opened it a short way and looked in at the dark. He heard her stir on the bed. "Dad?"

"If you don't want me right now, say so. I'll understand."

"No. Come on in. I'm not crying or anything. How is Davie?"

"He was falling asleep when I left the hospital. His color is good, and his eyes focus. They'll do X rays in the morning when he's rested. The doctor thinks the ankle might be cracked. But no signs of a head injury—a serious injury—thank God." Thomas went across to the bed and sat down at the foot. He had left the door open a little, and by the light reflected from the hall he could see Vicky, the shape of her under a quilt she'd thrown over herself, the paleness of her face, the gleam of her hair. Her eyes looked dark, enormous. There was a glimmer of wetness on her cheeks, so the part about not crying had been a lie to spare him worry. *The best kind of lie,* Thomas thought.

"Dad, I want to talk about Jeff this one last time. And then not again. But *why* . . . why did he have to get into Mr. Bowman's office? What could he have done if he had managed it? He surely couldn't have changed the will his aunt left or the provisions of the trust fund she set up for him—could he?"

Thomas was silent, thinking it over. "No, he didn't have a hope of doing anything like that. The only thing he could have wanted —that makes sense—was to get hold of the documents and go over them at his leisure and in privacy. I doubt if Jeff would have been naïve enough to think he could alter anything. All such documents are microfilmed, and the films stored in the bank. No, it had to be that he wanted to see just what the terms of the trust were, try to find some loophole. And of course there aren't any. It's Bowman's fault, in a way, all of it. Jeff has been in several times over the past couple of months, and Bowman was pretty curt with him. He dismissed Jeff with the thought that he should be satisfied, glad to know that his aunt had left him what she had. The roots of Bowman's attitude go back a long, long way. Bowman used to be engaged to Jeff's great-aunt. They were in love. I don't know why the marriage never took place; it just didn't."

"But Mr. Bowman felt possessive toward her."

"Yes. And protective. No doubt he felt that the woman had made him her watchdog, to see that the young whippersnapper didn't waste her money in disgraceful ways and so forth. He may even have advised her on the provisions of the trust. You can be sure *that's* ironbound."

"But Jeff had to see for himself."

"He had to get into that office somehow," Thomas agreed. "And it must not have seemed like much of a project, really. He'd scare Davie into giving him the keys; he'd use them, read what he wanted, perhaps photograph the documents—anyway, it was to be simple and quick and no harm done. Of course, to me the big question is: How could he say to Davie what he did, make the kind of threats he made, if he really loved you? These children are your brother and sister."

She turned restlessly under the quilt, drew herself smaller. "I've thought of that. I've forced myself to think of it, to face it, ever since I came home from Jeff's place. I saw him using binoculars over there—"

"Caldwell saw that, too."

"But he left before Jeff did it." She lifted her head in surprise. "Mr. Caldwell was there when I got there. I climbed in an open window and went through the house, looking for Jeff. I wanted to surprise him." Her voice took on a sudden ragged edge, and Thomas wondered for an instant just what had been the involvement between them. She lay back and covered her eyes with her arm. "I thought Mr. Caldwell went away."

"He stayed to watch for a while. Getting back to what Jeff told Davie over the phone—"

"Jeff had a—a sort of blindness about people, Dad. He told me many times that I was the only one who was real to him. And I know he meant it. I was his reality, and he wanted me, and he wanted the money his aunt had left him so that he and I could live in some world of our own, shut away from the ones he called paper dolls. He didn't think of Davie and Suzie as people I loved, people whose grief I would share. They were tools to be used to get what he wanted. Oh, there were times—tender times—when I think he tried to be different, when he tried to see how things might look to me."

"I guess there must be some explanation for his being what he was."

"I've thought of that, too. When Jeff was very small, his mother became ill and left him and spent a lot of time in sanatoriums—it must have seemed like the bitterest of rejections to a child that small. Then the aunt came, and she loved him, but again there was a change—the aunt left when his mother came back. Instead of bothering herself very much with her young son, his mother tried to become an artist. His father was away all the time. And then, when the aunt died, there must have seemed the bitterest rejection of them all. She left the money he wanted, the money he had expected, in the care of a tyrannical old attorney. But, Dad, I've just thought of something. That wasn't the crowning rejection. Jeff wasn't a killer, really, until tonight. You and Mr. Caldwell both have spoken of Grandma's death as an accident. And it was. Jeff didn't come that night to murder anybody. It was today, this last day of his life, that made him want to kill; it was *my* rejection of him. I wouldn't see him or talk to him, I'd made my hands into binoculars, standing in the driveway, facing his house, I'd let him know that I knew what he was doing, and then I—I threw him away. And that was when he really became a murderer."

She rolled over to bury her face in the pillows.

Thomas shut his eyes and rubbed them tiredly with his fingers. "You mustn't blame yourself."

She said, muffled, her voice choked, "I won't go to pieces, Dad. I think that Davie was incredibly brave, doing what he did to protect Suzie. Does he realize that he killed Jeff?"

"No. I've tried to think of a way that he need never know, that we might tell him Jeff had died of a heart attack, something like that. But there's an inquest to get through. And in the end, somebody at school, someone in Davie's classes, would bring it up. I don't see any way to keep the secret—and it would have to be kept forever. I wish there was a way he could get out of here for a while. For the school term, for instance."

She rolled over and sat up. There was a stir of fragrance as she leaned toward her dad. "Why don't you let him go to Arizona with me? I'd get an apartment instead of a room in a dormitory. And he'd be in school while I was; there'd be no baby-sitting problem. And we'd . . . we'd have each other for . . . for comforting." The tears were just under the surface. "And I won't think much of Jeff, and finally, I won't think of him at all."

"You're going to school? You're sure you want to?"

"Yes."

Thomas reached for her hand, pulled her across the bed toward him. "We hate to lose you right now."

"Are you and Mother going to get a divorce?" she asked anxiously.

"No. That isn't what I meant. We've talked things out pretty thoroughly. We've both been wrong, both been stubborn, both been blind. But we're through with accusing each other; we've discussed the past. And that's over. We won't fall in love again; this isn't a miracle. But we are going to be parents and be aware of you kids and provide a home for you. A good home, as good as we can make it. And this home will be here, Vicky, for you and Davie to come back to. What we found out is that in some way we all do belong together. It seemed that we didn't. It seemed as if each of us lived here in a kind of shell, neither loving nor communicating. We were a family that had lost itself. But really, it wasn't that bad. We're people who love each other. There's not one of us who wouldn't die for the others . . . and some of us have proved it. We're a family after all. And we won't be lost from each other again."

She leaned against him, and he put his arms around her.

"I love you, Father."

Thomas had a half-smile on his lips; he was grimly tired, but there was suddenly a little light ahead, and they were on their way to it.